WINDMEER

Robert Dornburg

Order this book online at www.trafford.com
or email orders@trafford.com

Most Trafford titles are also available at major online book retailers.

Printed in Victoria, BC, Canada.

ISBN: 978-1-4269-2328-9 (sc)

Library of Congress Control Number: 2010900248

*Our mission is to efficiently provide the world's finest, most comprehensive book publishing
service, enabling every author to experience success. To find out how to publish your book, your
way, and have it available worldwide, visit us online at www.trafford.com*

Trafford rev. 4/29/2010

 www.trafford.com

North America & international
toll-free: 1 888 232 4444 (USA & Canada)
phone: 250 383 6864 ♦ fax: 812 355 4082

To Mary Elizabeth, my first grandbaby.

To my sister, Emmy. Thanks for the memories.

As always to my wife for her assistance

I have faith but if I don't have
Love, I have nothing. Love is
Lastingly patient, and is tenaciously
Kind. Love does not envy, it is not
Jealous. Or easily provoked. And
now abide all faith, hope and love,
the greatest of these is love.

-1 Corinthians 13

CONTENTS

PREFACE

Life is eternal and love is immortal, and
what we call death is but a horizon and a
horizon is only the limit to our sight.
-Abraham Lincoln

As this novel is a sequel to *Thorn Castle*, I felt a synopsis would present the reader with a brief insight into the characters and the situations that had transpired until the end of the war.

The Third Reich was born on 30 January 1933 which Adolph Hitler optomiscally proclaimed would endure for a thousand years. In realty, it lasted twelve years and four months. During that period of violent change in history, it raised the German people to the zenith of power then thrusting them into death, destruction and desolation in a war that provoked a reign of terror over conquered countries unparalleled in the elimination of human life and spirit. To the majority of Germans, Hitler possessed the aura of a charismatic leader and followed his judgment for the next twelve turbulent years. The German armies invaded Poland and out of the sky aircraft unleashed death and destruction on bridges, railroads and cities heralding the beginning of World War II.

The war decimated the Lehndorff family. Heinrich von Lehndorff was the scion of an old and prominent family. He was the sole proprietor of the family business. When war became a reality his factories became a prime sub-contractor to Messerschmitt Aircraft.

Hanna, his wife, a patrician women suffered the oppressive life style she must follow in a country dominated by men. Germans were chauvinists. She gave birth to a daughter and four sons. Hilda, the first born, a precocious child would assert her right as an individual and attempt to escape the depressed values forced upon women. Graduating from the University of Oxford in England, she was accepted in die Firma over her father's initial objections. She survived the war prevailing over various obstacles. After the war, returning from a trip to the United States, she and her husband were passengers on a Pan American Clipper that crashed on the approach to Lisbon. They were listed as casualties due to a similarity of names, Fetters instead of Feathers. The erroneous list was corrected and they were listed as survivors. Her first husband was a German Army Infantry Major who succumbed to the winter on the Russian front.

The first son was expected to eventually follow the father in the family business but Herman's aspirations negated the idea. Much to his father's disappointment he became a pilot. He volunteered for service in the Condor Legion serving Franco's forces in the Spanish Civil War. When World War II began he participated in the Battle of Britain.

Hugo, the second son had then been tapped to assume the throne of die Firma at some later time. He was labeled as a misguided youth as were others of his generation, but unlike his contemporaries was content to follow a *derigueur* path of life. He spent a lot of time and money on expensive hobbies, but he who dies with the most toys, is none the less dead. Helmut, the third son was described by many adjectives-a paradox. He was a complex entity. In his youth he had the ability to appreciate the subtleties of life where as his father lacked that vision. His future was chaotic due to the inherent unpredictability of the natural system.

Hans, the fourth son envisioned a future of honor and glory. His father accused him of pursuing the frivolous and peripatetic life of a playboy. For a change in his life and future environment, his father suggested the idea of attending Harvard would be worth considering. After graduating, he returned to Germany, joined the Navy and served in the U-Boats.

Tom Korb and his family struggled through the austere conditions of the depression. He had a strong desire to learn to fly but the cost of lessons was prohibitive. An airline pilot, who had become his mentor suggested the Naval Aviation Cadet Program. Tom applied, was accepted and after receiving his Wings of Gold was commissioned a second lieutenant in the U.S. Marine Corps.

John Fairfield III came from an affluent, distinguished and respected New England family. His father was a senator and his mother was heir apparent to the Knox Plaza Hotels. John graduated from the Naval Academy, was commissioned a second lieutenant in the U.S. Marine Corps. He and Tom were assigned as room mates. A lasting friendship was formed during their flight training and continued through the years as they served as fighter pilots from Guadalcanal to Japan.

Beth, John's sister was enrolled at Radcliff College, her mother's alma mater. Majoring in drama, inspired her aspirations in becoming an actress.

Both Senator John E. Fairfield II R-Mass. and General Lundgren, Commanding General of the Marine Corps Air Station, Cherry Point, North Carolina served in France during World War I. The General assumed his son would graduate from the Naval Academy but much to his chagrin and surprise Lars announced his decision to enter the Citadel. His daughter, Kristin was enrolled at the University of North Carolina.

After completion of their flight trainng, Tom and John were assigned as flight instructors for a few months, then were assigned transition training on the F4F, the Navy's fighter aircraft at the time. When their qualification was complete they were assigned as replacement pilots to relieve some of the pilots who bore the brunt of the air war in the skies over Gualalcanal. Both received commodations and were returned to the states where were they assigned to a war bond saving tour. Velma Davison worked for the local newspaper and acted as cordinator of the events. It was love at first sight when she and John met.

Tom and his girl friend Mary Jane Evans were students at the same high school. They had marriage plans. Both couples faced uncertain futures as Tom and John were sent into harm's way with tours of duty from Guadalcanal to Japan.

THE MIGHTY HAD FALLEN

Nothing so needs reforming as other people's habits.
-Mark Twain

Some of the remaining collaborators from the Nazi regime, who were indicted for war crimes, lived to sit before the International Military Tribunal in Nuremberg. There had been a complete metamorphosis in the twenty one sitting in the dock. Attired in shabby clothes, slumping in their seats, they fidgeted nervously. They no longer resembled the arrogant leaders of the Third Reich. It was difficult to believe that these men had wielded such monstrous power and conquered nations and most of Europe. Of the twenty one facing prosecution, only Albert Speer, Minister for Armament and War Production, made the most straightforward impression during the long trial and spoke honestly and with no attempt to shirk his responsibility and guilt. Seven defendants at the Nuremberg Trials drew prison sentences, the others were sentenced to death.

Heinrich von Lehndorff was especially interested in the adjudication of the Tribunal. As a subcontractor to Messerschmitt Aircraft, utilized slave labor to meet production quotas imposed upon him by Goering's Luftwaffe (Air Force). In particular interest was the sentence imposed upon Fritz Sauckle, the boss of slave labor in the Reich. His main concern was how far down the ladder the Allies would go to implicate those who utilized slave labor. His confidence was somewhat shaken when he heard that Sauckle mounted the gallows in the execution chamber of the Nuremberg prison followed in intervals by six others of Hitler's collaborators who were judged as war criminals.

When the Third Reich emerged, a speech by Hitler made an impression on Heinrich and like the majority of Germans at the time

2   *Robert Dornburg*

joined the Nazi Party. Later on he became dissatisfied with Hitler when he realized the Fuehrer was leading the country into war.

At a meeting in Berlin that Heinrich had attended, Herman Goring, Commander-in-Chief of the Luftwaffe announced the hated Treaty of Versailles, virtually disarming Germany, had been repudiated and Hitler ordered a huge expansion in the armed forces.

Assuming the factories would be in operation twenty four hours a day seven days a week, "I'll need workers!" Heinrich exclaimed "hundreds of them. Where will I get them? In addition to raw material, I'll need menschen-human material."

Foreign conscripts continued to pour into the camps at an alarming rate. S.S. guards stood watch as Jews, Russians, Poles, Czechs, Ukrainians, French, Dutch and Belgian workman who had been volunteers were now trapped behind the barbed wire under compulsory extension of their contracts. Heinrich estimated he would require about a thousand draftees so to use the correct terminology slaves to convert the factories, operate a full schedule and expand the housing. All this in direct violation of the Geneva and Hague Conventions that stipulated no prisoners should be employed as such. The conventions covered a multitude of sins but were ineffective.

The German Labor Front had usurped the role and assets of the trade unions. All productive Germans were brought together with numbers in the millions when war began in 1939. This organization provided numerous functions for the labor group known as *Strength Through Joy*. As these organizations grew they were pressured into joining and participating in activities in the interest of their leaders but also in the administrative structure of the Third Reich and the Nazi ideology. Those who sought to undermine the commitment of the Nazi world views were ruthlessly suppressed. Although there was popular approval for rearmament and breaking the Versaille Treaty, the views were mixed with uneasiness about the possibility that Germany might go to war.

Several months had passed and Heinrich Lehndorff had not

been contacted by the International Military Tribunal regarding the utilization of conscripted labor for his factories. He viewed the situation with great trepidation but there was also a degree of optimism that the longer the denazification dragged on the process could be terminated and a greater portion of Germans would be classified as followers. As Heinrich utilized a large number of the workers, he was placed in the number two category and was liable to a term in a labor camp, the expropriation of his property and loss of state pension.

His anxiety reached a climax when he received notification that a trial would be held in regard to the degree of guilt that would be adjucated in the use of conscripted labor in his factories. It also stated that the trial would be held in Nuremberg where the major war crininals were tried and also lessor figures in the regime who were brought to justice that served to increase his anxiety.

THE TRIAL LOCATION

The history of conquest is littered with failed political dreams
-Unknown

The Allied Control Council exercised all government functions for defeated Germany. They decided that trials of the surviving Nazis would be held in Nuremberg, a war devastated city. It was chosen over Munich because the Nuremberg Palace of Justice could be restored in time for the trails, while it's cavernous virtually undamaged jail would house the Nazis awaiting trail along with the witnesses. Nuremberg was also the city where Hitler had evoked mass hysteria and venomous xenophobia and where Goering as president of the Reichstag, the German Parliament, had proclaimed the infamous Nuremberg laws, which terminated the civil rights of German Jews and demolished their ability to earn a livelihood.

Nuremberg had been heavily bombed by the Royal Air Force and captured after heavy fighting the few days before the war ended. Most of the city lay in ruins, sections were still burning and the streets were choked with rubble.

The Palace of Justice on the Furtherstrasse where the trial was held, in normal times the building housed the German Regional Appellate Court. It was a large heavily constructed complex including a jail, an office building and a courthouse. In the courtroom there were eight judges, comprising four voting and four alternate judges. Behind the judges were two interpreters to assist in discussion among the Russian, French and English speaking judges.

The table for the prosecuting nations and the defendants and their lawyers were in front. White helmeted armed guards stood against the wall behind the defendants. There was an up sloping gallery for the press and unprivileged visitors.

HEINRICH LEHNDORFF TRIAL

The quality of mercy is not strained , it droppeth as the
gentle rain from heaven upon the place beneath. It is twice
blessed, it blesseth him that giveth and him that taketh.
-William Shakespeare in
The Merchant of Venice

Several months had passed since the end of the war and Heinrich
von Lehndorff had been contacted by International Military Tribunal.
Since the time lapse had been so long, complacency had begun to
take effect and a trial would not be necessary. Nevertheless, it was
a severe shock when he was served the indictment. In part it stated
that charges have been filed against you in regard to the recruitment
and utilization of slave labor from among the German people. After
reading the indictment, Heinrich was totally surprised and angry that
the indictment was unconscionably false.

Documents did not proclaim that the conscripted hordes from
Russia, Poland, France and the low countries had joined the German
labor force voluntarily. Out of the five million workers who arrived
in Germany, 200,000 had not come voluntarily.Enslaved laborers and
Russian prisoners of war, in flagrant violation of the laws of war, were
forced to work on military armament or even used in combat.

Oberst Karl Feathers, his rank of Colonel was used, indictment
was equally damning. As a member of the S.S. Nazi organization and
their members will be charged, not merely with atrocious violations
of the laws of war, but with conspiring from the beginning of the Nazi
period in 1933 to commit such violations. The severity of the punishment
for individual members would be governed by evidence of the extent
to which they were involved in or were aware of the organizations
criminal activities in accordance with the decision of the jury.

The International Tribunal had set a trial date and Heinrich was notified to appear with his counsel. After the opening remarks the judge ordered the prosecution to call the first witness.

Prosecutor: You attended a meeting in 1934 held at the Bristol Hotel at which time Herr Goering announced the repudiation of the Versaille Treaty. Is that correct?

Witness: Yes, I sat at the same table as the defendants.

Prosecutor: You were acting in what capacity?

Witness: I was the chief engineer on the ME-109 project for the Messerschmitt Aircraft.

Prosecutor. How would you explain Herr Lehndorff's reaction to that announcement?

Witness: During the on going conversation with my boss Willie Messerschmitt, Herr Lehndorff welcomed the huge mobilization. It would be possible to convert his factories and become a sub-contractor for engines and parts for the ME-109.

Prosecutor: Any other action you could describe?

Witness: A project that massive would be a big business expansion and fill the coffers of die Firma with Deutsche Marks.

Prosecutor: To digress for a moment, you also attended a meeting at the Kaiserhof Hotel in Berlin. What was the purpose of that meeting?

Witness: Representatives from some of the largest industrial companies were present. One of the main topics discussed was labor.

Prosecutor: Was Herr Lehndorff in attendance?

Witness: Yes. The arrangement between Lehndorff Industries and Messerschmitt Aircraft was approved. Also, Herr Lehndorff, Herr Goering, C-in-C of the Luftwaffe and Albert Speer, Minister for Armament and War Production were there.

Prosecutor: What was the defendents opinion when he realized the scope of the operation?

Witness: He exclaimed! "I'll need workers, hundreds of them." His initial estimate was conservative. "Where will I get them?"

Prosecutor: Was his question answered?

Witness: Yes. He assumed and requested German workers but foreign conscrips poured into the camps. Many were volunteers but were now trapped behind the barbed wire.

Prosecutor: In your opinion what was Herr Lehndorff's reaction when he became aware of Hitler's huge expansion of the armed forces?

Witness: He was jubilant, especially when the agreement was approved to become a sub-contractor to Messerschmitt Aircraft. Two of his three factories could quickly be converted and utilized to begin production of engines and sub-assemblies.

Prosecutor: I have no further questions for this witness.

Witness: In my opinion, Herr Lehndorff should be tried and convicted in the death of Oberst Steiner, the previous Camp Commander at his factories.

Prosecutor: It was completely unexpected and the defense attorney shouted, "Objection, that is irrelevant to this indictment. He was tried and exonerated of those charges set forth in the German Peoples Court."

Judge: Sustained, and the witness is excused. The judge issued a severe reprimand.

When order had been restored from the unauthorized outburst, the witness was identified as Heinz Steiner, brother of Oberst Dieter Steiner, the Camp Commander dispatched by Herr Lehndorff upon hearing he had raped his daughter resulting in a pregnancy. Heinz harbored the grievance for a long time but was unable to figure out a way to act upon it. He heard that Heinrich would stand trial for using slave labor. Figuring it was as good a reason as any to air his complaint, he volunteered as a prosecution witness. Unfortunately for him he was not permitted to air his grievance and the plan failed. Regardless, if Oberst Steiner had lived, he would have been charged with rape. He was also under investigation for trafficking in the black market and most assuredly would have been indicted as a war crimnial for the brutal treatment he forced upon the slave laborers and also as a member of the S.S. a declared Criminal Organization and subject to prosecution. The judge declared a recess until the following morning.

THE SEIGE OF BERLIN

To perceive in the world intimations of the divine, to sense in small things the beginning of infinite significance, to sense the ultimate in the common and the simple to feel in the rush of the passing stillness of the eternal.
-Unknown

A break through of Germany's border in the east first occurred during the week of January 1945. By the end of the month another penetration by the Russians within forty eight miles of Berlin. The speed of the thrust took Stalin by surprise. He claimed the German Army was as vulnerable as perceived and insisted on building up his own forces for the attack on Upper Silesia and the Baltic. While he believed caution was the answer, German reinforcements arrived on the eastern front and strengthened the defense of Berlin.

In the west the allies had lagged. They had been overrun by the German counter-offensive in the Ardennes in December of 1944. An American patrol found a bridge intact at Remagen and the entire Allied Expeditionary Force crossed the river and enveloped the Ruhr. Advancing against the weakened opposition of the Ruhr, the German troops began surrendering by the thousands.

Realizing the war was over, they preferred a western POW camp to a transfer to the Russian front. By the end of March 1945 the Allies were two hundred miles from Berlin but the way was open. The Russians were only 35 miles from Berlin, but were being pummeled by ferocious German resistance. Stalin had not ordered a full assault on the German capital.

On 28 March General Eisenhower, thinking it was unnecessary to consult with the Allies or Washington, sent a telegram to Stalin suggesting their armies meet in Dresden, assuming the contact was purely a military matter. Eisenhower, the nonpolitical soldier, was unaware he was making a fundamentally political approach to someone who thought everything was political. Stalin's response was approving and mendacious. Berlin had lost its strategic importance while the Red Army was allocating secondary forces.

The British, learning of Eisenhower's telegram were outraged. They protested to the American Chief of Staff about the disregard for Berlin and Eisenhower's unilateral negotiation with Stalin. On 3 March Churchill urged Eisenhower to advance as far as possible to prevent the Russians from capturing Berlin. If Berlin is left to the Russians it will strengthen their conviction they had done everything to beat Hitler. Washington was fully persuaded by Eisenhower's strategic reasoning and resented criticism of their outstanding successful commander. Churchill was sensitive to their reaction and concerned not to damage the alliance directed at a crucial member. He penned a note of praise of Eisenhower but repeated a caveat emptor. "I deem it highly important that we should shake hands with the Russians as far east as possible."

The political crisis between the Allies was distressing to Eisenhower. His insistence to leave Berlin to concentrate on Dresden was for the best military reasons but admitted that war is waged in pursuance of political aims and only if the Allied effort to take Berlin overshadows the military consideration he would adjust his plan. But the combined Chiefs did not make that decision and a new directive was not sent to Eisenhower. The order to attack Berlin was given by Stalin to the Red Army.

Stalin had already decided on it when he gave the answer to Eisenhower and felt assured the Allied forces were about to launch an offensive against Berlin. He asked, "Who is going to take Berlin? Will we or the Allies?" His question was a signal for a race to Berlin between the Allies and the Red Army.

While the Red Army moved up its men and material, the allied forces in all ignorance continued to bomb Berlin for them. The first

American tanks reached the Elbe River. A combat group crossed the river and three more battalions had crossed and were digging in while more groups were crossing above and below them. The advance units were stunned to receive orders they were not to advance. Generals Bradley and Patton were completely surprised and said, "We had better take Berlin and quick." The British still urged Eisenhower to press on to Berlin but he flew to London to convince Churchill that it's best to leave the city to the Russians. At the time it was too late for Eisenhower to change his mind. On 1 April, three red flares signaled the beginning of a grim and bloody battle. By 20 April the first Red Army units had reached the outskirts of Berlin. Thousands of Berliners had attempted to turn back the assault but were overwhelmed by superior forces that had penetrated within 250 yards of the Reichstag (home of the old German parliament).

On 2 May the Red Army accepted the surrender of the city and Soviet guns remained silent. The city was in rubble. There was no electricity, transport and little drinking water or food. Their fear was not artillery but bayonets and rape. The first Red Army troops into Berlin had been disciplined. The second wave was a riot. They raped, looted and what they were unable to carry they smashed. The rampage was official policy. Factories were stripped and the contents carried away in Russian lorries. Anything was pillaged.

It could be explained the Russians had suffered the worst when the Nazi invaded the Soviet Union. They had experienced murder, robbery, extermination squads and gas attacks and other bestialities of the SS. It might be figured that they wanted revenge as well as victory even though they raped and looted other countries they claimed to liberate.

As the Russians continued to rape, burn and pillage, the military authorities did nothing to stem the violence. The military assault on Berlin was a disaster. It was the violation that followed which left ineradicable bitterness to Berliners and cemented their view of the Russians forever. The Soviet authorities planned to follow the actual siege of the city with a metaphorical military disguised as a political ceremony. Although superficially the campaign appeared successful at the time, severe limits had destroyed its effectiveness by the harsh barbarity of the troops in the horrible beginning. The Red Army also lost Berlin politically at the same time they captured it militarily.

WORLD WAR II ENDS

In the *Odyssey* Homer ascribed to the wonderings
of Odysseus after the fall of Troy, has come very
close to saying that one is what one has suffered and survived.

7 May 1945 at 2:41 marked the end of hostilities in World War II in Europe came to an end as Germany surrendered unconditionally. The guns and bombs were silent for the first time since 1 September 1939. The Third Reich had ceased to exist. In the intervening five years, eight months and seven days, millions of men and women were slaughtered on as many battlefields and bombed towns as were those in concentration camps.

A great nation and easily mislead people reached huge heights and then it all suddenly dissolved as there was no German authority they could turn to for comfort and consolation. Millions of men in uniform were prisoners of war in their own country. Also, there were millions of civilians governed by troops whom they had depended on, not only for law and order, but also food and fuel for the summer and winter.

Such was the folly of following Hitler with extreme enthusiasm that brought them to the fall of Germany. The people, dazed, bleeding, hungry and with the arrival of winter, shivering in their rags in the hovels that the bombing had made of their homes. The lives of the *Fluchling* (refugees) continued to be affected after the war. In desperation, carrying only their items remaining, they attempted to reach the west and the protection of the allies. Those who were unfortunate to fall behind, were taken into custody and received brutal treatment from the Russians. They were the human debris from a disastrous war. A vast waste land of rubble. The Third Reich was history.

When it became evident that the end of the Third Reich was in sight, the German High Command made an overture to the Allies to save Germany from further destruction by the advancing Bolshevik enemy. The achievement of this aim was impeded by the Allies and as such they continued to press for unconditional surrender. Germany was split in two as the American and Russian joined forces at the Elbe River. The plan was bitterly criticized by the British Prime Minister and the military chiefs for not beating the Russians to Berlin.

The German atom bomb project had worried London and Washington. It had not made much progress due to Hitler's lack of interest and Himmler's practice of arresting the atom scientists for suspected disloyalty or to work on some of his experiments which he considered more important. Before the end of 1944 the American and British governments had learned that the Germans would not have an atom bomb in this war.

Politics, the interference of politics in the affairs of science and the appointment of party hacks to important administrative posts was another grave error that would be foolish to suppose was purely a German monopoly. By putting politics first and science second, the Nazis contributed greatly to the deterioration of German scientific teaching and research. To be a good Nazi was not necessarily synonymous with being a good scientist and one can learn from their mistakes to leave science to the scientists.

The same thing applies to dogma, whether it be political, scientific or religious. The stubborn blindness of dogma and the free inquiring spirit of science do not mix, nor is there any such thing as Jewish science or Aryan science. The anti-Semitism doctrine of the Nazis was disastrous to the German physics not merely and even principally, because it brought about the exile of certain notable scientists. These men could have been replaced in due time by younger colleagues. But by the infusion of dogma into the body of scientific thought the Nazis tended to bring the whole subject of modern physics into disrepute with the result that the Jewish science of physics became unpopular at the universities.

Finally, there was the matter of hero worship. A young scientist wouldn't think of questioning the word of the master. But scientific research represents a collective effort. It's a matter of trial and error, of consultation and correction on the part of many minds.

Many scientific and military experts believed the United States was in a desperate race with Germany to develop an atomic bomb. The Germans were still discussing the uranium problem, one of the elements necessary in developing a chain reacting pile that would lead to an atomic bomb. Nor did they know how to produce plutonium from the uranium pile. The Germans figured if they couldn't make an atomic bomb nobody else could either, so they were not worried. The German arrogance received a huge surprise when it was announced an atomic bomb had been dropped on Hiroshima 6 August 1945 and a second bomb had been dropped on Nagasaki three days later on 9 August 1945.

The failure of the German scientists during the war was the mismanaged research. It was evident that the excellent Luftwaffe aerodynamic research under Goering produced superior results while the academic research contributed a minuscule to the war effort although the scientists in both groups were equally competent. And many were members of the same organization.

Complacency, deterioration of interest in pure science and regimentation in the administrative control of science were three German principle errors. Other mistakes were made also. For example, there was a lack of team work between the various scientific groups. An attitude of such does not promote successful research.

Hero worship was another attitude detrimental to progress. The uranium problem was too extensive in total to be absorbed by any one individual. A project of that magnitude needed ideas of many outstanding scientists. Finally, there remains the question of secrecy. However necessary strict secrecy maybe in war time, in piece time there are decided disadvantages. The present policy allowed for the publication of all basic scientific discoveries in regard to atomic research but it was difficult to know where to draw the line. The original secrecy in the United States atomic bomb project was not imposed by any military government ruling but arose among the scientists themselves. It was decided in scientific matters, the scientists were considered to be the best judges of what to keep secret.

Scientists mention the absence of international barriers in their work. During World War II astronomical information was exchanged via neutral countries. Secrecy would eliminate international cooperation in scientific matters. Pooling of scientific knowledge is essential for the progress of individual scientists and for scientists overall. After breaking the barriers of dogma, mistrust, fear and secrecy with the free exchange of ideas, can science continue to raise its level and the level of civilization?

After the German military collapse, suicide became a public phenomenon. A sense of helplessness and fear of what the soldiers of the Russian Army would do particularly to women. People shot, hanged, drowned and poisoned themselves. Entire families would kill themselves. After years of exposure to an ideology that described the world in apocalyptic terms in which evil would be destroyed and without a vision of the future to rebuild productive lives, to many Germans death seemed the only answer.

For the most part Heinrich Lehndorff's factories only suffered superficial damage from the Allied bombing. Thorn Castle, a prominent landmark miraculously escaped damage. With the end of the war in sight, an Allied fighter aircraft, a P-51 or P-47, searching for a target of opportunity on the return to England dropped a bomb on the far end of the third factory.

Hilda had received a phone call from the number three factory concerning a possible uprising of the conscripted laborers. Having success in the past defusing these tense situations, she was telling them to be patient as the end of the war was in sight and they would be liberated. She figured the crisis had passed and was about to depart when the bomb crashed through the roof. The atmosphere was permeated with dust, debris, smoke and falling pieces of the rafters.

Hilda was pinned under a section of the roof that was diverted by a rafter. In the initial examination her injuries appeared life threatening but after a thorough examination they weren't as severe as expected. After a short stay in the factory hospital, the doctor released her to further recuperate at home in the castle to repair of few broken bones.

At Allied Headquarters the German surrender was signed by the Allies, Russia and France. Heinrich was jubilant when the war finally ended but he viewed the future with mixed emotion, considering the utter chaos of life in general and to the people in particular who would suffer the most from shortages of fuel, clothing, housing and the other amenities that made life bearable.

In regard to his personal life, his thinking turned to a soliloquy of events that could have a serious impact on his future. It was almost a certainty the Allies would convene a legal system to assess the determination and degree of guilt and could end up in a death sentence for those adjudged guilty. It also occurred to him that he could be one of those who could stand trial as he utilized conscripted or slave labor in his factories albeit he had no say in the decision.

Robert Dornburg

WAR ENDS IN THE PACIFIC

The whole problem with the world is that fanatics are
always certain of themselves, but wiser people so full of doubts.
-Bertrand Russell

VJ Day 7 September 1945 marked the end of hostilities in the pacific. The war in Pacific, which began with the bombing of Pearl Harbor on 7 December 1941 by the Imperial Japanese Navy was progressing unrelenting from Guadalcanal, the first major offensive and subsequent island hopping until the capitulation of Japan.

Two major Islands remained on the road to victory, the islands of Iwo Jima and Okinawa. The invasion of Iwo Jima was necessary before the B-29's could gain real effectiveness in the raids on Japan. Damaged B-29's returning from bombing raids that were unable to return to their base in Saipan found a haven on Iwo. It also provided fighter aircraft cover that previously wasn't feasible due to the fighters limited range.

Okinawa, the last major island invasion was located 800 miles from Japan. It turned out to be the biggest and costliest single operation in the Pacific in World War II.

Kamikaze (divine wind), a suicidal attack by a Japanese pilot was the single most effective air weapon developed by the Japanese in World War II. Macabre, effective and supremely practical under the circumstances became virtually the sole method used in opposing the United States striking and amphibious forces and ships being the sole objective.

The *kamikazes* had dwindled before the atomic bombs were dropped on Hiroshima and Nagasaki thus ending the war. The Japanese were saving their aircraft when the homeland would be invaded. Operation Olympic was scheduled for 1 November 1945. When the invasion force appeared off Kyushu, the plan was to fly waves of 300 to 400 kamikazes every hour against the ships. VJ day was September 1945 when the official surrender was signed aboard *The U.S. Battleship Missouri.*

THE DENAZIFICIATION

Fire, water and government know nothing of mercy.
-Albanian Proverb

The predictable result of the denazification was that the majority who were exonerated were classified as followers and emerged as passive participants. Millions of Germans were compelled to fill out lengthy questioners from which tribunals determined the extent of their involvment in the Nazi regime. A bureaucracy was formed to operate the tribunals by placing those in question in one of five categories: followed by major offenders, offenders, lesser offenders and exonerated persons. The SS (Schutzstaffel) and the Gestapo, the dreaded Secret Police, an arm of the SS was placed in the first category as a war criminal organization. Those in the next two categories were liable to terms in labor camps, the expropriation of their property and loss of state pension. In the fourth category they faced the prospect of up to three years in prison which they were not permitted to occupy leading positions and financial penalties. The fifth category only faced financial penalties.

The idea that most Germans were followers made it easier to overlook the broad involvement in the Nazi regime and the degree to which a large number of ordinary Germans had profited from it, at least until catastrophe overwhelmed them at the end of the war.

The way denazification was accomplished left the Germans with a strong sense that the process was unfair and the wide spread perception among the Germans that they had emerged from Naziism and war as victims. Conversely, opinion pools taken by the American military government indicated that initially denazification met with considerable popular approval. However, only a small minority of the German public expressed satisfaction with the plan as administered.

Later on as the two successor states were established, there was widespread popular support for drawing a line under the past for declaring an amnesty so those with a checkered Nazi past would not have to worry whether the past would catch up with them. The way was clear for the reintegration of former Nazis into the West German society and a significant number were able to do so again in West Germany.

In the Soviet occupation zone and the German Democratic Republic, the process of denazification and the consequences unfolded with a different intent. The denazification process was used deliberately to achieve a structural change in the economy and society, not merely to remove former Nazis from positions of political influence or administrative power, but also to strip the economic and social elites of their power and property.

In the east the process ended sooner and less ambiguously. The Soviet military administration opened the way for the rehabilitation of nominal former Nazi party members restoring their civil and political rights and declared denazification in the Soviet Zone officially ended, but unlike what occurred in the west, there was no return of ex-Nazis to positions of influence in civil service or the economy. Instead, the denazification process was used to promote a social, political and economic revolution. Former Nazi party members who were not found guilty of war crimes or had not died in Soviet internment could not integrate themselves into the new antifascist democratic and then real existing socialist order. However, there was no question of public discussions of possible injustice committed in the denazification process and no question of a return by former Nazis to positions of influence and authority.

HEINRICH VON LEHNDORFF'S TRIAL CONTINUES

And the truth shall be known
Anonymous

After the illegal and unauthorized outburst from the prosecution witness, Heinz Steiner, the judge declared a recess to give both sides an opportunity to regroup. He was declared a hostile witness. The trial resumed the following morning.

Heinrich's lawyer decided in the best interest of his client, would be to have him take the stand and refute the accusation of the witness. He went right to the point of contention.

Defense: How did you feel about the massive expansion that was about to begin?

Heinrich: Actually I welcomed the news. Germany was in the throes of a depression. My three factories were having a difficult time showing a profit. I figured if it would be possible to become a sub-contractor to Messerschmitt Aircraft it would be a two-fold idea. Not only would it increase the factories income but also assist the Luftwaffe in the manufacture of the ME-109 fighter aircraft.

Defense: When the project was approved, the question of labor came up. In the indictment you were accused of recruiting and utilizing slave labor from the German people. How do you explain that?

Heinrich: When I was informed the factories initially would be operating fourteen hour days, seven days a week plus building new housing, I realized my labor force was grossly inadequate. Also, many of my workers, except key personnel were drafted into the army and there weren't any Germans available.

Defense: What was the alternative?

Henrich: I said I'll need workers. Where will I get them?

Defense: What was the final solution?

Henrich: The Office of Labor Allocation had been formed. Conscripted hoards from other countries joined the German labor force involuntarily along with Russian POW's.

Defense: This was all in flagrant violation of the laws of war.

Heinrich: Yes, that is correct.

Defense: Could you estimae the number of workers sent to you?

Heinrich: My initial estimate was very conservative. I figured a few hundred workers. Through the years the number was no doubt in the thousands. They were replaced as they died. The Office of Labor Allocation coordinated with the Camp Commander. It wasn't my decision. It was difficult to satisfy their demands. They constantly advised us to increase production especially at the height of the war.

Defense: In effect, there wasn't anything you could say or do?

Heinrich: That is correct. My daughter, who acted as liaison between the company and the Camp Commander attempted on behalf of the workers to improve their working conditions along with food and clothes. She and the Camp Commander had a volatile relationship about the situation.

Defense: Is that what Heinz Steiner was referring to in that outburst yesterday?

Heinrich: Yes, Oberst Steiner raped her resulting in the pregnancy. When I became aware of the fact, I choked him to death. Due to mitigating circumstances I was exonerated by the Peoples Court.

Defense: That's all the questions I have.

After the closing summations by the prosecutor and the defense, the case was turned over to the jury for the verdict. It was with great apprehension that Heinrich waited for the verdict of the jury. If found guilty his future would be in doubt. It wasn't of any great length but seemed interminable until the jury returned a verdict of not guilty on all counts.

RETURNING HOME

Home of the free because of the brave
U.S. Military

When Okinawa was secured, the aircraft carrier received orders to set sail back to Pearl Harbor. Tom had to return without his buddy, John who was shot down returning to the carrier from a raid on Japan. A bond had been formed between them since their flight training days at Pensacola, Florida. During the long trip back to Hawaii, Tom had time to reflect on the past and a much needed rest. No more takeoffs to engage the Japanese kamikazes or raids on the Japanese mainland. Flying in rough weather and landing on the carrier's pitching decks.

After several days at sea the skyline of Honolulu came into view with Diamond Head nearby. The Navy base bore the brunt of the Japanese attack on Pearl Harbor when the war in the Pacific had begun. A Navy tug eased the carrier to the dock and all lines were secured. With the gangplanks in place sailors descended en masse to receive a warm welcome at home. The Navy band played and the dock was crowded with sailors, families and friends. It was a joyous and at times a somber occasion. There were tears of joy mingled with cheers of happiness. The celebrations would come later. At long last, the war in the Pacific was over.

The first item Tom had decided, was call Mary Jane. He gave her an engagement ring the previous Christmas and they planned on a wedding when he returned. However, the telephone lines were long so he decided to have lunch on board and call later. "Mary Jane, this is Tom."

"Where are you?" she asked excitedly.

"In Pearl Harbor. We docked this morning but everything was so hectic, this is the first time I could get near a phone."

"You can't imagine how happy I am to hear from you. Are you okay?" She sounded concerned. "I mean physically. You haven't been wounded or anything?"

"No, I'm still in one piece. Just tired."

"Thank heavens. Its been a long time since I heard from you. I thought you were missing."

"We were busy dodging kamikazes."

"To bring you up to date, Sharon called Velma to tell her about John. I was saddened to hear that."

"We all were. I lost a good friend and I had to collect all his personal belongings to send to his parents.

"When will you be coming home?" She said looking forward to his arrival.

"At the moment I don't have any idea. The inevitable paper work and I'd like to make arrangements to enroll in college for the fall semester. Although the war isn't officially over its unlikely I would be assigned to further overseas duty."

She was apprehensive about his choice of college. She had high hopes he would opt for the inactive reserve and enroll in the University of Pittsburgh. His idea was to retain all the benefits of active duty and enroll at Georgia Tech for a degree in electrical engineering. As she wasn't eager to accept military life, it could prove to become a contentious subject. The news somewhat dampened her enthusiasm.

OBERST FEATHER'S TRIAL

Until you possessed dying and rebirth, you are a sullen guest of the
gloomy earth.
Goethe
-German Philosopher

The notification stated that Oberst Feathers, the Camp Commander
wore a black uniform as an officer of the SS and a member of a declared
criminal organization when the war ended and subject to criminal
prosecution. He was placed in category one. He was a member of the
Waffen-SS. Arguments were being investigated that they were part of
the Army and only nominally associated with the other SS branches;
that some parts of the SS were not involved in the atrocities and could
not be regarded as criminal; that many of the members were conscripts
rather than volunteers. The legalities of these arguments could not be
validated unless the organization of the SS as a unit was understood
and explained on the record.

The Waffen-SS, a fighting force, was a unit comprised of thirty five
divisions with about 550,000 men. The Waffen-SS incorporated from
two-thirds to three quarters of all members of the SS. It acquired the
reputation of not only spreading terror among enemy troops but also
civilians. The horror proposed criminalization of the Nazi organization
which the Waffen-SS was the prime target.

The prosecutions proceedings in general was an agreement that
an organization should not be charged unless most of the members
had joined voluntarily. Two witnesses, both from the German judicial
system had testified they had been drafted into the SS. They sought to
place the blame on the SS leaders and bring them to trial but Himmler
rendered their efforts ineffective.

A German report, "Total Strength of the SS," stated the total strength of 994,941. Waffen-SS 954,443 of whom 368,654 were members of combat divisions, most of the others were engaged in supported activities. However, 39,415 Waffen-SS were engaged in other SS occupations. The prosecution stated the tabulation proved the Waffen-SS was part of the entire SS. The defense countered that although they were labeled as Waffen-SS only nonmilitary duties were performed and therefore no connection with the Waffen-SS troops. The prosecution answered that all the men were carried on the strength of the SS. They were members of the Waffen-SS; wore the same black uniform and were part of the SS. The defense concluded: Everyone of the murderers and criminals who were members of the SS should be indicted. Conversely, thousands of those who served in good faith and who therefore only the morally and metaphysically, not criminally, the guilt which the German people must bitterly endure. The SS was the last and largest convicted organization. With the Waffen-SS and twelve main offices, the tribunal had a long list of the structure and component parts along with a long list of criminal activities. With such a variety of atrocities included the as yet unnamed holocaust, the declaration of criminality for the SS was a foregone conclusion.

A large group of men had been drafted into the Waffen-SS and as they had not come in voluntarily were excepted from the criminal group. Otherwise, in all but a few cases, the group included all persons who had been officially accepted as members of the SS, including the Waffen-SS. Oberst Feathers was a member of the group that had been drafted. The trial was held and subsequently the verdict was not guilty.

After the Nuremberg trial had adjudicated Fritz not guilty, with a sigh of relief he decided to visit his hometown, Schwabisch Gmund before heading back to Thorn Castle. His family had perished in the bombing. An errant bomb from one of the raids on Stuttgart exploded in the vicinity reducing the house to rubble.

He inquired to the whereabouts of a family he had known, named Lauderbach but to his surprise was told they had left Germany and moved to New York City in 1930. They also heard that one of the daughters returned to Germany in 1936 and lived in Mengen near Ulm. Life in Germany was hectic and unsettled at the time and envisioned the future to become even more chaotic. They operated a Gasthof.

The father, Alfred had died in 1928 so the widowed mother, Bertha and two daughters, Elsie and Gretchen and a son, Wilhelm gathered whatever possible and booked passage on a boat to New York and became citizens in 1935.

One daughter, who had returned to Germany, married a dentist and in the following two years, they had a daughter and a son. The family lived in a three story house utilizing the first floor as the dentist's office. When the war became a reality he was drafted into the medical corps. There were shortages of just about everything, especially food which was rationed. We kept in contact with them for awhile but when the war started it became impossible.

A unique facet of this story, we heard about later, the son was drafted in the U.S. Army and as the Allies advanced across Europe, he was stationed in Munich near Mengen. In the meantime time, French soldiers had commandeered their home and assigned the mother and the two children to a separate bedroom. She had to prepare the food for the French soldiers and also taste it before serving. They lived in fear what they might do to them, abduction, harassing, rape or other atrocities. For example, on one occasion when she was shopping for food in town, a soldier asked her for the time. Checking the time, she was ordered to surrender the watch. She reported the incident to the French Captain in no uncertain terms and much to her surprise the watch was returned.

Her brother, the U. S. Army soldier stationed in Munich decided to locate his sister if possible. It might be difficult for an Army soldier to locate a German civilian without asking questions. He succeeded somehow and they had a joyous reunion with her and the children. At first she didn't recognize him. He was a teenager the last time she saw him. She was in doubt until she made lunch and he picked out the onions from the salad and confirmed, indeed he was her brother. On subsequent surreptitious visits, he supplied her with various items that were difficult to acquire including food, courtesy of the U.S. Army. When the war ended, her husband the dentist was an American prisoner of war. He somehow managed to escape but traveling without papers or an ID was impossible. He traveled at night and hid in the garden. He threw pebbles at her bedroom window to attract her attention. The French were unaware that he was hiding in the bedroom and she was providing him with food.

On one of the visits to his sister, her brother suggested taking her husband to the French Commandant's office and persuade them to give his brother-in-law French papers and an ID. Without them he might have been shipped to France even though he had been released by the Americans. The French complied and her husband was free to go home.

The daughter who was living in Berlin was voicing concern for her daughter as she was approaching teenage. The cold war began when the Russians set up a blockade dividing Berlin into the east and west sector. She feared further Soviet advances in Europe and appealed to the family in New York to allow her daughter to live with them. Her grandmother went back to Germany for a visit and it was decided the daughter could spend a few years in New York to further her education. The other daughter who arrived in New York with the family in 1930, lived in New York several years and eventually moved to Florida.

MISSING IN ACTION

Joys are our wings: sorrows our spurs
-Unknown

John was shot down returning to the carrier from a raid on Japan. The Jap Zeros emerged out of the overcast and was surprised to see the Corsairs in front of them. Tom broke right and put the aircraft into a steep dive. John broke left and as it was cloudy no one had observed his aircraft.

Low on fuel, Tom was forced to return to the carrier. After landing he wanted to begin a search but the air boss squelched the idea. The aircrafts would have to be refueled and it would soon be dark. It's difficult to spot someone in daytime and almost impossible at night. Also, they didn't know where to begin the search. At the debriefing, one of the pilots said he saw something that resembled a smoke trail. They were all feeling the affect of fatigue so a search would begin the following morning. Where to begin was the problem. Whether he bailed out or ditched could be a difference of several miles. Also, if he had been successful in getting in his life raft he would have drifted with the current all night. After a disappointing search and nothing had been sighted, they returned to the carrier.

They were unaware that John was sighted in his raft and picked up by a Japanese destroyer limping back to their base in Sasebo on Kyushu after being attacked by a flight of Corsairs. Returning to the carrier and after the debriefing, John was officially listed as missing in action. The destroyer captain wasn't the typical sadistic Japanese officer. He and John had a cordial meeting. He told John that he had graduated from Yale University and majored in International Law. He also recalled the name of the Massachusetts governor at the time was Fairfield. It was indeed a coincidence.

After docking, John and several other prisoners were herded into a boxcar and sent to a POW camp in Yokohoma southwest of Tokyo. The boxcar was crowded so they had the choice of either standing or sitting on the floor. The only ventilation came from the loosely fitted door. As there was no sanitary facilities it soon became a foul smelling environment. John figured it had to be the worst trip in his life.

LIBERATED

Home of the free because of the brave.
U. S. Military

Dropping the atomic bombs on Hiroshima and Nagasaki was enough to convince the Japanese the continuation of the war would be an exercise in futility. The military mind was sadistic, arrogant, cruel and tortuous. Life was expendable and Hari-Kari (suicide) was the answer to failure. *Horryo* was the name given to soldiers who allowed themselves to be captured. They were subhuman and pathic, a disgrace to oneself and family. POWS were judged with great antipathy.

Fairfield, John E. III, Captain USMC, was liberated from the Japanese prison camp in Yokohoma after enduring four months of their tortuous interrogation. If the war continued he felt certain he would be unable to survive. During his incarceration he was awarded the Medal of Honor and promoted to Captain for the twenty nine aircraft he shot down. The award was posthumous as he had been listed as missing in action and presumed dead.

John's parents, Senator and Sharon Fairfild had all but given up hope and that their son survived somewhere. They were estatic when they received the news that John had been liberated from a Japanese prison camp and was being flown to Pearl Harbor for rehabilitation. Sharon in turn called Velma Davison, the newspaper writer John met at the War Bond Rally. It was love at first sight. Not expecting this preponderance of good news she gave vent to a cry of exuberance, for someone returning from the dead, that echoed throughout the entire building-at least on the floor where she worked.

John recuperated in the Naval Hospital for several days until the doctors decided his return to good health could be accomplished satisfactorily at home. He received a tumultuous welcome upon the airport arrival from relatives, friends and well wishers. Although it was only a matter of days, Sharon who was heir apparent to the Knox Plaza Hotels, was able to organize a welcome home party in the Crystal dining room for such an auspicious occasion.

Those in attendance were Tom Korb his ol' buddy from the flight training days. A bond had formed between them that would last a lifetime. Tom's fiance, Mary Jane Evans. Their engagenent was in jeopardy as she disliked military life. Velma Davison, John's love in his life. Nothing short of an emergency would keep her away. Harry Clark, Tom's mentor and his wife Grace. He suggested the Naval Aviation Cadet program to Tom and Kris Lundgren, the generals daughter. She and John grew up together as the two families remained in contact through the years.

It was a delightful evening for a celebration. The highlight of the evening of course was John's return. The dinner was exquisite with numerous champagne toasts, dancing with different partners to get reacquainted, reminiscing about the past, speculating about the future as the evening passed all too quickly.

When the orchestra began playing "*Goodbye,*" Benny Goodman's closing theme, the Senator stood up tinkled his glass with a spoon saying, "Customed as I am to making speeches," soft laughter, "I'd like to say a few words about this evening, a few hundred," groans this time. "Seriously though as politicians say," a knowing smile from the audience, "this was indeed a night to remember. The highlight of this evening was John coming back to us. It was a difficult for all of us but undoubtedly it was the worst period in his life and and we're thankful that it had a happy ending. It provided the opportunity for some of us to see those we don't see as frequently as we'd like, and speaking of visiting, next year we're going to organize the Windmeer get togethers again at Chatham on Cape Cod and Sharon and I hope to see all of you again. In closing, that might be a little over a hundred words, but whose counting. So best wishes for a healthy and happy future." Every one applauded. John's health was progressing rapidly and his thirty day furlough would soon be ending.

ORDERS

Commanding Officer
Marine Corps Air Station
Cherry Point, North Carolina
1. Fairfield, John E. III, Captain USMC
2. Above named officer upon completion of the thirty day furlough will report to USMCAS for physical and return to flight duty status.
3. Mil travel authorized. Report no later tnan 2400 hours 5 October 1946.

No delay en route authorized.
By direction:
Stryker, Frank C. Capt. USMC

IMPASSE

Take away from the heart of stone, and give me a heart of bless,
a heart to love and adore me, to follow and adore thee.
Ambrose of Milan

After Japan had capitulated thus ending World War II, Tom Korb, Captain USMC returned home to a joyus reunion. Relatives and friends met his flight at the airport and the celebration continued at home. Both families had contributed to a catered party for the returning hero. A foot high banner surrounded the room saying "Welcome Home Tom." Everyone had arrived at Mary Jane's home, Tom's fiancee. Among the friends and relatives, a special invitation was sent to Harry Clark, Tom's mentor and his wife Grace. Tom was overwhelmed with the extent of friendship and love. The dining room table was burdened with hors d'oeuvres, small triangular sandwiches, cheese and crackers and other tempting morsels. A punch bowl occupied the other end of the table with libations for those who were inclined toward something stronger.

Tom and Mary Jane were engaged prior to his departure for Okinawa. Now that he returned, a toast was proposed to the forthcoming wedding plans. "This is a pleasant surprise," Tom began in answer to the toast. "I didn't expect such a big welcome and my thanks to all of you. They don't serve food like this on aircraft carriers. As to our wedding plans, Mary Jane and I have a lot of work ahead of us."

The party was a huge success and time passed swifty. Tom had the opportunity to talk to everyone and answered numerous questions about his experiences. It was getting late and time for the party to end. The caterers cleared up everything and all the guests departed. Mary Jane's family drifted upstairs to bed after a busy and emotional day that Tom had arrived safely home.

When they alone, Mary Jane asked Tom if he was able to make any college plans. "Nothing positive as yet. When I left Eva, the CO said I'd be notified if I could make the September class."

"Did you request the inactive reserve status?" she persisted.

"No, this way I'll still receive medical benefits etc., the same as being on active duty? Not for certain, but will no doubt be Georgia Tech and I'll be able to fly out of Cherry Point or Jacksonville or some other field for the week end drills."

"I was hoping you'd opt for the active reserve and go to Pitt," she said sounding disappointed.

"The CO asked if I'd be interested in attending the Naval Academy. It would be to my advantage if I planned on making a career in the Marine Corps."

"You didn't accept I hope."

"No, I said it would be a big transition from an officer to a midshipman."

"I hate to be a wet blanket on your first night at home," she reluctantly continued.

"That's what Velma said," he interrupted.

"As you know," she began. "I'm still helping to maintain the old homestead and Ruth and Jim are saving to buy a house. I really like my job and I'm not too fond of the military life. I was hoping we could stay in Pittsburgh and I could still work while you went to Pitt."

"I'm sorry to be a odds with your plans. When we became engaged I thought everything would work out for us," he said at the swift turn of events. "Is this a *Dear John* type letter? Have you met someone else?"

"No, Tom. I still love you as much as ever. It's just that things aren't the same as when you left."

"I lost track of the times I thought about our future. I could finish college in three years if I went throughout the year. After graduation we could have our own house."

"Unless you were transferred to some ungodly place," she interrupted. "Why can't you get an airline job like Harry?"

"After this war and all these military pilots return to civilian life, pilots will be a dime a dozen. The airlines won't be hiring for years. Also, all the ATC pilots will be returning to their respective airlines."

"You could get a job as an engineer."

"If at all possible, I prefer to remain as a pilot. I enjoy flying and I've been told I do a credible job."

"I would think that with all the flying you did during the war you'd be tired of it."

"It's different if someone is shooting at you."

"I suppose so," she admitted.

"We could go on all night like this, and I didn't get much sleep since leaving Hawaii."

"Well I'm truly sorry, Tom to put you through all this on your first night at home. I should have waited, but you wouldn't want me to be in a situation where I didn't have a peace of mind. Would you?"

"Of course not. I don't think there's any rush to begin making wedding plans. Do you?"

"I think it best to hold off for awhile and reconsider our options," she agreed.

"Perhaps I'm being selfish without considering your options," he suggested.

"No but we're going in two different directions at this time."

"I guess there's not much else to say but good night."

They kissed without much enthusiasm. The evening ended at this unexpected turn of events. His home coming, which began as a joyous celebration, deteriorated into on ominous ending. All his thoughts about the future during the long months of combat suddenly vanished. Wedding plans would be put on hold. How to explain the problem to both sets of parents who were looking forward to a wedding. The only bright spot he figured would be his enrollment in college that ironically served to exacerbate the ideas put forth by Mary Jane. From the excitement and stress of combat flying to the good news that it was time to depart for home. Then to a joyous homecoming and a good feeling about the future. But after this evenings discussion with Mary Jane, he suddenly felt he had reached the nadir in his private life.

The following day as time passed into late afternoon, Tom's mother said, "Aren't you going to call Mary Jane today?"

"No, I think I'll just rest."

"You look as though you had a restless night. You feel alright?"

"I guess I'm just not used to all this peace and quiet."

Mary Jane's mother also observed her reticence. "I thought you'd be calling Tom."

"He said he was tired from the long flight home."

"You look as though you didn't sleep very well last night."

After the long separation both mothers thought they would be eager to get together and make plans for this evening. Suddenly, they both came to the conclusion that something adverse happened last night after everyone had departed.

Both Tom and Mary Jane believed their ideas were valid in regard to the impasse. Mary Jane staunchly defended her position. The two main points of contention; she didn't like military life, she and her sister were the financial support of their widowed mother and two younger brothers. She would have to resign from her job as executive secretary to the president of Continental Foods, but the company offered her a position in the Atlanta Office. Tom was already enrolled in Georgia Tech and offered support to the family as necessary. It appeared they would be unable to resolve their difference of opinion.

Tom would attend college courtesy of the Marine Corps and fulfill his obligation in the reserve at Cherry Point in North Carolina.

When John was liberated from the POW camp in Japan, a welcome home party was arranged by his parents in the main ballroom of the Knox Plaza Hotel.

It really disturbed John when Velma informed him that his ol' buddy and Mary Jane were encountering problems and the wedding was postponed. He assumed that everything was all settled when they became engaged. He figured there must be something he could do to get them together again.

He decided to call her. "Mary Jane this is John. Are you busy?"

"Not at the moment. Where are you and more importantly, how are you?"

"I'm able to sit up and take nourishment," he answered in jest. "Actually, I'm still a little weak but recuperating normally."

"We were all worried about you but it's great to have you home again."

"Mary Jane, Velma told me about the bad news that you and my ol' buddy are at an impasse and the wedding is postponed."

She was at her office. "Hold on a moment, John." A few moments later she said, "My boss just left for a meeting so there probably won't be any calls for awhile."

"I'd like to discuss the situation if you'd like to listen?"

"You have my complete attention."

"My experience in the POW camp was the worst four months of my life. I won't belabor you with all the details. After I was shot down I was rescued by a Japanese destroyer captain who was very cordial and in fact saved my life. When we docked at Sasebo, a group of us were herded into a cattle car to a POW camp in Yokohoma. Things deteriorated rapidly after that. We were interrogated, beaten with a truncheon, solitary confinement, sleep depravation, poor food and water. I never thought I'd survive if the war hadn't ended. I hope I'm not boring you too much."

"Not at all, John. It sounds terrible."

"After being liberated and cheated death twice, I vowed to live my life to the fullest extent possible. I sincerely hope that you and my ol' buddy can arrive at an agreement."

"When you're facing death you realize how tenuous life can be. Life is too short to watch it pass into what the future might be. The important thing is that you two had plans and you love each other. Don't let it slip away."

"You may wish I'd clam up and get off the line. Instead, why not reconsider and get your butt down here tomorrow, if you'll excuse the expression. That's an order, kidding aside, I've never seen two people like you and Tom who deserve to be together."

"You cast a different light on the situation, John. Perhaps, Tom may not be agreeable."

"I have a feeling everything will be getting back on course. Let us know when you'll be arriving and someone will be there to meet you."

Tom called the Fairfield's penthouse and said he would be arriving at four twelve. Mary called and said she would be arriving at four fifteen. It would be a big surprise to both of them.

The limo driver recognized Tom in his forest green uniform and said he was supposed to pick up someone else at the baggage area. Tom's first thought it would be Kris. "It's you," Tom said surprised. "I thought it would be Kris," as Mary Jane entered.

"You sound disappointed."

"No, actually I was not aware that you were coming to the welcome home party."

"John called yesterday and in his words he said, 'Get your butt down here and that's a direct order' "I can't disobey a direct order now, can I?"

"Absolutely not."

"He had a terrible ordeal as a POW. He mentioned that life is too short and live it to the fullest extent. I think he's trying to effect a reconciliation between us. You mentioned Kris. Are you specially meeting her? I'll go back home."

"That isn't necessary. Since they've known each other for many years, it's only natural she would be here to welcome John back home."

Mary Jane realized that if she dropped out of the situation, Kris was more than willing to fill the void.

"How's your family?" Tom asked changing the subject. They continued discussing situations up to the present. Tom thought it was pleasant just talking about things in general without attempting to negotiate their future.

They continued to chat and Tom, noticed a dreamy wistful look on her face. "What?" he asked.

"Maybe John's theory on life is valid. Live like there's no tomorrow. Do you think we could continue where we left off?" she said reaching for his hand.

"It involves a lot of change. Will they be acceptable to you without a strong feeling of remorse? I realize you will be the one to commit the most." The hotel came into view and suddenly she kissed him saying, "We'll have to talk later."

The driver, who had been listening throughout the entire conversation figured that possibly was the quickest change in a person's life that he ever witnessed.

In the past Tom and Mary Jane's discussions were more like a debate to defend their individual positions. Now that they achieved a different level of understanding, it was possible to reach decisions without bias and acquire a positive understanding.

Velma and John were in her room, also having some serious conversations. "When I first saw you I was concerned as you looked so vulnerable. Actually, John, how are you feeling?"

"Considerably better, stronger by the minute. I've been meaning to ask you something."

"Is it a multiple choice?"

"No, just one answer. What to you think about entering in a long term relationship?"

"You want to go steady for the remainder of our lives or have a legal entanglement?"

"Paraphrasing the words to Mary Jane and from my experience

as a POW, life is tenuous so lets make the best of it. What I'm suggesting is that we get married."

"I couldn't agree more." She kissed him exuberantly.

"Careful, I'm still fragile."

"Don't hurt yourself."

"Funny. I just had a thought. Why don't we announce our engagement at the party this evening. That should be a big surprise."

The mahogany room was reserved for the party. After everyone had a glass of bubbly, several toasts were proposed. John's return was the most noteworthy.

"We were going to delay for whatever reason, I forgot," John said. "Anyway, Velma and I are announcing our engagement effective now.

"It indeed was a surprise and another toast was proposed. With some more good news and a few more toasts, I don't think it matters if we didn't have dinner," Velma observed.

John agreed saying "I hope it's time for dinner. We've had enough champagne to float and aircraft carrier."

After dinner, the orchestra began playing again, Everyone chose a partner and Kris singled out Tom. "I'm glad that you and Mary Jane solved your dilemma," she said, "but if you hadn't I thought we might develop a relationship."

"I appreciate you being so candid. There are always a few detours in life until a satisfactory solution is achieved."

He thought she sounded somewhat disappointed. "As I said before, if you ever need a shoulder to lean on give me a call."

"I'll remember that, Kris." They were discussing her new job on the newspaper when the song finished.

After the party ended, John said, "I just had an idea, how about a double wedding? What are your thoughts on that?" he asked everyone.

"It's possible. Probably require more planning. We'll sleep on it, John."

Mary Jane was concerned there was something going on between Tom and Kris. They appeared to be having a serious conversation while dancing. Also, with all the goodbyes, hugs and kisses, it appeared she lingered longer with Tom more than the others. He tried to assure her there wasn't any reason for concern, but thought it best not to reiterate the remainder of their conversation as it would only increase her anxiety.

"What are your thoughts about John's idea of a double wedding," he asked Mary Jane, trying to change the subject.

"For starters it would be difficult to chose the location with all the families involved. Also, there would be quite a bit of traveling to consider. We'll have to discuss all these options with John and Velma."

"Also we'll have to discuss the housing situations in Atlanta. We'll be living there for at least three years," Tom added.

"Everything is moving so rapidly since I arrived today, I suddenly feel overwhelmed," she sighed.

"If you want to reconsider, I'll tell John we need more time to assemble all these items," Tom suggested. "It might be better if we delay the plans indefinitely until we can get some answers."

"These problems aren't insurmountable, Tom, but now you seem eager to agree to a long delay. If you have any qualms about us or anything going on with Kris, I wish you would admit it and we could call off the engagement and free you from the obligation."

He felt exasperated that she's back to Kris again. "You are reading things into this discussion that aren't pertinent. If there was anything between us, I'd level with you." Mary Jane realized if she withdrew, Kris would take her place in a heart beat.

Tom looked at his watch. "It's getting late. Why not sleep on the idea and we'll get together with John and Velma in the morning?" He wondered if they weren't heading toward another impasse.

THE WEDDINGS

If the love of what you're doing exceeds
the labor of doing it, success is inevitable
-Anonymous

John and Velma were waiting in the coffee shop for Tom and Mary Jane. They had agreed to meet for breakfast and discuss the pre-nuptial plans for the double wedding that John suggested. "Sorry we're late," Tom apologized. "We stayed up for a while and talked about the wedding plans and also our plans when we set up house keeping in Atlanta."

They made their choices at the buffet and when everyone was seated, John began, "Velma and I discussed it briefly last night also and came up with a few options. We could have a church wedding and the reception here at the hotel. Any thoughts on that?"

"Other than Pittsburgh, Tom's idea, would require quite a bit of traveling and the cost factors to consider."

"How about a military wedding at Cherry Point? It would be different and colorful. After the ceremony, walking through a canopy of raised sabers, but that would involve even greater distances," was Velma's input.

"What are your thoughts on all this, Mary Jane?" John asked.

"I hate to be a wet blanket, but wouldn't it be simpler if we just made separate plans?"

That brought the discussion to a momentary halt as they tried to evaluate the ideas. "Also, there's a date to consider. Tom and I have all the plans to consider for the move to Atlanta. When I came down here yesterday, I had no idea all this was going to happen."

"I can appreciate your feelings, Mary Jane. I believe a military wedding would be a memorable experience. Another thought, for those at home who would be unable to travel, we could have another reception some time later," Velma offered.

"That sounds like an idea worth considering," John agreed. "It would solve the problem for those who cannot travel."

"I think it's a good idea to slow down a bit and consider some of these options." Tom looked this watch. "Also we'd better think about getting to the airport so the flight doesn't leave without us."

"Lets all keep in touch and sort through all the options so we can make some decisions," John said,

Arriving at the airport, Mary Jane boarded a flight to Pittsburgh and Tom headed south to Atlanta. Mary Jane began to ponder the future. The same reasoning raced through her mind, the same ideas that created the original impasse; she didn't like military life, she would have to give up a good job, she and her sister were the main support of the family and she would have to move to Atlanta. To compound the situation, she now had all the wedding plans to consider. She was beginning to feel overwhelmed.

Velma called her friend the next day to see if she had any other ideas. "Mary Jane have you thought about any plans for the wedding?"

"Actually no, I was beginning to feel smothered by the situation and all the old problems returned. I was considering the idea of reverting to the status quo."

"Oh no," she said. "Have you talked it over with Tom?"

"No, but I had a long talk with my mother. Her idea was that life is full of challenges and some decisions are very difficult, but conversely a new direction in life can be very satisfying. Maybe I'm feeling insecure and I'm using the reasons as an excuse to call off the wedding. She also said, it would be one of the biggest mistakes in my life to cancel the wedding."

She had definitely resolved her problem after the long talk with her mother and they can continued in the planning mode. "Your mother has a keen insight into the future. I'll call John and we can proceed with the plans in earnest."

Velma called John. The phone rang several times and she was ready to hang up when he answered. "I was just talking to Mary Jane," she began without the usual banter and got right to the point. "She was so overwhelmed with everything and was seriously considering calling off the wedding. She couldn't subjugate the problems but used them as a reason for delaying the marriage. She had a long talk with her mother and as a result was able to view the future from a different perspective."

"She called Tom saying she was feeling more optimistic about everything and was ready to proceed with all the plans. We also agreed that a military wedding at Cherry Point was a good idea. If possible when you report for your flight physical, could you talk to the chaplain about the availability of the chapel and also check with someone about using the Officer's Club for the reception?"

"I'll do that but I presume we'll have to set a date for a definite reservation. It should be a Saturday. I'll call Mary Jane and we'll decide on a date that's suitable for all of us."

"What about the reception?" John asked. "For those that can make it will be attending the reception at the Officers Club. We previously discussed the idea of another reception in Pittsburgh."

"If everyone is agreeable, I'll check with the William Penn Hotel for an available date."

"I just got an idea," John said thinking ahead.

"Careful. Don't strain yourself."

"I'll get you for that. What do you think about the idea of filming the wedding and the reception. I think it would add a little authenticity to the reception."

"That's a great idea, John. We'll be talking to each other and get a confirmation on all the plans."

Tom and Mary Jane's transition to Atlanta was more involved. As Tom was already enrolled at Georgia Tech, Mary Jane had to make the biggest adjustment. She was able to secure a similar position with Consolidated Foods in the Atlanta office. They reached an equitable arrangement with the assistance of her sister, to support the family as necessary. Their housing problem was solved when Tom was successful in renting a house from one of the professors who would be taking a one year sabbatical.

With some of Tom and Mary Jane's major problems solved, they were able, with the assistance of John and Velma to concentrate on the myriad plans for the wedding.

Time swiftly dissolved and the wedding day approached.

The weather cooperated. It couldn't have been better if specifically requested. An azure sky dawned bright and clear. Later on a few strato-cumulus clouds slowly floated past as a gentle breeze wafted out of the west. It was a warm mild October eighteenth day for the wedding.

A Navy Chaplain conducted the double ring ceremony and everyone proceeded to the "O" club for the reception line and dinner. Coffee and the wedding cake would be served later.

The music began and the wedding party danced with each other, then everyone was invited to dance. Kris was John's partner. Before the song ended she asked John to switch partners so she could dance with Tom. They danced in silence for a few seconds. "Congratulations and best wishes, Tom."

"You really don't feel that way, do you?"

"Of course I do. I'm sincere about that."

"Why do I get the feeling that you would rather have the situation reversed." He attempted to explain their long term relationship.

"I realize that, Tom. You don't have to explain. Incidentally, there's a possibility of getting a job in Atlanta."

That was an unexpected surprise and his second thought that being in such close proximity might only serve to exacerbate the situation.

"Do you think you'll take it?"

"I haven't decided." The music stopped and it was time for the cake cutting ceremony. After all the guests were served the music began and as a change of pace the women were invited to choose a partner. Kris quickly chose Tom.

"We'll have to stop meeting like this," he admonished, hoping to add a little levity to the situation.

She shrugged. "I guess I'm the type who wears her heart on her sleeve. As I said previously, if you ever need a shoulder to lean on, ring my bell. I'm only a telephone call away." When the music stopped, she kissed him briefly without appearing too obvious, but inwardly accepting the fact that a relationship with Tom wasn't in her future. She felt there are times when the path in life isn't always smooth. She had experienced adversity along the way. Her father, a marine general was killed during World War II. Her brother, a navy commander would become involved in the Korean and Vietnam Wars and now an unrequited love with Tom.

John and Velma boarded an Eastern Airlines flight via Atlanta and continued the following morning on a flight to Nassau for their honeymoon.

Tom and Mary Jane had a reservation at the hotel. The honeymoon would be delayed as they both had obligations on Monday. In December, Mary Jane mentioned that she was feeling out of sorts whatever that encompassed. Tom suggested a visit to the doctor for a physical. It was confirmed, much to her chagrin that she was pregnant.

"Are you sure?" Maybe it's a mistake," Tom said hopefully.

"No, my figuring was faulty," she said trying to hold back the tears. He tried to console her as the tears flowed unabated. "We'll just become parents sooner then we expected."

As the new year progressed the two couples became engrossed in their individual pursuits. With the approaching of summer, the Senator and Sharon began making plans for the June get together. John called Tom to inform him about the get together, but they said it was near the delivery date and traveling might not be advisable. On July fourth

Mary Jane gave birth to a boy weighing six pounds, seven ounces and named him Robert Thomas Korb. Mary Jane's mother went to Atlanta to lend assistance until a workable routine developed, then returned to Pittsburgh.

The end of summer and the entrance of fall brought a chill to the air. A new baby as expected consumed a large portion of Mary Jane's time. Tom's first class didn't begin until two o'clock. They were going shopping. It was raining quite heavy at times. Mary Jane suggested rather than getting the baby all dressed for the inclement weather, Tom would stay home and baby sit while she did the shopping.

It was a fateful decision on that October eighteenth, their first anniversary when tragedy entered their lives. The rain intensified and she never saw the car that ran through a stop sign and hit her car broadside. The impact was so strong it pushed her car sideways through the intersection.

Tom checked the time thinking she was gone longer than usual but figured it was the rain and traffic. Shortly thereafter, he received a call from the police informing him that his wife had been in an accident and could he come to the hospital. His first question was, "how serious is it?" The doctor said, "she arrived at the hospital, DOA-dead on arrival. We believe she suffered massive internal injuries and a serious head injury."

Tom asked about the details of the accident. "The police report stated a seventeen year old boy ran a stop sign traveling fifty miles per hour in a thirty five mile zone. The boy survived with only minor injuries."

Tom called Mary Jane's mother and explained the situation. She asked if the baby was with her and was relieved that Tom was baby sitting. After the initial shock, she asked Tom some pertinent questions. How was he going to take care of a young baby, go to classes, have time for interrupted studying? She suggested bringing the baby to her and she would take care of his three month old son. Sounded like an excellent solution to him. She had solved things again. She lost her husband early in life and raised four kids. Now *de ja vu* was starting over again.

After the New Years Eve party, Tom and Kris were spending more time together when possible. They discussed the pros and cons of marriage. The wifely support plus companionship, sharing the decisions et al, and Tom would become a full time father. They both agreed that marriage would be beneficial and eliminate the long distance commuting and the expensive telephone calls. Kris was overwhelmed with ecstasy at the turn of events.

John and Velma suggested that they could get married at the get together in June at Chatham on the Cape. Velma began making elaborate plans for the wedding but Kris decided on a small wedding and they agreed-it's her day in the sun.

The ceremony took place in the gazebo. The weather appeared to be a problem for the outdoor wedding. A stationary front lingered in the area with strong thunderstorms. However, the rain moved out around noon, breaks in the clouds revealed blue sky. All those who were unable to attend the festivities in Cherry Point arrived in Chatham at the get together. The wedding followed the usual procession of events. As the evening wore on, Kris and Tom departed for Boston to take a morning flight to Buffalo for a brief honeymoon in Niagara Falls. Before departing, they thanked all the friends and relatives for coming and expressed there appreciation for everything John and Velma accomplished for them.

After the honeymoon they planned on a brief visit with both families before leaving on a flight to Atlanta.

Tom was somewhat concerned about Laura, Mary Jane's mother. His son probably thinks that she is his mother, but at some point in time she realizes he would be taking him now that he and Kris were married. Laura was happy that now Tom would become a full time father, much to their relief. He expressed his appreciation for everything she had done. It would have been a difficult situation without her. On the way to Tom's parents he said, "I feel guilty taking the baby with us. She had become attached to her only grandson. It would probably be a few months before they could arrange another visit.

Arriving at Toms parents house, he made the introductions again. They didn't remember Kris at the War Band Rally but did recall an attractive girl who they assumed was part of John's family.

"How do you feel about acquiring a ready made family, Kris?" they wondered.

"It will be a challenge but I'm sure I can rise to the occasion," Kris replied optimistically.

"I'm sure Laura will miss him," Tom's father said, "and so will we. She would bring him here frequently. We were discussing a one year old birthday party. Maybe we can plan a number two next year."

"We stayed longer at Laura's than anticipated, but it was time well spent. Sorry we can't stay longer. It's been a hectic week but we're happy we could spend some time with you, but we'll be back again for another visit."

They all said their goodbyes with hugs and kisses. "Come back again soon and stay longer." All considered they decided Kris will make a good wife and mother.

Arriving back in Atlanta, Kris and Tom occupied the house rented from the professor who was on a sabbatical leave. They quickly became absorbed in the daily routine of domestic living. Tom with his studies and Kris, now a mother to a baby who will soon be a year old. After the daily routine of diaper changing, bathing, feeding, etc., a bond was formed between Kris and the baby. He began to feel at ease with his new mother. Laura would assume the normal position as his grandmother.

THE BERLIN AIRLIFT

We are able to arise from the midnight of desperation to the daybreak
of joy.
-Unknown

On 26 June 1948 the Soviet occupation forces completed the blockade
of Berlin. The Allies had requested the western access routes to Berlin.
They wanted the right to use super highways (autobahns), three railroad
lines and two air lanes much as the highways and other transportation
routes would be used anywhere else in the world. The Russians
declared these requests were excessive; the necessity to protecting
these roads and lanes would pose for the Soviets an extremely difficult
and administrative problem. The Russians said that one central rail
line and one highway would me sufficient. Stalin's reasoning was
that the movement of Soviet forces in addition to the possibility of
other armies using the same route would be too congested and the
Allied Control Council could take a second look. There was nothing
signed as accepting specific routes that might be a denial of right of
access over all the routes. The Allies expected various problems but
did not anticipate any major problems as they were working with the
Russians not against them. The Allies had more immediate problems;
troop movements, refugees acquiring and delivering food to millions
of people for whom they held responsibility. No thought was given to
any future blockades of the city.

        After two days on 26 June the Soviet occupation forces completed
the blockade of Berlin. The question came up, where do we get enough
aircraft? At the time the Americans had only two transport groups in
Europe. The modest fleet included 102 C-47s and two larger C-54s
together with a few B-17s and other aircraft used for administrative

purpose. A small airlift was considered if it became necessary to evacuate the families of the U.S. personnel.

C-47s of the 54th Troop Carrier Wing served as a demonstration of American intentions not to give in under pressure. Some of that pressure came as a direct threat as Yak-9 Russian fighter aircraft buzzed the C-47s on the 275 mile flight path from the Rhine-Main base of the southern air corridor to Berlin. The airlift existed to maintain the U.S. personnel and was not able to sustain the people of the western sectors of Berlin. However, by June it was called upon to haul 500 to 700 tons of cargo a day to the city. The operation was not expected to last, possibly three or four weeks which would be sufficient but could not support the civilian population. It was regarded as just a threatening Soviet harassing tactic, the Russians would not seriously threaten 2.5 million people of western Berlin with starvation. If so, coal, food, potatoes, flour and other necessities would be depleted.

Observers in Berlin had the general impression that the Allies would consider leaving the former German capital if the suffering of the population became too great. The probable outcome if the Russians continued to maintain the blockade because the Allies could not supply 2000 tons of food and other supplies daily by air. The Allied decision to leave Berlin could be viewed as a diplomatic sacrifice undertaken in the interest of the German people. West Berlin had stocks of grain and flour for seventeen days, a thirty two day supply of cereals, a forty eight supply of fats, meat and fish supply for twenty five days, potatoes for forty two days and skim and dried milk for twenty six days. Before the blockade, Berlin imported 15,500 tons of supplies everyday. Now tight, but an adequate amount would require 5000 tons daily.

The crisis was a turning point for the U.S. policy. Three years previously, the Soviet Union had been an ally and Berlin was the target of American and British bombers. In 1946 Churchill had ignited protests by calling for an Anglo-American alliance against the U.S.S.R. The Berlin blockade made Churchill's *Iron Curtin* through Europe an inescapable realty. The Western Allies refused to back way from Berlin.

They developed an airlift, packing passenger planes with coal, potatoes, flour and other necessities. Even the Air Force couldn't believe the fleet could supply Berlin over a long period of time. The main airport was located among apartment buildings and autumn would bring heavy fog. It had never been tried to supply a city of millions by air. The Soviet leaders had planned their strategy to force a withdrawal of the west. It was a monumental task of perseverance and heroism for the Air Force. Flying heavy transport aircraft in all kind of weather that even grounded the birds and being harassed by Soviet fighters but never firing a shot. Crews took off every three minutes around the clock. Soldiers rushed to maintain the aircraft and runways, master a new radar system and even build a new airport. The operation depended on support from Frankfurt, London and the U.S. and on the sacrifice of German civilians in the success of *Operation Vittles*.

Just a few weeks after the operation began, Lt. Gail Halverson began dropping tiny bundles of candy and chewing gum to crowds of children greeting him and other C-54 pilots at the airport. Newspapers printed stories about this *chocolate bomber* and he began receiving packages of candy bars and handkerchiefs in the mail for *Operation Little Vittles*. Children looked forward to receiving sweet treats from these "candy bombers." Halverson said he was moved by the sight of German children at the airlift fence quietly watching his C-54 being unloaded from the airlift. They did not beg for candy or gum that he and other American fliers could give away as trifles. The children's polite stoicism in the face of need impressed Halverson. Soon he began tying candy bars to small parachutes made for handkerchiefs and raining them down where he figured kids would be as his C-54 passed low over Berlin on its way to landing at Tempelhof airfield. He was instructed at one point to stop the drops as a diplomatic measure. A retired fire station in Chicopee, Massachusetts, became an assembly line where volunteers attached candy to parachutes, delivering 15 tons of the goodwill bundles by the time the Berlin airlift ended in 1949.

The Berlin Airlift stopped Stalin's expansion in Europe and set the course of East West conflict for the next forty years. More than sixty U.S. and allied fliers died in the great operation keeping a besiged city fueled, fed and free.

The first flights were a token effort but the west began to believe Berlin could be supported entirely by air activity. But realizations when considering tonnage of prodigious amounts was beyond their capacity to operate. More aircraft were necessary. The Pentagon had arranged for a maximum airlift of seventy C-47s and two C-54 groups. The 600 tons would substantially increase the morale of the German people and seriously disrupt the Soviet blockade. A response like that would disturb the Russians. The airlift would serve primarily as a riposte, a tactical response to the Soviets initiative. They also requesed an immediate dispatch of fighter aircraft and a B-29 group in Germany and if possible B-29s should be sent to Britain and France.

Sensing a long haul, plans called for a forty five day operation. Important as this mission was, the west had to be ready for more logistics. If for some unforeseen reasons and shooting should break out between the Russians and the Allies, they wanted fighters and bombers available for immediate action. A squadron of Dakotas (C-47s) from the British Royal Air Force Transport Command arrived in Germany and planned to ferry about sixty tons a day. The R.A.F. commanders saw the endeavor growing rapidly and two more groups were quickly summoned giving a total of eight Dakotas Squadrons. All the time the Americans had only 102 C-47s available in all of Europe. Old C-47s gathered at the Rhein-Main and Wiesbaden airfields helped to break the blockade.

Calls for more transports yielded the first C-54s which came across the Atlantic from bases in the U.S. Originally intended for transcontinental passenger service, offered advanges over the C47. As an analysis, it would take more than five times as many C47s with more than four times as many crews flying four times as many hours at almost double the cost of gas to deliver 45 tons a day for one month.

In the first day of the airlift to bring as much tonnage into Berlin as possible, the British decided to utilize a lake formed by the Havel River just inside the southwestern border of the U.S. sector. The United Services Yacht Club offered to make temporary moorings and on 5 July the first flying boat splashed down. Another eight R.A.F. Sunderlands were engaged and joined by two civilian flying boats. These aircraft flew out of a former Luftwaffe station on the Elbe River near Hamburg.

Through hour-by-hour, day-by-day evolution rather than by any design, the airlift established itself. The operation represented a remarkable attempt by the Western powers to redeem a bankrupt political situation through technical and mechanical means. It also had a special meaning for the Americans, after what seemed like endless months of talking and arguing with the Russians and accomplishing nothing, a chance to show what people could do when they decided to hold their ground.

With an operation of that magnitude, inevitably there would be accidents. The first casualty occurred shortly after takeoff from Wiesbaden on its way to Berlin, crashed into a low peak in the mountains and plundged into a forest. The aircraft was destroyed by fire and the two pilots and a civilian died. Two weeks later, a C-47 approaching Tempelhof crashed into an apartment building killing both pilots. Condolence calls were made by the Mayor of the six boroughs in the American sector. The Berliners placed a plaque at the crash site. -YOU GAVE YOUR LIVES FOR US- Everyday the people brought fresh flowers and placed them by the plaque. Allied politicians and generals might question the idea, but the people of Berlin displayed no doubt.

As an overall observation the airlift had already become a giant. Material for the aircraft was being used in prodigious quantities. It was difficult to build a reserve supply of engines, propellers and other parts. Aviation gas to Frankfort arrived in cars from Bremerhaven and used immediately. At one point it was necessary to divert the fuel tankers at sea to keep the airlift from being grounded. By the end of June, the airlift appeared to have established itself as an effective operation. It became an official transport service although a variety of problems persisted, it acquired an independent status like a business with highly qualified personnel.

Operational and deficiencies arose from time to time in an operation of that magnitude. Flying in instrument conditions, altitude separation, take-off and landing conditions, holding altitudes without extending into Soviet airspace and if an accident occurred the aircraft were forced to return to their departure airport.

Discussions and contingencies continued between the Russian, the White House and the British. What had quickly become the greatest cargo operation ever imagined was buying time for the West as everyone agreed with varying degrees of faith but no one know how long this act would last. Sooner or later, it was obvious, the Berlin situation would have to figure out a resolution in a Western withdrawal, a Soviet lifting the blockade or war. The western leaders had not made any long range decisions.

The East-West continued in the ambassadorial sessions into August and on into September. For the third day the U.S. airlift had set a new tonnage record: in the past twenty four hours, 472 flights had carried 3572 tons to Berlin. Combined with the British for the first time the Allies delivered moe than 5000 tons in a single day. The Airlift would maintain the Allies in Berlin, but must have an even greater capacity. Washington was persuaded to send sixty-nine C-54s immediately and forty seven more by 1 December. Washington felt apprehensive about placing all their assets in one place. November fogs, Berlin's worst flying time lay ahead and after that the hazards of winter weather.

Aircraft require constant maintenance. Stresses from around the clock, the C-54s were being utilized for purposes other than those which they been designed-to carry people on long flights, not hauling heavy cargo on short flights. Engines straining to lift greater than anticipated loads and with increased frequency of take-offs and landings, components such as landing gear and tires receive greater wear. Two thirds of the heavy burden was coal with the dust sifting into various niches throughout the planes.

The maintenance problem was solved in a variety of methods. The 200 hour inspection was moved from the outdoor facility near Munich to Burtonwood in England where twenty five hundred men serviced the aircraft that required several levels of maintenance beside the attention at the squadron level. Periodic maintenance is required for every twenty hours of flight up to two hundred hours when a major inspection is performed. At twenty two thousand hours a comprehensive overhaul is due and the aircraft are flown back to the U.S.

November was the first and in some ways the worst of the months that gave the airlift the ultimate test. It wasn't the snow or the cold but the fog and freezing rain. To help reduce the interruptions in traffic, a series of high intensity lights were installed that helped to reduce some of the gloomy conditions. The airlift had interruptions due to the fog and low ceilings. As of 30 October a billion pounds of supplies were flown into Berlin on more than 67,000 flights. A negotiated settlement might be the policymakers desire but with diplomacy unlikely to settle the issue until the operation *Vittles* fliers had been tested by the winter, the airlift would continue.

Approaches were being made by GCA (ground controlled approach). A mobile radar unit operated by the controller broadcast corrections to keep the aircraft aligned with the runway and talked the pilot down to landing.

On 1 November in a standardization move, all the C-47s were grounded and all the loads would be flown by C-54s. That night impenetrable fog halted operation for ten hours. Again on 12 November the fog limited operations for two days. Berliners predicted this type of weather will predominate all November. On 16 November after a four day period of severe fog, the authorities said the airlift had passed the first test. On 26 November headquarters announced during the worst winter month, the airlift had delivered an average of 4051 tons a day. The pilots had achieved this level as they took advantage of clear days and delivered as much as 6000 tons to make up when few planes could land. On 28 November the remarkable achievement was celebrated by ordering a coal bonus of 28,000 tons to be delivered to Berlin families with a total tonnage of 113,588. The airlift survived the worst month of flying but there was plenty of fog and ice in the future.

Rumors persisted about the Soviet desire to end the blockade, contrary to the Russians belief, it brought the Western powers together and they succeeded in remaining in Berlin. It also served to develop the air transport system that would be useful in future conflicts. And also guaranteed that those in the western sector would develop an undying hatred of the Russians.

The West could not leave Berlin under conditions that would leave the Berliner subject to Communist oppression and revenge. Such a withdrawal would rattle the confidence of Europeans in the determination to hold the ground against the Russians. But, conversely Berlin could not be indefinitely dependent on the airlift for sustenance. The West had to recognize that the population of a large city in dire need of reconstruction could not subsist on the minumun of food and fuel.

It was believed that some sort of face-saving arrangement must be found before the Soviets would consider any new developments such as an East-West withdrawal from Berlin leading to a general end of the military government in Germany. High level diplomatic meetings between the West-East continued throughout the winter ending in a stalemate. The airlift continued with the crews coping with the fog and equipment chilled by the winter winds. Even though it was considered a mild winter, the people depended on coal for limited warmth and power for electricity that was rationed to two hours a day.

On Sunday in January, the Berliners who had repeatedly shown gratitude to the Allies, found an impressive way to honor their heroes. On the two hundredth day of the airlift they decided to celebrate by paying respect to the pilots who brought them their daily bread. Early in the morning the streets of Tempelhof district began to fill with people. They brought modest gifts-hand carved toys, old silver or china salvaged from the ruins of the city. Thousands rushed onto the field to personally present their gifts to the aircrews, who in two hundred days had performed an almost impossible feat-feeding and warming them and keeping the city alive from the air.

After what seemed to be endless negoitations, rumors were circulating that after further diplomatic discussions a reasonably factual statement, 26 April declared the Soviet government was prepared to lift the blockade. A three paragraph communique was released to the press, stating that all restrictions imposed since 1 March 1948 by the USSR on communications, transportation and trade between Berlin and western zones of Germany and between the eastern zones and western zones will be removed on 12 May 1949. Also, eleven days subsequent to the referred restrictions, on 23 May 1949, a meeting of the council of Foreign Ministers will convene in Paris to consider questions relating to Germany and problems arising out of the situation in Berlin, including the question of currency in Berlin.

The airlift would continue until an adequate stockpile is available and surface transportation can meet the requirements of Berlin. Already, in the first glimpse of freedom, the Russians showed they still controlled the roads and rails in their zones. Soldiers at checkpoints were turning back German trucks saying they didn't have the required licenses and also the trains required Soviet crews and engines. That the blockade was ending in anger would never completely disappear. Even though the blockade was lifted the Soviets in the east showed few signs of wanting to work with the west, Berliners or the Western Allies.

The airlift continued through the summer of 1949 stocking West Berlin warehouses. The final figures on flights and tonnage varied though not by much. Historians put the final flights as of 1 September 276,926, with tonnage of 2,323,006 tons. The official cost estimate was $300 million. The memorial carried a list of 65 persons killed, 31 Americans and 18 British crew members, 11 civilians and 5 Germans.

The airlift was a success story of two neglected sides of fighting forces, the air transport service and the engineers. Though the British played a large part it was essentially an American performance, organized people and equipment on a large scale to cope with an emergency without worrying about the precedents.

On 4 April 1949 a group of Western European foreign ministers in Washington were there to sign the North Atlantic Treaty and complete a resolution for the establishment of the German Federal Republic. The treaty encouraged American participation in regional and other arrangements for individual and collective self defense. What relation did for the airlift, both the effort and success, have in the creation of the new republic? The Western commitment to the establishment of West Germany antedated the imposition of the blockade as did moves toward the North Atlantic Treaty. Both sets of negotiations proceeded slowly, probably no more rapidly than would the case without a blockade. It was clear that this was the most critical crisis of the cold war. The airlift proved a technical, political and psychological triumph, building confidence in the United States among the people of Western Europe.

PAWTUXENT NAVAL AIR STATION

Great dreams contain inexhaustible truths and orient
us toward our future.
-M. Grosso

Marine 867574 was cleared to land at the Patuxent Naval Air Station in Maryland and thereafter a follow me jeep directed the aircraft to the parking area as a slight zephyr or breeze wafted across the tarmac. The pilot Fairfield, John E. III was now a Lieutenant Colonel. He was a test pilot at Pax River as it was called. The school provides instruction to experienced pilots in the processes and techniques of aircraft and system test evaluation.

The school was established in 1945 when the Navy's Flight Test Group transferred from the NAS Anacostia, Washington, D.C. to NAS Patuxent River. The selection process is highly competitive and applicants are accepted by a selection board. The school operates 50 aircraft of 13 types and a pilot can expect to fly between 15 to 20 different aircraft during their tour of duty.

The Navy relied on test pilots to advise if an aircraft performed to the contract specifications, the weapons systems were safe and what effect, if any, changes would alter the aircrafts performance. The test pilots had to evaluate all the changes before the aircraft was assigned to the fleet.

The Navy does not belive in permitting it's pilots to make a career out of test flying. The Navy relies on experienced test pilots to discover new ideas and tactics to be passed on to the fleet. Test pilots recognize their job is to keep their friends in the fleet and perhaps themselves when they return to a fleet assignment, from being blown out of the sky by there own bombs, from crashing and burning because the aircraft they were trying to land had flaws that were undetected before it went to sea.

The fleet is the *raison d'etre* (justification for existence). If the Navy did not go to sea with aircraft as well as ships, it would not need test pilots on shore. A test pilot flies with the fleet long enough to understand the demands of landing an aircraft on a pitching deck at night, but not remain in the fleet too long that the pilot forgets calculus, aerodynamics and other facets of engineering. The experiences in Test Pilot School enables the pilot to understand why testing aircraft for the fleet is different than flying with the fleet. After leaving test flying with all the experience and knowledge acquired, it could in the future, enhance one's Naval career in executive positions and possess the authority to enforce the decision.

John completed the mandatory paper work for the flight test and the debriefing. High cirrus clouds were forming in the west signifying the approach of a weather front. On the drive home, his thoughts began to occupy a subject that was taking a big portion of his time. He was agonizing over the best way to broach the idea with Velma, his wife. He realized it would be an emotional issue. After their initial meeting at the bond tour that he had been assigned after returning from Guadalcanal, their friendship matured rapidly. She almost became a basket case when he was assigned into harm's way after the bond tour. It's difficult to say goodbye to someone you may never see again. It was another difficult time in her life when he was shot down returning to the aircraft carrier from a raid on Japan. He was listed as missing in action and presumed dead.

Arriving home he still hadn't decided on his innocuous approach to the subject. Velma heard his car as he parked in the driveway. She greeted him at the door with the usual welcome home, a kiss and a hug. He removed his uniform jacket and hung it in the hall closet. After he was comfortably ensconced in his reclining chair she gave him a scotch and water saying, "How was your day, my dear?"

"Nothing too exciting," he answered uncommitted. "How was your day?"

"I asked you first."

They continued discussing non-controversial items. During their ensuing opinions, she sensed that something was bothering him. He wasn't in his usual optimistic frame of mind. "I've been pondering over a situation lately. As a test pilot I'm required to make snap decisions on occasion, but this is a far reaching decision that would alter our lives considerably."

"If it's that important, would you like to discuss it now?" she asked apprehensively fearing the worst. "Why not talk about it now and consider the pros and cons of the problem. Maybe clear up the anxiety. How about if I make us some hors d'oeuvres and freshen up our drinks?" She held up her glass in a toast and said simply, "To us, my dear whatever the problem."

"Remember during the war," he began, "when I returned to the Pacific, it almost became an obsession with you and I don't want to place you in that position again."

"That is very considerate of you John, but what did you have in mind?"

He hesitated. Reached for a cracker and cheese. Sipped his drink before beginning. "I've been doing some research lately and I've been thinking about sending in an application for the Astronaut program."

"That is a surprise." she said somewhat relieved. "I had dire thoughts that you met a young pretty Navy nurse at the Officers Club and was thinking about transferring to Hawaii. Does this have anything to do with our not being able to have a family," she asked as an after thought. The idea came out of the blue. She assumed he was content with his job as a test pilot and able to come home for dinner in the evening. No layovers.

"No, not at all," he replied sincerely. "You know my parents would like grand kids but they're content. We have each other and that's what matters. Acceptance is very competitive," he continued, diverting her thoughts about a family. She had three miscarries and felt it was her fault. "About five percent of all qualified applicants are interviewed, fewer than one percent would be hired," he explained.

"Would you be in the one percent?"

"I think my qualifications would suffice. Pilot qualifications differ somewhat from those of mission specialists. With my degree in aeronautical engineering from the Naval Academy, Masters from the University of Maryland, Naval War College in Newport, Rhode Island, would be acceptable. I can pass a first class flight physical but I realize the physicals for astronauts is considerably more extensive, in answer to your question."

"This is all so sudden and unexpected, John. I don't know else to say." She felt discouraged, "It's a difficult situation to resolve," she continued. "Our life style would be drastically altered. We love it here; the friendly local people, the golf course, the beauty of Chesapeake Bay and the Patuxent River." She paused to collect her thoughts then said, "and you enjoy flying as a test pilot?"

"It would be a big change." he admitted. "From my research, it would be a year of training, possibly two flights in the next three years. Four years and I'd probably be finished. Also we'd have to move to Houston."

She took a big swig of her drink trying to reorganize her thoughts. "We'd have to sell our house, resign from a job on the newspaper which I'm enjoying, buy a house in Houston. Also, we wouldn't be able to visit our families as often and leave our friends. Also there's an inherent risk in the space program. It all seems so experimental."

She ate a few hors d'oeuvres and took another big swig of her drink. Neither of them said anything for a few moments. She took another quick sip before beginning again. "I previously said I didn't know what to say now I'm chatting like as magpie. I thought for sure I'd lost you in the Pacific during the war. I don't think I could accept the possibility of losing you again in a program where there is considerable risk. It's true there is a risk in test flying but at least you have the option to eject as a last resort."

They sat there in silence for a few minutes, eating and drinking, attempting to perceive each others thoughts. "What you say is true," John conceded. "I thought in the beginning it would be an emotional issue that's why I hesitated to approach the idea. At least we can discuss it without malice."

"John, my love, I feel you would really like to become an astronaut, but there are also other conditions." She began to enumerate. "After four years, what are your options? Would you work for NASA in some capacity? Could you return to the Marine Corps and continue as a test pilot? I always thought the Corps would be your future. It's been rumored that someday you'll obtain flag rank like General Lundgren. Maybe you could receive a dream assignment and promotion to Brigadier General in command of the Naval Air Test Center. Your first star. In retrospect I feel like Mary Jane when Tom decided to attend Georgia Tech instead of Pitt and she had to give up a good job and move to Atlanta."

"Why don't we have dinner and sleep on it tonight. They say everything becomes clear in the morning," John suggested.

"I made one of your favorite dinners-meat loaf, macaroni and cheese. I put the oven on timer so it will be ready in a few minutes. Or if we have a couple more drinks we won't need any dinner and I'll entice you into my boudoir."

"One thing at a time, my dear." They were facing a profound decision.

ELIZABETH FAIRFIELD

Beauty is born of the coupling of life and love and its harmonies
with pain at life and its discord.
-Matthew Fox

Elizabeth Fairfield, informally know as Beth, graduated from Radcliff College in Cambridge, Massachusetts, her mother's alma mater. World War II was rapidly drawing to an end when she graduated and everyone was in a light hearted mood after four years of war.

There wasn't anything she really needed or wanted. Her parents were wealthy beyond description. Her education hadn't prepared her for anything specifically. Her future was in limbo. Beth joined the drama club in her freshman year and soon discovered she enjoyed acting. She participated in a few skits and began to think that acting might be her forte in life. She was able to join a repertory company gaining valuable acting experience and also did some summer stock around the New England area.

Senator Fairfield and General Lundgren families remained in contact through the years after their service in World War I. The Fairfield's had a son, John and a daughter, Beth. The Lundgren's also had a son, Lars and a daughter, Kristin. Growing up the kids viewed each other as cousins. The families assumed that John and Kris would marry sometime. But Lars, being older, the family hadn't considered a union as Beth was a young teenager.

Before the war, at the annual get together in Windmeer, the Fairfield's summer residence in Chatham on Cape Cod, Beth invited a German student, who she met at Harvard, to join them. Previously they had dinner and a show at the Schubert Theater. He became instantly enraptured with this vision of beauty as John labeled her. Realizing the German's interest in Beth kindled a dormant spark in Lars that made him aware that Beth had become an attractive young lady. Recognizing that he had some competition had captured his attention. She became more than just a family friend.

Lars remained on active duty after the war in the Navy and with the rank of Commander was a destroyer captain. He had decided to make a career in the Navy. He graduated from The Citadel Military College of South Carolina. As he wasn't a graduate from the Naval Academy some what lessened his opportunity to attain flag rank after a promotion to Captain. Lars had been talking to another group and excused himself to talk to Beth. "Hey vision of beauty as John called you."

"Don't you start teasing me again, Lars Lundgren," as he had been prone to do in the past. She wasn't aware of his transition from family friend to prospective suitor.

"Perish the thought. I agree with him. You become more attractive every time I see you." She had indeed blossomed into a tall young lady with blue eyes, light brown hair cascading to her shoulders and a photogenic smile. A black velvet ribbon around her neck was an accent to her fair complexion. "Can I get you a glass of punch? I'd like to discuss something with you." They touched glasses without toasting anything. "Growing up, I guess I always considered you just a kissin cousin," he admitted. "I realize we've known each most of our lives but would you consider spending more time together other than these family gatherings and get to know each other a little more in depth?"

"I guess it's possible," she agreed, surprised and somewhat bewildered with this sudden change in their relationship. "You're suggesting we begin dating? What brought about this sudden change?"

"Yes, if you think it's possible. And I'd like to become more than a kissin cousin." It would be a complete change in their involvement. Previously their association was light hearted with joking, teasing, cajoling. This would raise it to a different level. "It's something to think about. We'll talk later. By the way, what happened to your German friend from Harvard? I heard he would be here."

"He should be arriving soon, he's going back to Germany next week. Now that the war has begun in Europe, I imagine he is anxious to return to Germany if the U.S. becomes involved."

"I'd like to meet him." Lars had begun viewing Beth as a vision of beauty, possibly leading to marriage. In retrospect to a family friend, the German would have been competition to Lars.

KOREAN WAR BEGINS

Fire, water and government know nothing of mercy
-Albanian Proverb

When the Korean War started, Tom's reserve squadron was activated and he received orders to report to Cherry Point, North Carolina for transition training on the F9F-2. The Panther was a jet fighter aircraft. He had been flying the piston engine F4U Corsair in the reserve the past few years. After the training on the F9F-2, the squadron was deployed to Korea where they immediately tangled with the Russian MIG-15s. Tom was successful in downing four MIGs bringing his total to thirty three enemy aircraft destroyed, including the twenty nine in World War II.

The Korean War was winding down after General Eisenhower's campagn promise to end the war if he was elected president. The squadron received orders to return to the states. During the long months in Korea, Tom was giving serious thought to an airline career. He would remain in the active reserve but unlike John he chose not to make a career in the Marine Corps. During his absence Kris gave birth to a six pound girl and named her Greta Anita. Kris and Tom resided with her mother temporarily, pending a new assignment. Kris remembered that she was going to write a letter to Velma. "Speaking of letters," she said to Tom, "did you receive the poem I sent to you when you were still in Korea? I knew you liked the seasons and I saw this poem in a publication, but I don't remember where. I still have a copy of it."

SEASONS

Frosty air and northern lights,
Winter chills and daffodils,
Fields mottled by the winter mist,
Lie spent and waiting for the spring.
Lengthening days that hold back the night,
Meadowlarks soaring in the azure sky,
As clouds float by on gossamer wings,
A pictorial display of light and shade.
Warmer days loom on the horizon,
Fields of amber grains swaying in the breeze,
Watching over a summer day,
Lengthening shadows and falling leaves,
Trees standing silently like pawns,
Flights of geese in their seasonal migration,
Frosty fields portend a change,
Icy fingers drifting in the stream,
Higher clouds gather on the distant horizon,
A harbinger of approaching weather,
A winter wonderland of softly falling snow.
-Anonymous

"I don't recall receiving it," Tom said, trying to remember the letter.

Checking back into her file, Kris found a copy of the poem. She forget to insert it in the letter.

Scuttlebutt was making the rounds that the airlines were hiring and especially interested in military pilots. Tom and Kris discussed the situation and he sent an application thinking it would take sometime before anything transpired. Much to his surprise a letter stating in effect, an interview is scheduled, written tests and a physical. If successful, you will offered a position as First Officer (co-pilot) in a class beginning from said date, reporting to La Guardia Airport, New York. A confirmed space ticket would be enclosed.

After three weeks of ground school, then qualification on the Convair 240 a forty passenger two-engine airline aircraft utilized on short haul routes. The transition from flying a jet fighter aircraft to a piston engined airline aircraft was quite different but he rapidly adjusted to the change.

With the training completed, Tom was assigned Boston as his base.

Everything was progressing smoothly. They found a house in Hamilton, not as pretentious as the Fairfield estate of John's parents but within their budget.

Kris was busy with their son and daughter in addition to decorating the house. Tom was still flying the F9F in the active reserve at the Weymouth Naval Air Station in addition to his airline trips. In a ceremony on his first week-end drill, in addition to the four Migs he shot down in Korea, including the twenty nine that were destroyed in World War II, brought his total to thirty three confirmed kills. He was awarded another Navy Cross and promoted to the rank of Major.

He called John to bring him up to date on all the recents events in their life. And John in turn said he had completed the course at the Naval War College in Newport, Rhode Island and continued his duty at Pax River as a test pilot. They talked about an hour and tried to arrange a meeting but it was difficult with all their committents.

"Regards to Kris, ol' buddy. Hope to see you and Kris at the get together this summer."

"Our best to Velma also." The two old friends had survived everything that life had thrust into their paths. They would keep in touch, perhaps not as often but it was a life long friendship.

Tom's airline career was progressing much to his satisfaction. He was qualified on the DC-6 and DC-7(dual qualification), the main long range aircraft in the fleet and was also certified as a check airman. He had the authority to check out pilots on their initial qualification and also proficiency and line checks. In due course, the chief pilot in Boston retired and Tom was named as the replacement. He was chosen, not only for his natural pilot ability, but he had also been an instructor and the management experience he acquired through the years.

Kris and Tom had settled into a workable routine, enjoying all the aspects of married life with his son, who was born shortly after Mary Jane's untimely death in an automile accident, and their daughter who was born when Tom was in Korea.

They managed to meet John and Velma at Windmeer for the annual get together at the Fairfield's summer residence in Chatham on Cape Cod. They were also able to visit the Senator and Sharon on occasion when they spent some time at the Fairfield estate in Hamilton.

The jet age in the airlines began in 1959 when the Boeing 707 was inaugured into airline service. It was a long range four engine turbo-jet. Also, the Lockheed Electra, a four engine turbo-prop (a jet engine geared to a propeller) entered airline service. It was planned as an interim aircraft between the piston engine and the turbo-jet. Boston was one of the first cities to offer Electra service so it became necessary for Tom to become qualified. Through the years the airline management became aware of Tom's ability and he was considered for another promotion. Due to another retirement, Tom was transferred to New York and assumed the title of Superintendent-Flying Eastern Region.. The airline was divided into four regions-Eastern, Central, Southern and Western. The cities the airline served were under the jurisdiction of that region. Also, the cities that served as flight crew bases utilized a chief pilot who reported to the superintendent of that region. There were those who speculated that Tom's next promotion would be Vice President-Flight with an office at company headquarters.

When offered the promotion which involved moving to New York, Tom and Kris agonized over the decision. They were enjoying the years in Hamilton and it came as an unexpected surprise. They had established roots and it was the first house they owned. Also, Boston being a small base, they were on a first name basis with most of the people from the other departments.

Contrary to that line of reasoning, if he refused the promotion his future career would be negated and he would remain in Boston until he retired or bid into another base as a line pilot. Reasoning in regard to the promotion prevailed and Tom accepted the move to New York. The next big decision-deciding where to live. They looked at several places in New York area but all considered they were favoring Connecticut. As his office would be in La Guardia, which was more convenient than at the time, Idlewild(changed to Kennedy) or Newark. After looking at several houses, they decided on Greenwich for their future home. Due to his position, he was entitled for qualificaion on the highest paying aircraft at the station, which was the 707, regardless of seniority.

Another advantage he just realized, it would enable him to visit his mentor, Harry Clark and Grace. Harry had been responsible for pointing Tom in the direction of the Naval Aviation Cadet Program. Tom was eternally grateful and they had also developed a life long friendship.

POSTWAR GERMANY AND REORGANIZATION

THE MARSHALL PLAN

The chain of human life as limitless as the waves in the sea
that lap the shores. It is good to know of those who went this way
before to think of those who will come after.
-Richardson

Germany had been extensively damaged by the bombing and the street fighting of the war. The country had lost some four and a half million people, but nine million people arrived into the western zone as refugees from the east. After World War II Germany was divided into two separate states. The East section became a satellite of the Soviet Union with other European countries. West Germany was allied to Western Europe and the United States. It received aid from the west and began to build its economy.

Germany had the industrial potential to feed the people and even pay reparations. However, without raw materials it could neither produce nor support anything. The lack of raw material led to hardship, disputes, strikes and further economic chaos. The country needed aid to buy raw material and a currency reform to restore confidence in the German mark and terminate the bartering system and the black market.

The Marshall Plan was formed to restore economic aid to Europe's economy. It would help to rebuild their economies so they could provide a market for American products as well as somewhere for America to invest money. The plan was also political. It was aimed at containing communism and promoting free economic growth. Stalin boycotted the plan as he viewed to it as an American attempt to dominate Europe. It did serve to help Europe's economy after the war.

The United Stated and Britain introduced a German currency reform so the western zone had a stable Deutsch mark. The Soviets walked out of the Control Commission and ended the Allied rule of Germany.

After the war, Heinrich was attempting to reorganize Lehndorff Industries against what appeared to be overwhelming odds. When World War II ended in Europe, cities had been demolished. The economics, financial and commercialism of Europe were in shambles. Europe's communist parties were flourishing, the Soviet Union emerged as the only superpower on the continent. The Marshall Plan was a four year, thirteen billion dollar plan to provide assistance for Europe's economic recovery.

Inflation had reached absurd proportions. Hoarding was rampant and the German mark had essentially lost it's efficiency as currency declining to about one five hundredth of it's official value. The military governor in the American occupied zone of Germany announced a currency reform. A German economic official called it a climate of stagnation in misery, hopelessness and despair that could not endure. The Marshall Plan would control their own destiny with a greater sense of political autonomy.

It was an alarming turn of events for the Soviets. They wanted to keep the west weak and divided. Stalin didn't want a revived Germany, allied with a western bloc in opposition to the Soviets. Also, they feared a prosperous West Germany would attract Germans from the east and ally them with the west. It was a strategic thought and the Soviets wouldn't let it happen without a fight.

In spite of the Soviet's resistance, the West German economy was becoming rehabilitated thanks to the Marshall Plan and Heinrich's factories would become solvent. The Marshall Plan was more than an aid program. It also sought to modernize Western Europe's economics and launch them on a path to prosperity and integration. It also sought to restore Western Europe's faith in democracy, capitalism and enfold the region firmly into the western economic association, eventually ending the military alliance. It was also designed to deter or meet the Soviet threat. The two Germanies were finally reunited after forty five years. The union was greeted with jubilation but stresses became apparent when free market principles were applied to the aging East German industries, resulting in many plant closings and unemployment.

West Germany prospered in spite of the Soviet threats in the cold war. Heinrich was well pleased with the present conditions as compared to the runaway inflation and currency devaluation prevalent after the war.

The Marshall Plan had a profound effect on the economy in Germany which in turn helped the Lehndorff factories to reorganize and ultimately to become profitable. The company remained a sole proprietorship because Heinrich wanted sole control. His banker urged him to incorporate but he wouldn't consider the idea. He wanted to utilize his own capital to expand when he could have sold stock for expansion without using his own capital. It would also make his factories more competitive not only in local markets but also in the international marketplace. He was content to continue as he had done for years and no amount of explaining would change his mind.

REORGANIZATION

Ability is what you're capable of doing,
motivation determines what you do,
attitude determines how well you do it.
-Lou holtz

Heinrich von Lehndorff was completely absorbed in reorganizing his company-Lehndorff Industries. There were a myriad of items to be accomplished in the organization from the production of aircraft sub-assemblies and engines back to the original products-a wire drawing plant, nail and screw factory, electrical products and small machinery. He was also interested in developing other products that could be utilized in the mass rebuilding program of the homes and cities that would be necessary after the war.

The third factory suffered major damage from a direct bomb hit and was rebuilt. The other two factories only received collateral damage. There were numerous contracts to be negotiated for construction and supplies. Another important factor was the financial arrangements with the banks for the economic aid from the Marshall Plan.

Hilda Lehndorff Holtzmann, Heinrich's daughter was an active member of die Firma during the war. She acted as the liaison between the factories and the camp commander that supplied the conscripted labor and also between Goering's Luftwaffte (Air Force). In the new reorganization Hilda would head the activities in the marketing department. She received a degree in economics and business management from Oxford University in England before the war so she was qualified.

There wasn't much information about Oberst Feather's background. It was know that he entered the Officers Corps before the war and through the years attained the rank of Oberst (Colonel).

He was a member of the Waffen-SS which was part of the army. He had been wounded and was unable to serve in an active unit so was appointed Camp Commander as Oberst Steiners replacement. He escaped prosecution as a war criminal when it was proven that he was drafted into the Waffen-SS and did not join voluntarily. From his experience as an Army Officer and Camp Commander, he was a logical choice as Director of Personnel. He and Heinrich worked long hours checking back through the files that were still available, attempting to find previous employees of die Firma. Some of the previous personnel had been drafted into the German Army and replaced by conscripted labor. Now they needed people from laborers to middle management experience.

Heinrich and Fritz had been begun work at the break of day. They were thinking about taking a break when Hilda entered his office with a tray of coffee and biscuits. Erna, her secretary had prepared the tray but was intercepted by Hilda. "Let me do the honors, Erna, I need a few words with my father anyway." Heinrich cleared the middle of his desk that was cluttered with files. "I think both of you need a break."

"Danke," Fritz replied, "I was getting drowsy and beginning to read things that weren't there." Hilda poured the coffee for all of them and they briefly discussed the progress of the reorganization. "Looking through the files, I made a list of some of the previous personnel who may want to return if they're available."

"I'll take the list and Erna and I will make a few calls or mail a note to them." Hilda set her coffee mug on the desk. "Speaking of mail, I was looking through the morning mail and Erna called to my attention one letter in particular." She leafed through the folder and retrieved a letter in a plain white envelope. "No address on it except your name." She hesitated attempting to fathom the reason, and her father was eager to see the letter. She gave him the letter saying, "What are you thoughts, Father?"

The letter contained one piece of white paper with the printed words, YOU WILL BE SORRY. Heinrich looked at her for a few moments trying to determine a reason for what had become a perplexing situation. "Any comments or ideas," he asked.

"In the absence of a post mark it might be a good idea to check the mailroom," Fritz suggested.

"That's a good beginning," Heinrich agreed. "And it also might be a good idea to advise security if we can't solve the problem. It appears to be an internal problem."

They finished the coffee and biscuits and Hilda said, "I'll do all that and keep you advised. You both are so busy. One thing we don't need now," she said resignedly," is more problems. It could be someone holding a grudge for some reason or a malcontent who is trying to get recognition. Or in the other extreme, a misanthrope who hates or distrusts all people."

RELOCATION

The future you trust determines the present you experience
-Unknown

Tom an Kris Korb bought a house in Greenwich, Connecticut. It had three bedrooms and another room that could be utilized as a den, dining and a family room, two and a half bathrooms, one in the master bedroom and a walk in closet. A two car garage, they both would need a car and a breezeway leading into the kitchen. It was more house than they needed and the price was also outside their range but the cost would be commensurate with his future position. Also they liked the house of all that was shown and it had a good location.

Tom's son was only three months old when Mary Jane was killed in an automobile accident. Laura, her mother, to Tom's ever lasting gratitude took over as a surrogate mother until he graduated from college and he and Kris were married. At the time, John pledged a trust fund from the Fairfield Foundation for Tom's son's education at the college of his choice or the Naval Academy. He chose the Naval Academy and would enter in the fall class. Their daughter was born when Tom was serving in the Korean War. She would be a sixth grader.

Moving at best can be described as a hectic operation. Tom had already been scheduled for 707 qualification and was in Los Angeles for the ground school when the moving van arrived. The time they chose did not coincide with the mover, but they had to vacate their house so it was necessary to accept the movers schedule. Tom was able to come home for his forty-eights but Kris was forced to initially decide the location of the furniture and most of the home decorating.

Tom was listed on the first flight out of Los Angeles non-stop to New York after completing the three week ground school. The flight training would be accomplished at Idlewild (renamed Kennedy) as the runways at La Guardia aren't long enough to accommodate the 707. The flight training schedules were predicated on the availability of the aircraft. The regular scheduled flights had priority. Centralized training had not been implemented as yet, then all the training would be accomplished at Fort Worth, Texas. Kris and the kids met Tom at the airport.

THE VIETNAM WAR BEGINS

Anger is the way things are and courage to see
that they do not remain the way they are.
-Unknown

The Gulf of Tonkin Resolution authorized presidential action in
Vietnam after North Vietnamese boats reportedly attacked two
United States destroyers on 2 August 1964. President Johnson ordered
continous bombing of North Vietnam below the 20th parallel. Bombing
of the Hanoi area of North Vietnam by U.S. planes in June 1966. By
December 31st 38,500 troops were stationed in South Vietnam, plus
60,000 offshore and 33,000 in Thailand. Vietnam was a winless war.
The military was saddled by an absurd ROE (rules of engagement)
guidance on targets, tactics and weapon use. The defense department
devised this absurd situation in one of the greatest blunders in a
century full of military misfortune. They failed to listen to on-scene
commanders about how the war should be fought. Instead they tried
to *micro-manage* the war from afar and turned it into one of the worst
military fiascos in America's history.

Tom had been flying in the active reserve in addition to the airline
flying since the Korean War ended in 1953. He had been flying out of
the Weymouth Naval Air Station in Massachusetts until he received
an appointment as a Squadron Commander in Cherry Point in North
Carolina.

Kris and their daughter, who soon would become a teenager
accompanied Tom when he flew to Cherry Point for his monthly drills in
the reserve. Their son was entering his first year at the Naval Academy
in Annapolis, Maryland. Kris' mother was still living at Cherry Point
after her husband Lieutenant General Lundgren, was killed on Okinawa
when the aircraft he was flying in was shot down by a Japanese, who

somehow managed to elude the radar screen, returning from a meeting with General Buckner, the tenth Army Commander. They all enjoyed the monthly reunions.

Now that war with North Vietnam was a reality, Tom and Kris discussed at length the possibility that Tom's squadron would be recalled to active duty. "Looks as though you'll definitely be recalled," Kris said resigning to the fact.

"Fraid so," he agreed. "There's some scuttlebutt making the rounds that it's just a matter of time."

"You survived two wars. You'd think that would be taken into consideration and not sending you into harm's way again." Kris grew up in a military life but it didn't make the separations any easier. Now that she has a family, it's a different viewpoint although her daughter was born while Tom was in Korea.

A thunder storm was in progress and the rain was pelting against the windows. "We just got home in time. Not a good night for flying," Tom observed.

The phone rang and Kris answered. "I'm Ruth, Mary Jane's sister. You must be Kris," she introduced herself. Tom wondered how she got their new number. "How's everything with the both of you?" she continued.

"Things have been moving along smoothly until now that Tom believes he will be recalled for the Vietnam War."

"Sorry to hear that. How's your son?"

"He has been a wonderful son. In fact, he just began his first year at the Naval Academy. We also have a daughter who is almost a teenager. Do you have a family?"

"No we don't, I'm sorry to say." She didn't explain any reason.

"Did you find a house? I recall you were looking."

"Yes we did. I'm surprised you remembered. I finally found a house we liked and were able to afford. Well, nice talking to you, Kris. Is Tom there?"

She passed the phone to Tom. "Hi, Ruth this is a surprise. I've been sitting here listening to your conversation with Kris."

"Sorry to hear you're going to war again."

"I stayed in the active reserve so that's what happens. How's your two brothers?"

"Bill went to Pitt medical school. Currently he's in the Navy based at the Naval Hospital in Hawaii. Ricky works in the medical field also. He's a biologist with a research company. He also had polio if you recall. It has a slight affect on his left ankle so he was exempted from the military."

"My regards to both of them."

"The reason I called, Tom, is that I have some bad news, Laura died about two weeks ago. Thought you would like to know."

"Thank you for calling, Ruth and I'm really sorry to hear that." Mary Jane died in a car accident when their son was only three months old and Laura was a surrogate mother til Tom finished college and he and Kris were married. "What happened, Ruth?"

"She had pancreatic cancer. By the time it was diagnosed it had developed too far and life ended soon thereafter. We sure miss her. She did a remarkable job raising four kids without a husband."

"After the accident I was in a difficult situation. When I called to tell her about the accident and without further discussion or hesitation she said, 'Bring him up here, I'll take care of him.' I was relieved beyond description. She was a jewel. I would write or call her" he continued, "but lately I've been remiss," he admitted. "Our life has been hectic the past few months. I was transferred to New York from Boston and we're living in Greenwich, Connecticut and I had to go to Los Angles for the 707 ground school."

"She always mentioned it when you called or wrote and she enjoyed hearing from you. We will miss her and I'm sure you will also. Best wishes, Tom if you're recalled. Let's keep in touch."

"Thanks again for calling." Kris said before Tom ended the conversation.

A FLIGHT TO REMEMBER

The clock of life is wound but once, and no man has the power to tell just when the hands will stop at late or early hour. Now is the only time you own. Live, love, toil with a will. Place no faith in time, for the clock may soon be still.
-Unknown

After their move from Massachusetts, Tom and Kris were settled in their new home in Greenwich. Kris decorated the home to their satisfaction, their daughter was enrolled in school, Kris was able to free lance a few articles to her known contacts and Tom was completely involved in his new job as Superintendent Flying-Eastern Region. He was instructing pilots for their final flight check and also flying with them for the twenty five hours of line flying but the job required more administration. As he wasn't actually flying the aircraft, to maintain his current qualification required three landings and take offs within the ninety day period. It was possible to replace a pilot, he would be paid for the trip, and take his place. Tom was internationally qualified so he chose a trip from New York nonstop Hawaii, with a layover, then on to Fiji and Australia which would satisfy the current qualification.

To fly nonstop New York to Hawaii it was necessary to advise dispatch of the FOB or fuel on board 75.0 pounds, before departing the west coast for the overwater portion of the flight. The fuel burn was calculated in pounds to arrive at or below the aircraft's max landing weight. About half way to Hawaii, the Coast Guard stationed a ship called *Ocean Station November* to verify position or anything that might occur that the Coast Guard could offer assistance. On one occasion, several years previously, Pan American was having a problem and realized at the reduced speed they would be unable to reach San Francisco. As it was night, so the decision to ditch would be less chaotic at day break. The Coast Guard was standing by for any assistance and when the ditching occurred the aft section of the fuselage separated at the trailing edge of the wing and the Coast Guard assisted the passengers. All survived.

Airline crews crossing the Pacific would contact the Coast Guard crew to chat with them or perhaps just to relieve their boredom. They would take periodic fixes with celestial navigation to establish their position and compare them with the airlines INS (inertial navigation system) position.

"Let's give the ocean station a call. We should be in their area," Tom suggested.

"Ocean Station November, Flight One, how's everything down there?" The co-pilot asked.

"Overcast, the sea is running about four to five feet and the wind is out of the northwest at ten to fifteen knots. Appears to be swinging more to the west. What are your conditions?"

"Clear and smooth. We can see forever." They compared positions. "I'll put on the number one flight attendant. They're serving dinner so she can't say too much, although she's a fast talker, ten words a second with gusts to fifteen. I shouldn't of said that, probably won't serve us dinner now."

"Hi, guys we're serving dinner to the passengers, filet mignon. What are you having?"

"I'm not sure, I'll have to ask the cook. He said something about going fishing."

"Maybe he can catch some mahi-mahi for you. Duty calls. Enjoy your dinner whatever it is."

As she was leaving the cockpit her parting words were, "For what you said about me being a fast talker, you guys are going to get leftovers."

When all the frivolity ended, Tom asked, "Say again your celestial position?"

"We're reading N311518, W1374523."

"We don't have you in sight due to the clouds but it's close to our INS reading. We'll sign off for now, call you on the way back to Los Angeles." Tom finished his dinner. The Flight Attendent didn't make good her threat about leftovers and he was served a filet mignon. One pilot and the flight engineer ate at the same time. "That took the edge off and should hold me til we get to Honolulu. When you call for your dinners, would you ask her to bring me some coffee, cream only?"

Tom checked the wind readout on the INS and received a surprise. "Ocean Station said the winds were swinging to the west." It showed the wind did indeed shift to the west at one hundred fifty knots. "With that much wind on the nose we may have a problem. That wind wasn't forecast. I think we're in the jet stream. Highest recorded winds in a jet stream was 200 MPH. I hope they don't increase to that extent. If so ditching would be necessary. What's our fuel?" He asked the flight engineer.

He made a quick calculation of the fuel gauges. "We have 56.5 thousand pounds remaining. According to the flight plan, we should have 21.5 thousand pounds after landing, but at this fuel burn we will only have 7.0 thousand pounds on landing. We'll be 2.0 thousand pounds into our 9.0 thousand pound reserve.

"Recalculate the flight plan," Tom said to the co-pilot," and we'll switch to long range cruise. Maybe that will help to conserve some fuel. We're beyond the point of no return (enough fuel to return to the departure airport). If the possibility exists that we can't reach Honolulu and forced to ditch, we can reverse course and head back to the ocean station. We would have their assistance with the passengers. It's ironic that we were just discussing Pan Am's ditching and we may be facing the same problem."

"Tom, according to my calculations, assuming the winds persist, we'll have about nine thousand pounds of fuel on landing which isn't much, possibily forty five minutes. It wouldn't be enough for a missed approach."

Tom began contemplating their options. "We'll burn more fuel at lower altitudes and the wind will no doubt be as strong. Higher altitude, we'll use more fuel in the climb. Tom asked the flight engineer if flight level 390 was a habitable altitude?"(Aircraft can maintain level flight in regard to the weight and temperature).

"It is, but we'd have to climb four thousand feet which you realize."

"Reviewing our options," Tom said, "I think the best decision for the moment is to continue at this altitude. At the next check point we'll have a better idea of the fuel burn. It's critical but reaching the airport is better than ditching near the ocean station. Any other ideas," he concluded. The other two members agreed.

"The possibility of a ditching hangs over us like a shroud," he continued to discuss the situation. "I'll explain it to the number one flight attendant. "Hey, how are you guys doing up there?" Without waiting for an answer, she said, "we have some ice cream sundics with strawberries or hot fudge sauce. Anybody want one?"

"Sounds good to me," and the other two shook their heads in agreement. "A situation has developed that we have to discuss, I want to talk to you first so it won't be a big surprise."

The smile on her face diminished somewhat as she asked. "Is it serious?"

"Yes, we picked up a very strong headwind on the nose that has reduced our speed considerably thus increasing our fuel consumption. We will arrive according to our latest calculations with minimum fuel. Also, the possibility exists that we may have to ditch if the wind increases. I'll make a PA to inform the passengers later on but I don't want to unduly alarm them. In about two hours we'll have a better perspective on the situation. If conditions deteriorates, I'll make the PA and you can prepare the cabin for ditching well in advance. I want to avoid panic. We have to make a position report shortly and we can get a wind forecast. I'll keep you informed."

"When you send our position report," Tom said to the co-pilot, "advise them that we expect to have minimum fuel on board at destination."

"Oceanic Control Flight one."

"I read you five square. Go ahead with your report."

"Our position at 0848Z (Greenwich Mean Time) was 311518 north (latitude), 1374523 west (longitude), ETA (Estimated Time of Arrival) Honolulu 1053Z, FOB(Fuel on board) 56.5, FL (Flight level) 350, SOB (Souls on board) 97, encountering CAT (clear air turbulence). Our INS (Initial navagation system) is reading 155 knot wind out of the west. Request the latest wind reports?"

"All the flights are reporting strong winds at all altitudes. The weather bureau forecast the strong winds to continue possibly increase slightly."

"The INS just indicated a five knot increase to 155. Would you call our dispatch and tell them we expect minimum fuel at destination."

"Will do hope conditions improve."

"That doesn't sound encouraging," Tom said. "Our only option is to stay at this altitude and hope the winds will abate. I'll make a PA. I think it best to keep the passengers informed and hope they don't become too agitated." The Flight Attendent had previously brought up their sundies as promised. "Anyone for coffee before I make the PA." Good idea they agreed. "Give her a call." he said to the Flight Engineer." Also tell her I'll be making a PA in a few minutes."

The Flight Attendent delivered their coffee. "Any good news?" she asked hopefully.

"We just made our position report. The winds are about the same with a slight increase, so we lost a few more minutes and used more fuel. We'll let you know if there's any change. We're about two hours behind flight plan."

"Ladies and gentlemen, this is the Captain speaking. This slight turbulence, I'm sorry to say will continue on into Hawaii. Oceanic control said that flights at all altitudes were reporting clear air turbulence. We're encountering very strong head winds and as a result we're about two hours behind flight plan and using more fuel and therein lies our problem. If the winds remain constant, we will arrive at Honolulu with minimum fuel. However, if the winds increase it's possible we may not have enough fuel to arrive at the airport. I don't want to unduly alarm you but as a precaution when we are closer I will advise the flight attendants to prepare the cabin for a possible ditching. I would appreciate you cooperation and I'll keep you informed."

The passengers reaction to the news varied as expected. The flight attendants answered their questions hoping to allay any apprehention that may have developed. Some of the passengers displayed a strong reaction while others more or less accepted their fate hoping for the best.

Tom pushed the call button three times indicating he wanted the number one flight attendant to come to the cockpit. She was a twenty two year veteran with the airline and had dealt with a myriad of problems and situations involving passengers, but ditching was not one of them. She had retained much of her youthfull appearance and from her experience would be reliable in an emergency. "What's happening, Tom? You called for an aerial tanker and they're going to give us some fuel," she said adding a little levity to a serious situation.

"If it were only possible. What were the passenger's reactions?"

"Mixed," she began seriously. " One woman began sobbing hysterically saying, 'We're all gonna die.' Her husband was trying to placate her. Another woman asked us to send a message to her baby sitter. 'I have two kids.' Some were talking quietly to each other. Another couple were arguing, it was their last trip before divorcing when they returned home. Some were praying, one woman was reciting the rosary. One of the more belligerent passengers loudly announced he was going to sue the airline for negligence if he survived. His wife vociferously agreed with a strong epitaph of doom."

"Some people believe that money is their *deity*," Tom interjected.

"I think most are apprehensive but have a wait and see attitude. What's the situation now, Tom?"

"The wind has shifted slightly to the west north west but sad to say increased ten knots. Our latest ETA is three eighteen local time."

"And the fuel," the Flight Attendent finished.

"Don't ask." he said. "Actually, our estimated fuel on arrival is only seven thousand pounds. It's like running on the fumes. I'm going to discuss it with the company to get their viewpoint of the situation. We'll keep you informed."

"Will the fuel tanks be empty then?" she asked wondering how much time would be available before the aircraft sank. The empty tanks would increase the buoyancy.

"There will be some unusable fuel below the standpipe level."

Tom called the company and they discussed the pros and cons of ditching. The ramifications involved in ditching are obvious. As he has all the facts, it was agreed that Tom would be in the best position to make the decision. A pilot-in-command is responsible for everything. The known and the unknown, the seen and unseen and everything in between. That responsibility cannot be delegated or self-abrogated. They would deal with all the problems involved in a ditching, the press, TV and the families.

It was important to keep the flight attendants informed. They would be a big influence in helping to prevent panic if ditching became a realty.

THE DEBRIEFING

Wisdom is the reward you get from
a life time of listening.
-Aristotle

Tom and Kris were very happy with the move to Greenwich, Connecticut. They made many new friends and enjoyed the social life in town. Their son was in his second year at the Naval Academy. Their daughter would be a thirteen year old teenager trying to cope with all the teenage problems. Tom easily settled in with his new job as Superintendent of Flying. Everything was proceeding along smoothly with a few glitches which were to be expected. Monday morning he reviewed the week-end activities. Most incidents were minor and easily solved.

Being the captain of the trip it would be necessary for him to debrief the incident involving the possible ditching. A hearing would be held to determine if any negligence was involved. The flight was computer generated and the required amount of fuel was figured to the destination, an alternate and forty five minute reserve. That amount was verified by the flight engineer's reading on the fuel quantity gauges and agreed with the fuel slip. The fuel burn across the country was normal for the forecast winds. The required amount of fuel was on board when the report was sent to the Los Angeles dispatch in regard to the standard procedure before departing the coast for the overseas portion of the trip.

Although it wasn't a compulsory reporting position, most crews contacted *Ocean Station November* to check their position with the celestial navigation system of the Coast Guard and weather conditions. The crew reported the surface wind was shifting to the west and increasing. The winds aloft had increased to 160 knots from 270 degrees on the inertial navigation system readout whch considerably reduced the forward speed with increased fuel consumption.

The flight plan was recalculated based on current forecast winds and under those conditions it could present a problem reaching Honolulu with the amount of fuel on board. I reported to the flight attendants that a possible ditching existed. At that point we were about two hours from the mainland and they will be kept informed.

The co-pilot made a position report to oceanic control and they confirmed that all flights were reporting strong winds at all altitudes. During the ensuing time, conditions remained about the same except with an increase in the wind of ten knots and it appeared that a ditching was inevitable. I made a PA to inform the passengers of the situation and also notified the flight attendents to prepare the cabin for ditching when they were notified.

I also informed the company that the fuel on board could be less than seven thousand pounds. Obviously, a ditching presents many problems and if at all possible to be avoided. After discussing all the ramifications of ditching as opposed to trying to reach the airport, the captain has all the facts and is the logical person to make the decision. When he signs the flight release, he became responsible for everything involved when the engines are started until they're shut down at the destination.

At the hearing, the details of the flight were reviewed. The company meteorologist stated the unforecast winds were caused by the jet stream that was forecast to remain north but made a sudden dip coming out of the west. The flight was dispatched with the normal procedures. There weren't any maintenance problems. The hearing ended as there wasn't any negligence involved. Also, as there wasn't any aircraft damage or injury to the passengers, it was classified as an incident rather than an accident. The cause of the incident was a weather phenomenon over which we have no control. In his stream of conscious, Tom was attempting to speculate about the debriefing and the hearing upon the return to New York. His thoughts quicky returned to the immediate problem.

"It's decision time, guys." Tom turned to the co-pilot and flight engineer. "Any ideas, comments, suggestions?"

"If we have to ditch with fuel tanks almost empty would aid the buoyancy," the flight engineer offered. "It would give us more time to evacuate the passengers before the aircraft sinks."

"In descent with the throttles at flight idle, we should save some fuel," the co-pilot's suggestion.

"Obviously the company would like to avoid ditching due to the notoriety it would precipitate once the press became involved followed by the lawsuits. My first priority is the passengers welfare. A ditching can become very chaotic. I had to ditch twice during the war at Guadalcanal, " he recalled. "It's an anxious experience and sometime the unexpected happens. A wave lifted my right wing and submerged the left wing and flooded the cockpit. Fortunately, I was able to get out before it sank. I decided the best choice is to try for a landing at the airport. If the fuel gauges are accurate we may be landing on the fumes but all considered it's a better choice of the two options." The co-pilot was an Air Force reserve pilot flying out of Newburgh, New York. The flight engineer began his airline flying career in 1948. All three had logged many hours in the air.

"We concur with your decision, Tom," they both agreed.

"I'll call the number one first, then make a PA. Last chance for coffee. They might be too busy to serve the passengers unless a complete coffee service can be accomplished. This is the captain again. Previously, I mentioned the possibility of ditching and it's still a possibility but I decided we are going for a landing at the airport. All the passengers cheered in regard to his decision. The 707 is the worlds biggest glider. I don't think anyone wants to go swimming anyway. It would be more enjoyable for a swim at the hotel. However, as a precaution I've asked the flight attendants to prepare the cabin for ditching. They will instruct you in donning the life vests, opening the emergency exits etc. Upon landing there will be two impacts-we'll enter the water at a slight nose high position so the nose won't dig into the water. We'll try to land between the swells. The second impact occurs when the aircraft is committed to the water and deceleration is rapid. Hopefully that won't be the case. This will probably be my last PA. When we begin descent we'll be busy with our check lists and radio communications. So please cooperate with the flight attendants. Stay calm and we'll all get through this together."

"The company had advised the control center about our situation so we'll get priority handling. Call approach control," Tom said to the co-pilot.

"Honolulu approach, Flight One."

"Flight One, you are cleared to descend at your discretion. You have a clear track to the airport. Advise when you begin descent."

"The fuel gages will be reading upon landing about zero, Tom," the flight engineer advised. "The landing check list is complete except for the landing gear and flaps."

"Guess we didn't have as much fuel as we figured. Hope the gauges are accurate in the lower range. Advise approach we're beginning a slow descent and have the field in sight. We'll try to keep as much altitude as possible and still land. Initially I'll begin descent at 1000 feet per minute. It maybe necessary to adjust the rate. The INS readout is still showing the ETA at 3:53 local. We don't want to overshoot the runway, we don't want too much altitude either." He wondered if anyone had ever tried to slide slip a 707. A maneuver accomplished by using opposite controls, left aileron and right rudder, for example, to loose altitude without increasing airspeed.

"Contact Honolulu tower on 123.0," approach control advised.

"Honolulu tower, Flight one descending."

"The fuel gages are reading almost empty, Tom." The engine instruments indicated they were still operating.

"Advise the tower we may have a complete engine flameout and we'll try to stretch our glide to the field. How's the landing check list?" Tom asked again.

"Complete except for the gear and flaps."

Tom called the number one flight attendant. "Have everyone braced for landing, it's a touchy situation."

"Tower, we're on a high final. Everything is looking good," the co-pilot advised.

"The emergency equipment has been notified and moving into position," the tower answered.

"This might be an aircraft carrier landing as I want to be sure I can clear the threshold, then plop it on the ground," Tom advised.

"Let us know if we can do anything. We're cheering for you."

"Thanks," then to the co-pilot. "Lets use the speed brake as necessary to dissipate some of this speed. After the landing gear is deployed the drag will be increased considerably." When the flap extension speed is reached, the flaps are partially extended to further reduce the speed and increase lift. Feeling sure he would reach the runway he called for gear down and full flaps. They had to wait for what seemed to be a few interminable seconds until the three green lights indicated the landing gear was down and locked in position. They all breathed a sigh of relief simultaneously that the landing would be successful. At that moment, a light aircraft taxied into position for takeoff and all four engines flamed out. Tom exclaimed! "Oh no, we can't make a go-around anyway."

The co-pilot grabbed the mic and forcefully said, "Get that aircraft off the runway!"

"Not enough time," Tom said. "I'll have to fly over him and hope the landing gear clears him."

The distance between the landing gear and the light aircraft could probably be measured in inches as the 707, traveling at 135 knots touched down safely on the runway, thereby averting what could have been a disaster. Speculating the possibility if the landing gear hit the light aircraft, it would have demolished the aircraft and killed the pilot. The landing gear could have separated from the aircraft, and inboard engines would have contacted the ground and separated from the pylon as the aircraft veered off the runway. Although the fuel tanks were empty, the unusable fuel at standpipe level presented a fire hazard and was sprayed with foam by the fire department.

As they were taxiing to the gate Tom said. "Recalling my previous experience in ditching, everything can proceed according to plan unless something happens at the end." The landing wasn't a grease job (smooth) but was gratefully accepted in contrast to a ditching.

After the successful landing, the cabin erupted into cheers as the passengers released the suppressed emotions of anxiety and fear. They hugged and kissed each other even if they weren't acquainted didn't matter, although at the time they hadn't realized they just survived another situation that could have been a disaster and lived to fly again for another time and enjoy their Hawaii vacation.

Tom, the co-pilot and flight engineer stood at the cockpit door and the flight attendants gathered in the forward galley as the passengers, some rubbing tears of relief deplaned expressing their appreciation for a job well done. The number one flight attendant gave Tom the thumbs up signifying a great job.

What could have been a disaster and made headline news in the paper was covered in a short article on the second page of the second section. Fate is the hunter but will have to continue to search for future situations.

In regard to the light aircraft involved in the near catastrophe, a violation was filed against the student pilot and his medical certificate was revoked pending the disposition of the incident.

A NEW DIRECTION

In the depth of winter, I finally learned
there was an invincible summer.
-Unknown

The year was 1966 and Vietnam was still a young war. It was a mistake. Who could prophecy saying the war would drag on until 1975. The U.S. launched evacuation of Americans from Saigon was a humiliating withdrawal as the communists forces completed the takeover of South Vietnam and the government officially surrendered.

Tom and Kris again discussed the possibility that his squadron would be recalled to active duty. The scuttlebutt making the rounds that it would be announced in the immediate future. In fact, he received notice of a scheduled appointment with the commanding general at Cherry Point during his week-end drill.

Entering the general's office Tom engaged in the usual protocol, "Korb, Thomas J. reporting as ordered, Sir."

"At ease, major. Pull up a chair. I'll call you Tom. Less formal that way. Would you like some coffee?"

"Yes, Sir. Sounds like a good idea."

He buzzed the sergeant in the outer office. "Two coffees please, one black and one with," he looked at Tom, "just cream."

"I've been reading your file, Tom. Quite an accomplishment. You've been in the corps since 1941. Served at Guadalcanal, the central Solomoms and carrier duty with Task Force 58. Awarded several decorations-Silver Star, Air Medal, Distinguished Flying Cross, Navy Cross and again in the Korean War bringing your total kills to thirty three, Purple Heart and the Medal of Honor. Very impressive. By the way, do you keep in touch with your buddy, John Fairfield?"

"Yes, Sir. We call each other occasionally but its difficult to arrange visits. He's a test pilot at Pax River which you no doubt know."

"Yes, he was promoted to Lieutenant Colonel after attending the Naval War College in Newport. He has a bright career in the Corps, no doubt will achieve flag rank in the future." Their coffee arrived. The sergeant, knowing the general's preference handed the black coffee to him and the other to Tom. "Thanks, sergeant that will be all. We were discussing John Fairfield. He is one of the finest individual I've ever met."

"His father is a Senator. He comes from an old, respected and affluent New England family. His mother is heir apparent to the Knox Plaza Hotels. Her brother was Frank Knox, Secretary of the Navy in the Roosevelt administration."

"That I didn't know."

"I was fortunate to be able to spend sometime with John and his family. Also, his father served with General Lundgren during World War I. The families grew up together, you might say and the general was like a father to John."

"I wasn't aware of that either. He is well connected." They had been talking for awhile and the general asked, "Would you like more coffee, Tom and how about a danish?"

"Sounds like a good idea, Sir, didn't have much for breakfast. All the years I've know John, he never abused his position of affluence or influence to accomplish an objective. He did it on his own initiative."

They were finishing the coffee and danish. "How does the saying go?" the general reflected, "we learn something new everyday. That was very interesting, Tom. The reason for this meeting is to inform you that your squadron is being assigned to active duty. I realize you've been a fighter pilot but a new squadron is being formed with the A-6A Intruder, an attack bomber. We think you would be an excellent choice as the squadron commander. I realize fighter pilots don't relish the idea of becoming a bomber pilot."

"Is this an assignment, Sir?"

"Actually, it isn't, Tom. You have the option to remain with your squadron but this new direction carries with it a promotion to lieutenant colonel and of course you would have to get checked out on the A-6, it's a two man aircraft with a bombardier-navigator in the right seat. The squadron would be deployed on a carrier. How does that grab you, Tom."

"I would miss the freedom of a fighter pilot. Would it be possible to think about it?"

"I can't let this drag on. Normally it would be an assignment. With your experience in carrier flying and also your airline experience in management you would be effective in forming a new squadron, I would need a decision by tomorrow. That is the best I can do."

"Thank you for your consideration," Tom replied simply, "and I'll definitely give you a decision by tomorrow morning."

After Tom departed, the general's adjutant, a colonel entered the office. "Did the Major jump at the offer, Sir?"

"Not exactly, in fact I don't think he was enthused about the choice. He was grateful but there are a few reasons why he was reluctant to make a decision today. He was a fighter pilot and they don't like to give up their freedom as he mentioned."

"What about the promotion?" the colonel interjected.

"The Marine Corps isn't his career so he doesn't have to rely on advancement. He has a great future with the airline. He's in management now and when he returns to civilian life the job will be available to him. In regard to salary, as an airline pilot, his salary is probably greater than mine now. It will be interesting to hear what his decision will be tomorrow."

Tom vacillated between the pros and cons of the general's offer. They both had merit. It was a difficult decision. Recalling his conversation with the general about his buddy John, he thought it would be good idea to call John. Maybe help with his decision. The phone was answered by a familiar voice. "Velma, Tom here. How's my favorite girlfriend?"

"Same old, same old."

"You sound as pretty as ever."

"You're always so gallant. Where are you?"

"We're at Cherry Point. Kris and Greta came with me for my monthly drill and Kris has an opportunity to visit her mother."

"That's nice and convenient. What's new with you?"

"Everything was great until yesterday."

"You have some problems?" she sounded concerned.

"The squadron is being deployed to Vietnam."

"Oh, Tom I'm sorry to hear that. How does Kris feel about it?"

"We had discussed it previously and accepted the fact it was only a matter of time. It doesn't get any easier."

"John just get home. He's upstairs freshening up for our pre-dinner cocktail. When are we all getting together again? It's been a long time."

"I'll probably get a few days before I leave. Maybe we can get together for a going away party."

"Sounds good. Looking forward to it. Here's John."

"Hey ol' buddy, from the gist of the conversation I'd guess the squadron is being deployed."

"It isn't official as yet but I had a meeting with the general yesterday, how about that? He verified the squadron would be deployed but gave me a choice. I could remain with the squadron or a new squadron is being formed and they need a new CO. I was chosen because of the carrier experience and also my management experience with the airline."

"That's unusual. Giving you a choice that is. Normally these slots are assigned."

"Anyway, we had a nice chat previously and he asked if I kept in touch with you. He sent his regards."

"I don't recall ever meeting the general. Possibly, he has some connection with Pax River."

"The new squadron will be flying the A-6 A Intruder. I'd be a bomber pilot. I mentioned the fact that I had been flying fighters all the time and most recently the F9F Couger. Incidentally, he said it would carry with it a promotion to lieutenant colonel."

John took a sip of his pre-dinner cocktail and ate a pig-in-a-blanket before answering. "Well ol', buddy it sounds like you have a big decision. What do you think about it?"

"Right now, I'm on both sides of the fence. They say it's the Navy's newest and smartest bomber. Have you had any experience with the A-6?"

"I've never flown the A-6 but during the initial testing for acceptance, if there are serious problems with a particular aircraft type it becomes known throughout and won't be released to the fleet."

"The meeting ended with the general saying he couldn't let this drag on and he wants a decision by tomorrow morning. You have any thoughts on the situation, John. Frankly, I'm undecided. I'd miss flying fighters. The promotion would be great but my future lies with the airline."

"It would be a challenge flying a new aircraft," he reasoned, "and that's a part of my job that I enjoy. In regard to the promotion, it could be quite awhile before you come up for a promotion being you're in the reserves. You might retire as a major and your pension would be greater but I'm sure your airline retirement would be more than adequate, but who can foretell how long this war will continue and you could possibly come out of it as a colonel. Remaining where you are is stagnating. Accepting the offer is progress to the future. If I were you I'd take it. It will also be entered in your record that you declined a command position, although it was voluntary with a promotion in rank to lieutenant colonel."

"I appreciate your valued opinion, John. I hadn't considered it in that direction. I'll let you get back to your libations. Have one for me. As Velma suggested, maybe we can all meet somewhere and have a going away party before I ship out."

"Looking forward to it and whatever you decide, I'm sure it will be the right decision. Regards to Kris, Greta and the Mother."

The following morning Tom was scheduled for an 0700 meeting with the general. He was an early riser. "Have you had your second cup of coffee yet?" Tom answered in the negative. The general called for some coffee. "How about an apple cinnamon muffin? They're delicious."

"Sounds good to me," Tom replied. " Haven't had any breakfast yet."

"What time are you scheduled to fly?"

"I have a 1000 departure. It's a navigation refresher."

"My wife keeps telling me that I shouldn't eat all these calories, but the only thing I can't resist is temptation. Don't tell her about this."

Tom figured the chances of meeting his wife were remote but the general seemed to be in an unusually good mood this morning maybe because he doesn't have to leave for Vietnam. "Are you staying in the BOQ, Tom?"

"No. My wife and daughter are here and we're staying at her mother's home. She is the widow of General Lundgren."

"So your wife is the general's daughter. I didn't know that either. Do you have other children, Tom?"

"Yes, my son just began his second year at the Naval Academy. My daughter will be thirteen. She was born when I was in Korea, my son's mother died in a car accident when he was only three months old. My mother-in-law took care of him until Kris and I were married. I was still in college at Georgia Tech."

"Do you think your son will choose the Navy or Marine Corps after graduation?"

"He hasn't made a decision as far as I know."

"You've had an interesting life, Tom. Speaking of decisions, what have you decided about our situation?" They both finished their muffin and coffee before the general turned to the reason for this meeting.

"I think it best to accept your generous offer and I appreciate the opportunity I was permitted to make the decision."

"I think you made the right choice now and for the future. The sergeant will cut your orders and you'll have to get checked out on the A-6 before assuming command of the squadron. Also, congratulation on your promotion to Lieutenant Colonel, Tom. It isn't official yet but will be shortly." The general walked around to the front of the desk shook hands and wished him good luck in this new facet in his life.

Tom didn't think it necessary to tell the General about his conversation with John.

ORDERS

Bureau of Personnel
Washington, D.C.
Commanding Officer
Marine Corps Air Station
Eva, Oahu, Hawaii
Korb, Thomas J. Lt. Colonel, USMC
1. Upon completion of transition training on the A-6A Intruder will report to MCAS, Eva, Oahu and assume command of VMFA-312. Squadron has previously boarded the USS CVA-19 and will depart in re: the Capt's orders.
2. Mil travel authorized. Report no later than 2400 hours 18 Oct 1966. No delay en route authorized.
By direction:
Devereau, James P. Major USMC

FAREWELL VISIT

This is my wish for you and for all who care for you.
This is my hope for you now and forever that you always
have a friend who is worth that name. `
-Irish Blessing

When Tom received his orders, he thought he'd have more time before departing, he called John and Velma hoping they could arrange a get together on such short notice. It was a beautiful autumn day, Tom's favorite season. A few clouds scudded past in an almost clear sky. The trees welcomed the fall as the sun reflected off the changing foliage with a slight crisp in the air. Colder weather would soon arrive. I wouldn't be here anyway, he mused.

Velma answered the phone. Tom said, "How's Velma since our last conversation?"

"Everything is about the same. What's new with you?"

"My orders arrived and I'll be leaving on the 18th. Would it still be possible to have a get together?"

Checking the calender she said, "That's this Monday. I'll have to check with John. He will be home shortly. No sooner had she said that, John walked in. "Tom is on the phone."

"Hey ol' buddy, what's happening?"

"I just got my orders. I'll be leaving on th 18th."

"That doesn't give us much time. Actually only Saturday unless you could arrive Friday evening," John said as an after thought.

"I have some last minute legalities that I have to conclude, but I think it's possible."

"I really hope so. We want to get together before you leave. Let me know when your flight arrives and I'll meet you at the airport. Or if I can't Velma will." John was delayed at Pax River, so Velma met Tom and Kris at the airport. Greta remained in Greenwich with a babysitter. When they all finally arrived home, Velma whipped up some munchies and John made the drinks. John raised his glass saying simply, "To the future." They hadn't met since last June at the usual get together at Windmeer, the Fairfield summer residence in Chatham on Cape Cod.

They reminisced about past events, families and other pertinent items.   Tom mentioned that Laura, Mary Jane's mother had died.

"She stepped in at the opportune time to take care of your son when Mary Jane died in that auto accident," John mentioned.

"I'll always be grateful for that," Tom said seriously. Speaking of Mary Jane, I'll be shipping out the same day she died, October 18th 1946, twenty years ago. Isn't that a coincidence?"

"It sure is," Velma agreed, "where did all the time go? Dinner will be ready in about fifteen minues if anyone wants to freshen up a bit."

"What's for dinner?" Kris asked.

"Standing rib roast, scalloped potatoes and a green bean casserole consisting of French style green beans, mushroom soup and topped with French style onion rings. The dessert is German chocolate cake and coffee. I made it all except the cake, especially for this occasion. Hope you like it."

"I'm sure we will," Velma, I didn't have any lunch and I'm famished. It sounds like the United Nations."

"You had to say that, Tom Korb, didn't you? You and John are incorrigible."

"I didn't say anything," John innocently replied with a slight grin at Tom's description.

"No, but you were thinking about it the way you two always agreed in the past." The old friends enjoyed all the good natured bantering through the years.

As they were enjoying the delicious dinner, Velma said to Kris, "How's this guy been treating you through the years?" referring to Tom.

"I keep a short rein on him. Seriously, though we've had a wonderful life. As you know Tom's son is beginning his second year at the Naval Academy thanks to John's father for the recommendation. Our daughter will be thirteen and developing into a young lady. We've had a couple of bumps in the road. The Korean War and now the Vietnam War."

"Tom is resilient," Velma said, "and think positive. When John was reported missing I always felt deep down that he would return." However, both Tom and John at times seriously wondered if they would survive World War II. "Now its *déjà vu* all over again."

John said, "Hey this is a happy occasion. Not that I want to change the subject, but what's your opinion of the A-6, Tom?"

"As you know it's the Navy's newest technology designed to deliver weapons on targets completely obscured by weather or darkness. I'll miss the freedom of flying the fighters but it will be a different type of flying. Also, there will be a bombadier-navigator in the right seat so I won't get lonesome." The girls chuckled about that.

"You're probably not aware, but John has to make a decision also." As she was opposed to the idea, she was hoping to enlist at least some token support from Tom and Kris. "Are you going to tell them, my dear?"

"Yes, I was just waiting for the opportunity. I've been thinking about it and we discussed it at great length, applying for the Astronaut program. Velma frowns on the idea."

"That is a big decision," Tom said. "My decision was comparatively easy. It would involve a few years from what I know about it."

"About four years. One year of training and possibly one or two years as commander. I feel I'm qualified and they prefer test pilots plus my engineering background. On the negative side, we'd have to sell the house and move to Houston. Leave all our friends and an area we really enjoy. I'd have to resign from a job I really enjoy. Sounds similar to the decision Mary Jane faced. Plus there's an inherent risk in the space progam. It all seems so experimental was Velma's idea."

The conversation turned serious again. "What's your opinion from the woman's point of view, Velma?" Kris asked.

"Both of you survived the war but this is voluntary and although John and I weren't married at the time, I worried about both of you. Now, Tom has made a decision and yes I'm concerned about him. With the space program, it's like putting yourself in harm's way again. What's you opinion Tom?"

"Both sides have valid view points. My personal opinion is that I wouldn't want to be an astronaut. I'm more attuned to my future with the airline. But I think you visualize it as being somewhat like a pioneer with new frontiers to explore and conquer. So my best wishes with whatever you decide."

"Well that was a serious discussion. How's the Senator and Sharon doing, John?" Kris inquired.

"Very well for the most part. A few minor problems attributed to aging."

"Is he considering retirement?"

"Not unless the people vote him out of office."

"I always think of them as another mother and father," Kris reminisced. We visited them on occasion when they were in Hamilton for a few days. Best regards when you talk to them again. You still like your job at Pax River, John?"

"I can say one thing for it. It isn't monotonous. We fly several types of aircraft. Check them out for initial acceptance to problems that arise in the fleet. It's quite different than flying the same aircraft all the time."

Time was racing inexorably toward the end of the evening. Tom and Kris had reservations on a 0745 flight in the morning. The two couples had developed a life long relationship, kept in touch and visited when possible, their schedules permitting. They all weathered the aging process gracefully. A few gray hairs were visible. They kept their weight within reason, although the girls figures were not as svelte as they had been in the past, but were still considered attractive. The guys, being in the military, remained in good physical condition with exercise and diet control.

"Just a thought, ol' buddy, what about your airline job?"

"It will be there when I return."

"That was a nail biting trip you had a while back when you figured that ditching was a possibility."

"We've been down that road before. The difference being this time we had 97 passengers. The pucker factor was in the stratosphere."

John said, "You did a tremendous job in calculating the long glide with engine power still available and averting a disaster when that light aircraft taxied into postion. I hope the company appreciates your effort."

"I received a letter from the president expressing the company's appreciation. I'll call the cab company and arrange for a pickup tomorrow morning," Tom said.

"Wouldn't consider it ol' buddy. Velma and I will drive you to the airport. We don't mind in the least getting up early. Being Sunday the traffic won't be heavy." Arriving at the airport they engaged in the customary goodbyes, handshakes hugs and kisses. Let us hear from you when possible and best wishes and good hunting," both John and Velma said in unison.

AN IMPASSE

Beauty is born of a coupling of love and life and it's
harmonies with pain at life and its discords.
-Mathew Fox

Elizabeth Fairfield (Beth) graduated from Radcliff College with a
degree in Liberal Arts. She was undecided what path in life she would
follow and had joined the drama club. She enjoyed acting and decided
on drama as her major. She enjoyed all the physical attributes of an
actress. Tall, with blue eyes, light brown hair and a photogenic face.
There were those who would describe her as a young Grace Kelly.

It was the German student's interest in Beth that kindled Lar's
awareness that she had developed into an attractive young lady. As
the war was responsible for the German student's return home had
removed the competition and Lars had an open field. He suggested
to Beth that they raise their relationship to the next stage. She was
surprised since it was always platonic, but she agreed.

Beth was living in the family estate in Hamilton and managed to
become involved in summer stock. It was valuable experience for an
ingenue. With that experience she was able to join a repertory company
performing at various locations during the fall season.

Lars was in the Navy and Beth was on the road with the company
so their relationship had an inauspicious beginning when he was at
sea for the six month cruises. In the meantime, Beth was becoming
recognized as a potential starlet and was receiving prominent roles
and accolades for some of the movies. She was commuting between
Hollywood and Washington where she stayed at her parents penthouse.
The Senator and Sharon had ambivalent feelings about their daughter's
choice of a career. They were happy with her success but felt a career as
an actress can be fleeting.

During his shore leave, Lars would stay at the penthouse on the weekends. On occasion, Beth would fly to Norfolk where he was based. She agreed providing they had separate bedrooms in his condo. After these commuting arrangements had been on for quite awhile, Lars suggested they get married. They discussed the consequences of the future situations. "Considering, after my six month sea duty, I get a thirty day furlough so it would only be five months we wouldn't be together. Between movies you could fly back to Washington or Norfolk."

"That doesn't sound like an equitable solution, Lars. I can't determine when movies begin. Also, some movies are shot on location. Another alternative," she suggested, " you could resign from the Navy."

Lars frowned on that idea. "I hope to be promoted to Captain in the future and command a bigger ship, possibly a cruiser. It's unlikely I could be promoted to flag rank, not being a Naval Academy graduate. I've been in the Navy all these years and I don't particularly want to resign now."

"I don't want to give up acting now either that I'm being offered some good scripts." They discussed the pros and cons at length of long distance commuting without reaching a viable conclusion. It was a perplexing problem. They decided to think about the situation for awhile before making a decision.

Beth decided to call her brother, John. He was instrumental in getting Mary Jane and Tom back together when they reached an impass. She was staying at the penthouse. The Senator and Sharon were attending a luncheon. Lars had week-end duty at the base. She had finished filming a movie and attended the premiere before flying back to Washington. The movie received good reviews in the *L.A. Times* and *Variety*. Velma was working as a volunteer on occasion at the local hospital. John was wrestling with his own problem, whether to apply for astronaut training.

"John this is Beth your little sister." He usually referred to her as my little sister or magnanimously as a vision of beauty.

"I recognize your voice. How's things in show business and where are you?"

"Show business is great, but my personal life is unsettled and at a low point. I'm at the penthouse to answer all you questions. I caught the red-eye out of L. A. last night. I have a problem, brother."

"I hope its not serious?"

"Not earth shaking, but without a solution in sight. Lars wants to get married."

"So what's the problem?"

"Getting married isn't, it's the logistics, to use a military term, that's the problem. Being in the Navy he has sea duty for six months and lately I'm spending more time in L. A. Even if he's ashore, which he is now, I have to commute to Norfolk to see each other. I just finished shooting a movie so we could connect this time. We've discussed it at length and failed to reach an equitable solution."

"You do have a problem," he admitted.

"You got Mary Jane and Tom together," she said hopefully. "You have any ideas?"

"Those six month cruises are a real bear," he concluded. "Unfortunately, it's part of the Navy. Now that you're working in L. A. for the most part exacerbates the problem. Have you asked any of the Navy wives how they handled the situation? Would it be possible for him to request a ship based in San Diego. At least you'd have the six months together. L.A. is only about a hundred miles from San Diego in round figures."

"That's a wonderful idea," she said excitedly. "Also, I'll talk to some of the wives to see how they handled the situation, and it's a simple solution. Why didn't I think of it? You came through again, brother. I hope Lars makes a good husband like you are to Velma."

"I think you're biased but thanks anyway."

"I'll have to call Lars and tell him the good news. Hope we can get together sometime. Regards to Velma."

About a week later an item appeared in the society page of *the Washington Post*.

RISING STAR TO WED NAVAL OFFICER

By Laura Thurston
Staff Writer

Senator John E. and Sharon Fairfeld announced the engagement of their daughter, Elizabeth to Cmdr. Lars Lundgren, son of Ingrid and the late Lt. General Lundgren, USMC. Tentative nuptial plans are scheduled for June at the summer residence in Cape Cod, Massachusetts. Elizabeth or Beth is a rising star in Hollywood movies. Lars is a Navy Commander. They plan to reside in San Diego, Los Angeles or Washington depending on their schedules at the time.

PROBLEMS

Sadly, the song I wanted to sing has never happened.
-Unknown

Two of the Lehndorff factories had been converted from the production of aircraft sub-assemblies and engines to the manufacturing of the wire drawing plant, nail and screw factory, electrical parts and small machinery. The third factory, had suffered the most damage inflicted by an Allied fighter aircraft that dropped its bomb before heading back to England. The three factories would play a vital part in the rebuilding of Germany.

Labor wasn't an overwhelming problem although many of the original employees had been drafted into the German Army never to return and replaced with conscriptive labor. However, many of the Germans were looking for jobs to help rebuild the country. Fritz Feathers, who had been the previous camp commander, was head of the personnel department that required several hundred employees to fill jobs ranging from laborers to management positions.

Hilda Holtzmann, Heinrich's daughter was marketing manager. She graduated from the University of Oxford in England before the war began with a degree in business management and economics. The company hospital, utilized for the most part by the military was renovated. It was just worn out and completely updated. The conscripted laborers were not treated. They were expendable. Hanna, Heinrich's wife took an active part in the hospital and employee housing. The castle had also received a complete refurbishment. Before the war, the castle was the center of many social activities, local meetings, banquets and weddings. During the war it served as a meeting place for the military on occasion. Heinrich and Hilda weren't too enthused about the meetings but it wasn't their decision.

Since the factories were producing sub-assemblies and engines for the ME-109, both the representatives from the Messerschmitt factory and the Luftwaffe stayed there. Even Herman Goering, the Commander of the Luftwaffe was in attendance at times to prod the factories into increasing production.

Also, Willy Messerschmitt who was the namesake of the factory, would make an occasional trip to the castle with his representatives. It wouldn't have surprised Heinrich and Hanna if Adolph Hitler with his Charles Chaplin moustache arrived for a visit much to their chagrin.

They had been working diligently to convert the factories and were tired. They had been operating for several months and Hilda was congratulating herself that everything was operating smoothly except for minor glitches. No sooner had she figured that the time of the *cause celebrae* had passed, one of the department heads rapped on the side of the door to her office which was open but as a courtesy, "Got a minute?"

"Sure, come on in. Pull up a chair. I was just about to ask Erna for some coffee. Want a cup?"

"Yes, danke."

"I hope you have good news, however my intuition tells me otherwise." Erna arrived with their coffee.

"It maybe a mistake," he started with some uncertainty, "but some electrical parts are unaccounted for or missing during inventory. We thought they might have been misplaced or mislabeled so we checked the invoice and they should be there and there wasn't a signed removal."

"Our only option at this time," Hilda figured, "is to have a wait and see attitude. Maybe they'll turn up somewhere. Keep me informed. Perish the thought they were stolen. Thanks for coming in."

"I'll let you know if anything else is missing." During the ensuing weeks the electrical department again reported a timing device and a switch were missing. The wire factory reported a roll of wire and tape was also missing.

Hilda scheduled a meeting with her father. She explained the problem with the missing parts and the notification from the department heads and also the rechecking had been accomplished. In summation, she said, "I think we have a thief in our midst."

Coffee time again. Erna placed a tray of coffee and biscuits on his desk. Just when they thought everything was running smoothly. "I guess we were too optimistic," he offered between bites of a biscuit. "Were there any notes this time?"

"Not that I'm aware, only the two departments are affected so far."

"I think we should get security involved."

"Just a random thought, Father. As electric parts were taken, do you think whoever it is might be planning on making a bomb."

"That's a possibility. Good thinking. Let's call security. Check if they have any further Information?"

IN HARM'S WAY

One more daily wish, that you
Successfully defy the storms of daily life.
-Celtic Blessing

Tom and Kris spent a quiet day before his departure the following morning. This was the second time Kris sent him off to war. The first time was the Korean War in 1952 and their daughter was born before he arrived home. This will be the third war he had served in since he became a Naval Aviation Cadet 1941.

Tom finished packing and doing other chores around the house. It was a rainy, dreary day as the rain drummed against the windows driven by a fifteen knot wind, a small nor-easter. It matched the mood in the house. Their daughter stayed in her room for the most part attempting to stem the flow of tears fearful that she may never see her father again. Tom and Kris reviewed their enjoyable trip to Pax River at the get together with John and Velma. It was difficult remaining upbeat with Tom leaving and John thinking about sending in an application for the astronaut program. "I hope he doesn't go through with it. Velma would be a basket case when it was launched," Tom said.

"Would you like a glass of wine before dinner? I retrieved a leg of lamb from the freezer and its roasting in the oven. Should be ready in about half an hour."

Greta joined them with a soft drink and some hors d'oeuvres.

"Why are wars necessary?" she asked Tom. "They disrupt peoples lives and with all the killing."

"Wars are fought for various reasons whether real or imagined. World War II was fought to stop a tyrannical dictator who had conquered almost all of Europe until he invaded Russia. Korea was dubbed as a police action and in the end nothing was accomplished. Vietnam is a young war and its anybody's guess how long it will last. Wars are immemorial," he continued, "and there will always be dissension among people and countries."

"I don't see why you should go. You already served in two wars. You should get an exemption," she said emphatically.

"It's my job, the same as the airline except I'm in the active reserve and subject to recall as necessary if and when the need arises," he tried to explain.

"I think it should be changed," she said trying to stiffle a few tears.

"I'll be home soon and watching your soccer games."

Kris announced that dinner was ready. They tried to discuss anything but the war. Kris grew up in a military life and her father Lt. General Lundgren was killed on Okinawa. That evening, Tom made and received several calls from friends and relatives including a call from his son at the Naval Academy. "I wish I was going with you," he said.

"By the time you graduate, hopefully the war will be history." Little did he realize the war would drag on for seven more years. He called John and Velma, his lifelong friends. Harry Clark, his mentor, Grace and his family. Kris called her mother and Tom talked to her after they finished. The following morning when Tom was ready to depart, Greta came down, still half asleep to kiss her father goodbye. She gave him a kiss and a hug and began sobbing, reluctant to let him leave. Kris said, "These goodbyes aren't getting any easier." They held each other for a fleeting moment and after a brief kiss, admonished him. "You come back, Tom Korb, this family needs a father and a husband, to laugh, to love, to work with and play. Also we need you to help us look for the green flash as the sun disappears at sunset." It is caused by the light rays from the sun being bent as they pass through layers of differing temperatures of air.

The military transport flew non-stop to Hawaii, a ten hour flight. "I'll be back," he promised. But thinking in the past from his experience in the war, he wasn't sure that he could fulfill his promise. Speculating about the future, he briefly wondered what pitfalls he would encounter on the road to survival in this war. He checked in with the C.O. according to the usual protocol at Ewa, Oahu. He received a warm welcome but the C.O. said he was sorry they didn't have time to chat but the ship was waiting for him. "I'll let them know you're here and on the way. Good luck, Colonel." Being addressed as Colonel was a surprise. He would have to adjust to that.

Tom boarded the carrier, saluted the flag and returned the salute from the sailor on duty. The gangplank was removed, the lines cast off and the carrier was ready for the sea. He was escorted to the bridge and met the captain and the air boss, who were beginning their six months of sea duty. Normally there aren't many marines on board but this time there's an entire squadron. They all shook hands and the captain said, "We're about to get underway." A navy tug eased the huge ship away from the dock and then got underway with it's own power. "The orderly will escort you to your cabin so you can get settled in and we'll visit for dinner."

It was a beautiful day in Hawaii, as much as he was able to see after the whirlwind arrival and departure. A clear sky, light winds, a splendid day for any outdoor activity if it was possible to have the time to enjoy it. He had been hoping to play some golf or tennis for a little exercise. It would be a long trip on the aircraft carrier.

Tom had been settled in with all his gear in the appropriate places. He even had time for a nap to brush away all the cobwebs from the early departure and the long flight. He wanted to be sharp figuring the captain would be inquiring about his ability and experience. They don't like incidents on the flight deck when the deck is active with departing or landing aircraft.

"You all squared away, colonel?" the captain asked at dinner. They dined in the captain's quarters as he wanted more or less a private meeting and was eagerly looking forward to working with the squadron. "As I understand it you have to renew your carrier qualifications." He gestured to the mess steward to begin serving dinner. It would consist of several courses from appetizer, including choice of entrée, to dessert and coffee.

"Yes, Sir. When I finished the A-6 checkout it was decided to accomplish it en route as you will be conducting operations at the time."

"Have you had much experience in carrier flying?"

"Yes, Sir. I flew F4Fs off the *Copahee* en route to Guadalcanal. Then the Corsairs from the *Ticonderoga, Essex* and the *Bennington* with Task Force 38 and 58 in the Linayen Gulf and later Okinawa."

"You never flew jets from a carrier?"

"No, Sir. I don't expect any problems."

"You sound optimistic."

"I always approach something new with the thought in mind that I'll succeed."

"I requested a copy of your service record. I like to get an idea about the people I work with. Very impressive, Colonel. You have thirty three confirmed kills and decorations coming out your kazoo."

"My buddy, John Fairfield and I have similar records until he was shot down when we were returning from a raid in Japan. Presently he's a test pilot at Pax River. He graduated from the Naval Academy. We were cadets at Pensacola in 1941."

"There's a Senator with that name. By any chance are they related?"

"He's John's father."

"Then John was in a class prior to 1941? Are you a Naval Academy grad?"

"No, sir, I graduated from Georgia Tech with a degree in electrical engineering."

"Then you no doubt had a social relationship with the family?"

"We've had some memorable occasions when we were able to get the free time. After Guadalcanal we were assigned to a War Bond Tour. There John met his future wife Velma. My wife is General

Lundgren's daughter. He was killed on Okinawa, returning from a meeting with General Buckner. The Senator's wife's brother was Frank Knox, Secretary of the Navy in the Roosevelt administration. Sorry, Sir, I'm sounding like a name dropper but I've met some wonderful people through John. Presidents, Senators, Generals, Admirals. I was just a young kid who had never been far from home. John opened the doors. I felt like a stranger in paradise."

"As you're in the reserve, colonel, what's your job in real life?"

"I'm an airline pilot. I was flying the 707s. When I was hired the airlines were flying the Convair 240s and the DC-6 and DC-7 piston engine aircraft."

"Will you be able to return to the airline?"

"Definitely, the job is there waiting for me when the war is over or some other reason."

"Airline flying must be dull compared to military flying."

"For the most part. Airlines don't like bad publicity. It isn't good for business. You mentioned airline flying is dull. A few months ago, I displaced one of the captains on a flight from New York to Honolulu to renew my qualifications. We talked to *Ocean Station November* and they mentioned the wind was shifting to the west. We checked our INS and the wind was coming out of the west at 150 knots. The wind wasn't forecast. We refigured the flight plan and fuel was going to be a problem with the probability of ditching. To shorten the story, I kept our cruise altitude and figured a descent rate if the engines did flame out and they did, just pror to landing we were able to glide to the airport. The 707 is the worlds biggest glider.

It almost ended tragically. A light aircraft taxied into position for take-off when we were on a short final and to our relief the landing gear cleared the aircraft. Airline flying has its moments. Fortunately, incidents like that are infrequent."

"That was an exciting trip. The possible ditching was a major problem and had you collided with that light aircraft would have been a disaster. They say accidents are caused by a compounding of failures. Out of curiosity, how do you replace a pilot?"

"As Superintendent of Flying-Easter Region, I'm also a check pilot, and I have that option and the displaced pilot gets paid for his trip."

"That's interesting. I wonder if the Navy could adopt that system," he said facetiously. "Well you've had quite a career, colonel. We'll begin your carrier qual tomorrow. The air boss will give you a briefing."

"I've enjoyed our conversation, sir. The dinner was excellent, my compliments to the chef," he said smiling, "and I'm looking forward to flying the A-6 tomorrow."

The following morning the captain filled in the air boss about their meeting. "He's had a career you wouldn't believe. To top it off, he's an airline pilot in civilian life and also a check pilot. I'm sure he can become adept to carrier flying again."

As the A-6 was a two seater with a bombardier-navigator occupying the right seat, the air boss took his place as they were staying in the traffic pattern for the checkout. Previously he had briefed Tom about the checkout. "You've had previous carrier experience so we'll fly three traps and if everything is go, we'll save the taxpayers some money and call you qualified."

The aircraft's tow link was attached to a lock on the catapult. Tom pushed the throttles to full power but the aircraft was restrained by the holdback fitting. It was designed to snap apart when the catapult sent the 25 ton aircraft down the deck. After the final check, Tom saluted the deck officer signaling he was ready to be launched. The cat officer touched the deck, a signal to the sailor at the end of the deck to push the button, activating the rotary valve that sent a gigantic charge of steam into the catapult. The arm slammed forward separating the holdback fitting and sending the aircraft from a stop to 135 MPH in two seconds. A sudden quiet told them the aircraft was off the carrier and within a few seconds delay the engines took over sustaining flight. They flew three traps and Tom caught the usual third arresting wire for the final conclusion.

Reporting back to the captain, the air boss said, "That was one of the best flights of precision flying I've ever seen. The guy is good and lives up to his reputation."

"At dinner yesterday he said he felt certain there wouldn't be any problems. That's the kind of confidence I like."

The squadron consisted of twelve A-6 A aircraft and twelve pilots in addition to the other personnel necessary to operate a squadron. Tom met and talked to the pilots, bombardier-navigators and mechanics who would be directly involved with the aircraft. Then the other groups. What he expected of them and conversely what they expected from him. He had excellent qualifications from his experience as a squadron commander and the airline operation as superintendent of flying.

The captains orders were to patrol the South China Sea off the coast of Vietnam with preemptive strikes on the main lands as required. Tom's first target with the enemy was the insurgent Khmer Rouge, a growing number of hard-core guerrillas, supplied with weapons from Communist China and the Soviet Union. Although Cambodia was officially neutral, the territory served as a vital link in the Ho Chi Minh trail, the north-south supply line through Vietnam.

It was the dry season, January to June and the Khmer Rouge attempted to strike a mortal blow against the Cambodian government forces in Phnom Penh.

As it was their first flight into enemy territory, Tom elected to lead a three aircraft flight to the target. At 25,000 feet and 450 MPH it didn't take long to go feet dry over south Vietnam. At that altitude they were above the Vietnamese AK- 47 rifles and the 37 and 57 MM guns. It was to be a barrel roll attack. Dive at the target in tandem, drop the bombs and return to the ship.

Their five Mark 82, 500 pound bombs wouldn't cause much damage even if they hit the middle of the road, the objective being to disrupt the supply road to South Vietnam. The old bombs had contact fuses in the nose, not the hard casing or contact fuses that would make a crater by exploding after penetrating the road. The bombs also had obsolete M-990D-2 electrical fuses in the tail that was supposed to prevent the bombs from exploding close to the aircraft.

Tom dove at the road in a 50 degree angle. They had to keep 3500 feet between them and the road, shrapnel from their own exploding bombs might knock them out of the sky before they could pull up from the dive.

Tom pushed the bomb release button on the left side of the control stick, ejecting the bombs from the under side of the aircraft. A loud explosion rocked the aircraft. He realized later that one of the 500 pound bombs on the right wing had only dropped five feet before exploding. At the time they suspected anti-aircraft fire. The blast pushed up the right wing sending shrapnel through the aircraft. The spinning compressor blades were sending out lethal pieces of the engine. The engine was mortally destroyed.

"We've taken a hit!" Tom exclaimed. The red fire warning light glowed on the instrument panel. Then all the warning lights came on simultaneously. Glancing in the mirror on the right side of the cockpit revealed a disturbing sight. Fuel was flowing from the right wing. It could erupt in a fire at any moment and explode. Tom shut off the fuel to the engine but the fire warning light remained on. The engine was no longer functioning and the left engine bore the brunt of keeping the aircraft in the air. Tom pushed the left throttle to the firewall in an attempt to gain altitude. The engine struggled, the engine fire warning light came on and the engine ceased to function.

"We're on fire!" Tom said to his right seat mate. "Left engine has failed also." Bomb fragments had penetrated the hydraulic lines and Tom couldn't move the flight controls-ailerons, elevators and rudder. He attempted to move the stick with as much strength as he could muster but to no avail. The right side did not have a control stick. The aircraft was locked in a 12 degree left bank. They were in an uncontrollable aircraft falling like a brick if it didn't explode in the air. "What was the heading and distance to feet wet."

"090 degrees and 280 miles. That's out of the question anyway."

Their only option remaining was to eject. Their minds flashed back to the ejection procedures. They lowered their seats in the first item to improve their posture. They decided it was better to eject through the canopy than trying to jettison in case it was damaged and couldn't be opened manually. The top of their high backed seats had cutting edges that were designed to open large holes in the plastic canopy. Pulling the ejection lever under the seat would trigger the explosive charges that would propel them through the canopy along with the seat.

The aircraft was plunging earthward from 13,000 feet. They quickly reviewed the remainder of the ejection procedures: keep arms down and close to your sides, press your head and back into the seat, put the underside of you legs flat against the seat, pull down your helmet visor, reach down and give the yellow and black ejection lever a good yank upward.

Tom slapped his fellow crewman's knee. It was the signal to eject. He motioned for Tom to go first. It was a selfless gesture. He reasoned that Tom had a wife and family and he was single. Tom yanked the ejection lever. The charge under the seat exploded against his butt and shot him and the seat through the enclosed canopy. The ridged back of the seat had failed to make a big enough hole in the canopy. His gloved hands jammed against the jagged edge of the small opening. Pain from his cut and bruised hands stabbed him as he hit the atmosphere at 230 MPH winds and began flopping him around like a department store manikin. The onrushing air battered his lip microphone into his lips splitting them. As blood flowed from his lips, he heard a "hump" as the parachute opened automatically at 12,000 feet. The sudden jerk from the parachute wrenched his shoulders and ripped his 38-caliber Smith and Wesson from its holster and swung around hitting him in the face.

Looking down, he was still several thousand feet from the ground.

He felt the blood from his lacerated fingers coagulating in his gloved hands. He was becoming concerned about the loss of blood from his fingers, lips and nose bleed when the holster hit him in the face. He was wondering how much blood he could lose and remain conscious.

As Tom floated to the ground he began to reflect on the promise he made to Kris that he would return and watch Greta playing soccer. Now the possibility existed that he may not be able to full fill his promise. If he survived the landing he could get captured and tortured or killed by the Vietcong. Also the thought passed through his mind when John was sent to the Japanese POW camp and tortured by the vicious captors. He wondered if he would be able to survive that kind of treatment. He glanced at his watch that had some how managed to survive the ejection. He would be forced to travel at night to avoid capture. The time was 2:28. His thoughts flashed back to a saying familiar to aviators-to fly west into the sunset is a flight we all must take for a final check.

Kris usually stayed up to watch the eleven o'clock news. Greta went to bed about nine. Kris thought about Tom, subconsciously at times, wondering if he was okay, where he was and what he was doing. News about the war came on. It was all bad so rather then being depressed further, she shut off the TV and went to bed.

Kris woke up from a thunder storm in progress. A clock projected the time on the ceiling. It read 2:28. She had a disturbing dream and when she recalled the contents of the dream, she began to sob as the tears began to flow. Greta was also awakened by the rolling thunder and heard her mother crying. "Are you afraid of the thunder or did you have a bad dream?"

"It was more like a nightmare. The dream was about your father. He was involved in an accident and was seriously injured. I don't recall anything else about it," she said dabbing away the tears with a tissue. "I've heard of incidents like that I hope it isn't true." Ironically the time was 2:28, the same except for the twelve hour difference in the time zones.

"It's probably only a bad dream." Greta said attempting to console her mother, "maybe when you go back to sleep the dream will continue and you will know what happened."

" I don't think dreams can continue, dear. We'll have to wait to hear if the dream is a reality. When the dream is a nightmare, it might be better if it didn't continue."

The thunder storm continued unabated as the lightning flashes briefly lit up the bedroom. "Can I sleep here tonight, mommy?"

Kris gave her a hug and patted the bed beside her. "What if daddy doesn't come home?" she asked, her voice quivering in disappointment.

Kris hesitated, trying to fathom words of consolation rather than the harsh facts of reality. "But life will continue and we'll plan for the future. After college and whatever career you chose to pursue." A streak of lightning lit up the room again. "The storm is close," Greta exclaimed, as the lightning reflected off the walls.

"We still have each other, your brother and plans for the future." They both slept fitfully, with the possibility that Tom might not return, until the alarm went off. Time for Greta to get ready for school. The dream did not continue.

THE MYSTERY

The only thing necessary for the triumph of evil
is for good men to do nothing.
-Edmund Burke

When Heinrich and Hilda were notified that parts, mostly electric were missing from the factories inventory, they decided to get security involved. This was all precipitated by a letter addressed simply to Heinrich Lehndorff. It wasn't postmarked so it had to be internal company mail. The people who worked in the mail room couldn't shed any light on the situation. Quite a bit of the mail was simply addressed only to the recipient's name.

All the departments were asked to report any missing parts and when they were taken to put a time frame on them. If, in fact a bomb was being produced it might add some urgency to the plan. A meeting was scheduled by Heinrich and Hilda with the security department. When she entered his office she thought something was different. "You have a new desk, Father," more of a statement than a question. "I just got tired of looking at the old desk. It brought a plethora of memories from the past."

"I've been thinking of refurbishing my office. If these offices could talk, they would reveal a lot of history that had transpired here in the past six years."

"Go with the flow, Hilda."

Two men from the security department arrived at the appointed hour. They prided themselves with being punctual. Their uniforms were dark gray with a Lehndorff Industries patch on the right shoulder. They were also armed with a Luger. From their demeanor, it was obvious they served in the military. The taller and slighty heavier was senior of the two. Without any preliminaries he got right to the point. "Herr Lehndorff, can you think of anyone in the past, possibly someone during or after the war who would be holding a grudge against you?"

Heinrich pondered the question, ribbing his chin. "I can't recall anything of significance." He paused momentarily, "There was an incident that maybe remote but occurred during the Nuremberg trials."

"Would you like to elaborate, Herr Lehndorff?"

"When the prosecutor said he had no further questions for the witness, he created an outburst by saying, 'I should be convicted in the death of Oberst Stiener, the camp commander.' "

"I'm not familiar with the situation. Would you refresh our memory?"

"Stiener raped my daughter with the resulting pregnancy. When I became aware of the situation I literally choked him to death."

"That was reason enough for his animosity. Can you remember his name?"

"Definitely. It was Stiener's brother, Heinz."

"Assumimg it was Stiener's brother who sent you the two notes, have you had any other contact with him?"

"None at all."

He pulled a pack of cigaretts out of his breast pocket. "You mind if we smoke? He offered one to Heinrich who refused. "As the notes don't have a postmark, it's possible he's working in your factory or he has access to your company mail system. It's also possible he isn't using his real name but an AKA."

"What's that?" Heinrich asked.

"It means, *Also Known As*, like a fictitious name. I really doubt he would use his real name, but it might be a good idea to have personnel check the names of all the employees. Sometime they use the same initials, just change the name. There's not much we can do now. You might advise the mailroom to be aware of any unauthorized people entering. In the meantime, let us know if there are any further developments."

THE SEARCH

How shall freedom be defended? By arms when it is attacked by arms.
By truth when it is attacked by lies. By democratic faith
when it is attacked
by authoritarian dogma. Always, and in fact, by
dedication and faith.
-Archibald MacLeish

Tom had a general idea which direction to travel if possible. He also realized that civilians and soldiers from miles in the area could see the billowing parachute. He saw the burning A-6 hit a mountain and explode. Tom's fellow crew member had a comparatively painless ejection from the burning aircraft. He feared that he was floating rather fast to earth and would break something on landing. He was drifting toward the center of a village and noticed people looking up at him. Some had rifles and presumed they were soldiers. He attempted to manipulate the risers on the chute to steer him away from the village, but to no avail. The saint that looks after pilots interceded and a gust of wind carried him away from the village.

Both guys buried most of the items from their seat packs. They kept a compass, knife, signal mirror, emergency rations and radio. Tom had accidentally set off the small carbon dioxide bottle used to inflate the life raft and an orange blossom began to rise that would reveal his position. He managed to puncture the tough fabric and the raft deflated. Tom landed about half way on the other side of the hill. Suddenly he sensed an eerie quiet. Then the noise grew louder and more distinct. He heard dogs barking. The men would probably kill him if he was captured. We're in trouble he figured. He began running through the high grass. The shouts of his pursuers grew louder. He crossed a stream and became mired in a rice paddy, reversed course and climbed onto the hard dike of the rice paddy and ran toward the woods on the far side. He ran along a trail then entered the deep jungle growth. He tried not to brake branches that his pursuers could follow and at times crawled on his hands and knees to get through the thickest growth. He saw an animal den and decided to hide in it pulling brush over the entrance.

A group of men approached. He could hear them beating through the woods to flush him out of his cover. They knew he was near as his parachute had caught in a tree but walked past. Like a scared animal he remained hidden and silent.

Night came at last. He decided it was safe to leave and search under the cover of darkness for a suitable area where a rescue helicopter could see him in the morning. The jungle was too thick and the trees too tall for the copter's horse collar to reach the ground if he was located. He continued to hunt for a more suitable pickup area. He kept moving eastward until he came to the top of a hill but the trees were still too high. He walked back to an area of thick underbrush and decided to remain there for the remainder of the night and hope for rescue in the morning. He tried to sleep but the adrenalin in his body kept his senses alert.

The bombardier-navigator, except for a few bruises came through the ordeal relatively unscathed. He stopped running at ten P.M. He was on a hill still dangerously close to the village. He could hear dogs barking but he needed a rest. His throat was dry but hadn't stopped to sip the water from the streams. He picked out a few Charms candies from his survival vest that created a little moisture for his dry throat.

The moon was full. This would have been welcome as it made it easier to land on the carrier at night. Now it made it easier for the soldiers trying to find and kill him. He decided his best odds were to hide someplace where a helicopter could land. He found thick brush near a lone tree he could use as a marker for the copter to land. He buried himself in the underbrush and waited for the dawn. He was overwhelmed with loneliness, but like Tom he couldn't sleep.

During the night they both heard trucks entering the village with troops that spread out looking for the hated Americans. They stayed in their hiding places listening and worrying as the soldiers passed so close they could have touched them.

In the light of the pre-dawn they heard the engines of an Air Force C-54 transport aircraft circling at 10,000 feet over their last known position. Tom's partner in the disaster called the aircraft on his pocket radio but wasn't sure if the call had been received.

About an hour and a half later they heard the distinctive wop-wop-wop from the two Sikorsky UH-34D helicopters. They figured that each of their radios was partially disabled. Tom's radio could transmit but not receive. The other radio could receive but not transmit. The listened to each others radio.

Looking across the valley at the choppers shuttling over what he assumed was Tom's hiding place but they couldn't locate him. Later, four Skyraiders, piston engine aircraft armed with rockets and 20 MM cannons arrived. Tom called on his radio but no response was received. He called again and asked the pilot to rock his wings if they were receiving his transmissions. They did and it made Tom feel a little better about being rescued.

One of the choppers asked Tom, "Where am I from you?" Although Tom couldn't receive he sensed why the pilot paused. "Back here," he flashed his pocket mirror at the hovering chopper. It was dangerous because at times the gunners fired at the light believing it was from enemy rifles, but the pilots turned around and headed for Tom. Small arms and the staccato sound of machine guns opened fire on one the choppers. The wingman was hit and fuel streamed from the chopper. The pilot said, "I'm losing fuel and have to get out of here."

Without helicopters in sight, the two aviators were concerned their frantic radio contact and the mirror had revealed their hiding places to the antagonists. Tom heard a man approaching and laid as flat as possible, expecting to feel the jab of a bayonet or the butt of a rifle. Instead the man walked to within about eight feet, then turned around. He would always wonder whether the soldier did not want to kill him or didn't see him in the under brush.

The bombardier figured it would take at least two hours for the choppers to refuel and return for another rescue attempt. Although it was mid-morning it was going to be a hot day. He decided to climb the hill and go down the other side where the soldiers who fired at the choppers could not see him. He figured it would be safe on that side for the choppers to land if they returned.

Pushing on through the thick brush, he stumbled on a grass flatland. Just before noon, more fixed wing aircraft and choppers arrived. He set off an orange smoke flare. None of the aircraft saw it. He hurled a second flare into the air. An Air Force pilot flying a T-28 saw it and dove on the bombardier. He felt relief at first, then terror as he thought he might get strafed rather than being rescued if the pilot figured he was an enemy soldier. He looked up when the aircraft was passing and the guy in the back was waving at him.

The chopper followed the same route as the T-28 had flown. He stood up and raised his arms in a cross signifying he was friendly. The chopper pilot slowed to a walk as he brushed the bombardier who made a running dive for the open door and landed in a heap on the chopper's deck. The pilot immediately pulled up sharply out of the area with Tom still in the brush.

The chopper flew around the area where he figured Tom would be but couldn't see the downed pilot in the brush. Tom set off a flare when the chopper was overhead but he kept on flying past. He couldn't stay there now that his position was revealed. He went deeper into the brush and radioed his rescuers that he was directly up hill at the tall tree with the big round top. The pilot headed for the spot and saw Tom.

The down wash from the chopper made it difficult to stand, but Tom saw the horse collar on a steel cable being lowered to him. Then the down wash blew it into the branches of the big tree stopping it's descent. The chopper's crew couldn't place the collar any closer than three feet above his head and downhill from him. Tom backed up the hill about ten yards, stripped off the remainder of his gear and prepared to make the jump for his life. If he missed he was dead. He sprinted downhill and leaped. He thrust his right arm through the collar but was unable to get his left arm into it. In desperation he locked his left hand over his right wrist and hung on for his life.

The crewmen looked out the door at Tom but could not reel him in. Dragging him through the tree branches the pilot backed the chopper away from the tall tree. He didn't want to stay in a hover position until Tom was aboard. Soldiers in the valley had already hit his wingman and more were still firing at the chopper. The rescue aircraft tried to form a shield of fire between Tom and the valley but he was a target for any rifleman on the ground as he hung precariously to the rescue collar as he was pulled through the sky at 60 MPH. He dangled that way until the chopper climbed to 2000 feet. Only then did the chopper slow to a near hover so the crewmen could reel Tom through the door. The bombardier watched anxiously as the rescue proceeded. At that point he didn't know if Tom was dead or alive. When he saw the horse collar, Tom's head wasn't in it. "They were unable to get him!" he exclaimed. Then he saw a tree branch, followed by Tom's head then the rest of his body as the crewmen pulled Tom through the door to the floor of the chopper. The two hugged each other as they realized how fortunate they were in escaping what appeared to be certain death.

Back on the carrier, the Captain had assembled a band to welcome Tom and the bombardier-navigator. Every sailor and marine not on duty was standing on the deck cheering when they departed from the E-1B aircraft on the carrier's flight deck. It was an emotional moment as the two rescued airman crossed the fight deck, acknowledging the cheers. "WELCOME HOME."

NAVAL HOSPITAL-HONOLULU

O Good shepherd, seek me out, and bring me
home to thy fold again.
-Unknown

Tom was unable to fly due to his injuries after he and the bombardier-navigator ejected when a bomb exploded after leaving the aircraft. His right seat-mate hadn't received any serious injuries so he was to remain with the squadron. Tom was scheduled to fly back to Honolulu for treatment at the Naval Hospital.

After arriving at the hospital and his injuries were diagnosed, Tom put in a call to Kris. He didn't know if she was in Greenwich or at her mother's home in Cherry Point. "Kris, I wasn't sure you'd be at home."

"Here I are," she said facetiously, hoping the call wasn't something serious. "Where are you?"

"I'm at the Naval Hospital in Hawaii."

She started sobbing anticipating the worst. "Are you," she hesitated, "are you okay? I mean are you in one piece?"

Greta was standing beside her mother listening to the conversation. "Has daddy been hurt?"

"Yes, dear but I have to find out how serious. What happened, Tom?" she asked rubbing away the tears.

"A bomb exploded leaving the aircraft. After that the aircraft wasn't functional so we had to eject. The ridged back of the seat failed to make a big enough hole in the canopy. My hands jammed against the ragged edge of the small opening. The force of the air hit my lip mic and battered my lips then tore my pistol from its holster and swung around and hit my face. I landed in a tree and I thought my shoulder was dislocated by a branch but I guess it was only bruised."

"Oh, Tom I'm so sorry to hear that. The main thing is that you survived."

"We thought that capture by the Vietcong was inevitable but we were rescued by the helicopters. I can't say enough for the chopper pilots. They risked their lives under fire to rescue us."

Greta talked into the phone with Kris still holding it. "Daddy, when are you coming home. We miss you."

"I have to stay in the hospital for awhile but I'll be in touch. See you soon."

"Kris, a nurse just came in and I have to take some evaluation tests. I'll call you later."

Greta shouted into the phone, "We love you, Daddy."

"Love you too, Daddy," Kris added. Kris held Greta for a few moments overwhelmed by the news but thankful Tom survived.

Tom called Kris after the evaluation was completed. "Kris, guess who?"

"I always remember your voice. Any news with the evaluation?"

"As to the face wounds, the swelling will disappear and there aren't any problems that will linger, just be a matter of time. The hands are another problem that is not as simple."

"Will you be able to fly?" she asked concerned about his job with the airline.

"They took some X-Rays and it showed three fingers on each hand are lacerated but not broken but will take awhile for them to heal and recover complete flexibility. It may require some therapy."

"Do you know when you will be coming home?"

"From what they said, I'll only be here a few more days to see how the fingers are heeling and then I'll be released to recuperate at home. I'll let you know. I'm going to give John and Velma a call. I'm sure they would like to know what happened and also John would be interested in the A-6 problem. How's Greta doing?"

"She's happy you'll be coming home soon. She's doing her homework in her room. Do you want me to call her?"

"Don't interrupt her. Tell her I called and I'll call you when I'll be coming home."

"Really looking forward to it. Love you!"

The following day, which was a week-end, Tom called John. He picked up the phone after the third ring. "John, Tom here. Figured you would be home today."

"Hey ol', buddy how's everything and where are you?"

"I'm in the Naval Hospital in Hawaii."

"That's a surprise. What happened?"

Tom went on to explain his visit to the hospital. The bomb exploding within seconds after leaving the aircraft and the necessity for ejecting. "That was a thrilling experience in itself."

"Could you fly the aircraft." John interjected.

"No way. The right engine was throwing parts and streaming fuel. Then the left engine failed, and we lost all the hydraulics and the aircraft was in a 15 degree left bank. We thought it would blow up so we punched out at 13,000 feet. The cutting edge of the seat didn't make a big enough hole in the canopy and my hands were jammed against the small opening." He went on to explain about the mic hitting his lips and the pistol which was yanked out of the holster hitting his face.

"You said the bomb exploded seconds after you pushed the button on the control stick?"

"Yes. They were the Mark 82- 500 pound bombs and they also had the obsolete M-990-D2 electrical fuses in the tail that were supposed to prevent them from exploding close to the aircraft. I landed in a tree. We thought we'd be captured by the Vietcong but managed to elude them. The chopper pilots rescued us under fire. I couldn't begin to say enough for them. They did a tremendous job. I imagine the A-6 will undergo some scrutiny, although it wasn't the aircraft but an ordnance problem."

"I think the ordnance problem will be handled somewhere else as it wasn't an aircraft problem. How long will they keep you in the hospital?"

"They haven't set a time on it. My hands I think will be the question."

"Keep in touch ol', buddy and let us know what you'll be doing when they release you. Things didn't work out as planned. Hope you have a rapid recovery."

"Thanks, John and regards to Velma."

A nurse arrived and guided Tom into one of the examining rooms. The sun was shining directly into the room and she adjusted the slats to deflect it to the ceiling, "How are you today, Colonel?"

"Well, I've felt better. I guess I'll survive."

"I'm sure you will." She was a Navy Lieutenant so she had several years of service in the Navy. She was all business, not prone to engaging in any small talk, possibly intimidated by his rank. "I'll do a few tests-blood pressure, temperature, pulse." She entered the results on his chart. "The doctor will be in to see you shortly," and promptly departed. Tom speculated that one of the doctors gave her a hard time.

Tom became engrossed in a *Popular Mechanics* magazine and the doctor arrived about fifteen minutes later. "I'm Doctor Evans," he said extending his hand. He was more cordial than the nurse. "I'm here to do a follow up on your evaluation check." The name sounded a familiar chord to Tom as his deceased wife's name was Mary Jane Evans. They studied each other for a few seconds before recognition arrived. They both said almost simultaneously. "Tom?" "Bill?"

Tom said, "The name caught my interest. It's been a long time, Bill. In fact Ruth, your sister, called to tell us that your mother had died. She was a special person."

"That she was. I wasn't able to attend the funeral. By the time I was notified the service was over and the distance was a factor."

"Ruth said you were a doctor and based at the Navy base here. This is a coincidence."

"It must be almost twenty years, Tom. By the way, how is your son?"

"He's in his second year at the Naval Academy. We also have a daughter. She was born when I was in Korea. Do you have a family, Bill?"

"I married Shirley who lived in the corner house below us. She was a nurse then became an airline stewardess until we got married, then she had to resign. Her father was a builder. We have twin girls. They both attend Pitt."

"I'm sure I met her on occasion but I don't remember."

They continued discussing the past for a few more minutes when Bill said, "I have a few more patients before lunch so we should get on with the evaluation. As this is a follow up check from your initial evaluation, everything is improving, Tom. Your hands will be stiff for awhile but will return to normal. I don't imagine you'll want the experience of ejecting again. I have a break between one and two, how about I buy lunch and we'll continue to reminisce about the past."

"You're the doctor," Tom said smiling. "When I get home I'll call Ruth to tell her we had lunch."

GOOD NEWS

Sometime, no news is good news, but when
news is good, that's satisfaction.
-Anonymous

John and Velma enjoyed living in St. Mary's county. The friendliness of the people, the beauty of the base, the fishing, boating, golf, tennis and the beauty of Chesapeake Bay and the Pawtuxent River. Inside the gate, there was plenty of evidence to remind everyone that airplanes were the king at Pax River. Roads pointing to the left and right from Cedar Point Road were named after those who died testing aircraft. Further evidence, that the airplanes ruled the domain, was clear when the stop light signaled the cars to stop when an aircraft was crossing the road on the way for takeoff. It was one of the few bases in the country where carrier aircraft and cars could collide at an intersection.

John was still wrestling with the decision to apply for the astronaut training program. He and Velma discussed the situation at length. With his background and being a test pilot, he felt certain he would be accepted. They loved the area at Pax River but it would be necessary to relocate to Houston for the next three years. Velma preferred to stay but if John really wanted to become an astronaut she could accept his decision.

He finished his flight for the day and completed the debriefing. On the drive home he began thinking about Tom's close brush with death and possible capture by the Vietcong. He reflected on his own ordeal in the Japanese prison camp during World War II. If the war continued he wasn't certain he would be able to survive the brutal treatment dealt to him by the Japanese captors. Both he and Tom had managed to survive all the pitfalls they encountered throughout their lives. He wasn't superstitious but continually placing one's life in precarious situations greatly reduced the odds for survival. Fate is the hunter in determing the final outcome.

Velma greeted John at the door with the usual kiss. He hung up his forest green jacket in the hall closet and sat in his reclining chair. "And how was your day, Marine?" she asked handing him his usual before dinner cocktail.

"Ordinance is trying to figure out the reason the bomb exploded after leaving Tom's aircraft. I flew the A-6 today and the aircraft performed normally. It has to be the bomb. There will be a flight test of the armament system. How was your day?"

"Same old, same old."

John sipped his drink before beginning. "It's about the astronaut program. After considering all the angles," she interrupted, 'You decided to send in your application.'

"I have a surprise for you. I'm not going to send in an application."

"You just made my day. Thank you. I really wasn't enthused about going to Houston." She gave him a big hug and kiss. "Now I have a surprise for you."

"You just made my favorite dinner? "

"No!"

"Your mother is coming for a visit."

"No, it begins with a P."

"You have to pee?"

"No silly I'm pregnant!"

"You're kidding. On second thought you wouldn't kid about that. That's wonderful. We've waited a long time. How long have you known?"

"Ever since you began thinking about the astronaut program. I didn't want that to bias your decision." They hugged and kissed again.

"That was very considerate of you," John said, pleased with the happy news. "I have to call my folks. They'll be thrilled to hear that finally they will be grandparents. Also call your folks."

"Now if it's a boy," Velma speculated, "he will be able to carry on the Fairfield name."

"Does your mother know?" John asked.

"Yes, but I told her not to mention it until after the astronaut decision? My folks also know."

"I have to call Kris. I want to call her anyway to see if she has any further information about Tom."

CALLING TOM'S MENTOR

The best thing a father can do for his
children is to love their mother.
-Unknown

Kris had a thought that Harry Clark, Tom's mentor, would be in interested in what was happening to Tom. He always felt somewhat responsible for Tom's involvment in the war. Realizing his interest in flying but couldn't afford flying lessons, he suggested the Naval Aviation Cadet Program which led him into harm's way during World War II.

A pleasant voice answered the phone. "Hi, Mrs. Clark, I'm Tom's wife. Remember me. We met previously."

"Of course, I remember you and you don't have to be so formal. Just call me Grace."

"It's such a pleasant fall day, I thought you might like to hear about Tom's adventure."

"Just a moment, dear and I'll have Harry pick up the extention. It's Kris, Tom's wife."

"How's Tom and your family?"

"I just heard from him yesterday. Did you know he was in Vietnam?"

"I hope this isn't bad news!" Grace exclaimed. "What happened to him?"

"A bomb exploded as it left the aircraft and it wasn't flyable and on fire so he and the bombardier-navigator had to eject. His hands were jammed against the jagged edge of the canopy. The doctors evaluated his condition and determined that his fingers will be stiff for awhile but will return to normal."

"He's had more problems than anyone should have to cope with in a life time." Harry said, "I thought he was flying fighters."

"He was, but a new squadron was formed and he was given command of it and also promoted to Lt. Colonel. He was flying the A-6A Intruder an attack bomber."

"Do you know where he was based."

"He was flying off a carrier. That's one of the reasons he was chosen, for all his carrier experience. Also, it was their first flight after arriving in Vietnam waters so Tom led a three aircraft flight to bomb some roads."

"What happened after they punched out?" Harry asked.

"They landed in hostile territory and Tom said they felt certain they would be captured by the Vietcong. They managed to elude the soldiers and were rescued by the choppers who were operating under fire. He said, 'You can't say enough for the chopper pilots who risked their own lives to save us'."

"I sincerely hope for a speedy recovery and his hands come back to normal. It could affect his airline career," Grace speculated, "he has served in three wars, I think he would be exempted from harm's way before his luck runs out."

"I'll let you know when I hear something definite about his homecoming."

"We hope everything turns out for the best. He sort of replaced our son who died at a young age."

"I'm sorry to hear that. Tom never mentioned it. I can imagine how you feel. I'll be in touch."

"Thanks so much for calling, Kris. We appreciate your thinking of us."

FURTHER THREAT

There comes a time when the risk to remain tight in the bud
is more painful than the risk it takes to blossom.
Unknown

Erna entered Hilda's office carrying a plain white envelope with single message also on plain white paper that read: TIME IS RUNNING OUT. Hilda gave the message to Heinrich who had just received a call from the electrical department saying that more parts were missing. Heinrich in turn, notified security about the latest developments.

Security contacted the personnel department if Heinz Steiner was listed as an employee or if the initials H. S. were used in a bogus name. Everything came up negative. They asked what Steiner's job was at the Messerschmitt factory. "He was an engineer," Heinrich replied, "and as such he had the knowledge to design a bomb."

"We're dealing with a determined assassin here who, if in fact it is Heinz Steiner, wants revenge for his brother's death at the hands of Heinrich. We'll increase surveillance, Herr Lehndorff. Would you like us to post a guard outside your office?"

"I don't think that's necessary. If he is making a bomb I believe he would figure out someplace to hide it in the office."

"If anything looks suspicious, notify us at once."

"This situation is becoming very disruptive," Hilda offered. "It's also very suspenseful." Erna arrived with some coffee and muffins. "Let's have some coffee and continue business as usual. We can't let this threat become an obsession," Hilda said and Heinrich agreed.

Several days passed without any overt activity and Heinrich and Hilda began to feel more positive that the threat had passed. Maybe it was just a hoax to cause anxiety without a real threat intended. He succeeded in that respect. They had become complacent.

Heinrich had a new desk installed in his office. Solid oak, eight by six and superbly finished. The middle drawer did not carry to the end so there was about a two foot space remaining. Large enough to accommodate a bomb. The office doors remained open at night so the cleaning women had access to all the offices. The security guard would make the rounds every hour, so anyone would have adequate time to plant a bomb unobserved and it also provided enough time to seek out a place that wasn't suspicious.

At nine o'clock the following morning, Heinrich scheduled a last minute appointment with Fritz. The personnel department required more space due to the increase in hiring. He wanted to discuss the plans with Heinrich.

At nine twenty, Heinrich received a call from security. They had apprehended a man they thought might be Heinz and asked Heinrich to come to the office to identify him. "This shouldn't take much time. I'll be back in a few minutes."

"I can make a few calls, no need to hurry," Fritz answered.

K-boom! The explosion occurred precisely at nine thirty, shattering the peaceful calm of the morning and instantly snuffing out the life of Fritz who was sitting at the desk where the bomb had been attached. As Hilda's office was adjacent to Heinrich's, the wall partially collapsed pinning her under the debris. Hearing the explosion, Heinrich hurried to the scene realizing the bomb had been meant for him but fate intervened.

Hilda was injured, it wasn't known how serious and Fritz was dead. It was the third time Hilda's life had been threatened. When the bomb from the Allied fighter went through the factory building; approaching Lisbon, the Pan Am Clipper crashed on the approach and she and Fitz were listed as casualties due to a similarity of names, Fetters rather than Feathers and now this explosion for the third time escaping the grim reaper. Hilda was not immune to disappointments in her life. Her first husband was a Major in the German Army and died from hypothermia in the Russian winter due to lack of suitable clothes.

Now, Fritz her second husband who survived the war and died in an untimely incident.

Security inspected the remains of the desk and figured the bomb was attached to the open space behind the top drawer. They also assumed the perpetrator had checked Heinrich's appointment calendar to see if there were any other scheduled appointments between nine and ten o'clock. He was not interested in eliminating anyone else as Heinrich was the prime target.

Hilda was rushed to the company hospital to determine the extent of her injuries. Due to an early appointment that the bomber had not anticipated, an innocent person was killed. When Heinrich arrived at what remained of his office, the area was in complete chaos. The fire department responded although there wasn't a fire. Hilda was strapped on a gurney and taken out to a waiting ambulance. Fritz was declared dead by the doctor and his body was removed to an ambulance. Erna, Hilda's secretary was also taken to the hospital for further examination. Several employees from other departments had arrived after hearing the explosion. Security had cordoned off the scene until they searched for other clues.

After semblance of some degree had prevailed and a calmer atmosphere restored, Heinrich called Hanna, his wife to inform her about the tragedy. He previously mentioned the threats he had received. In the excitement, he began telling her what had happened before she asked. "There has been an explosion at the office. Hilda and Erna were taken to the hospital and Fritz is dead."

"Are you alright?"

"Fortunately, yes. Ironically I was discussing some plans with Fritz when I was called to the Security Office when the explosion happened."

"I feel so sorry for Hilda and Fritz. Hilda has experienced more than her share of problems during her life. It doesn't seem right that one person has to endure all that tragedy."

"I'll call the hospital," Heinrich said mentally exhausted from the disaster. "It maybe too soon to have a complete evaluation of Hilda and Erna's conditions. I'll call you if I hear anything." Erna was like a member of the family. She began working for the company before the war.

GOING HOME

I am the loving bread that
came down from heaven.
-John 6:51

Tom was recovering in the Naval Hospital in Hawaii from injuries received when he and the bombardier-navigator were forced to eject from their burning aircraft. The medical department decided he could further improve from his injuries at home so was released from the hospital on a thirty day leave. He called Kris to relay the good news. "Kris, how's everything on the home front?"

"Just great. Greta and I miss you, Will you be coming home soon?"

"That's what I'm calling about. I've been released from the hospital so as soon as the paper work is completed I will be on the way."

"It's a long trip. Are you well enough to travel?"

"The flight will be on a commercial aircraft with a stop in California. I still feel sore and I look like a walking wounded but everything is improving. My fingers are still bandaged. My lips are still puffy and my shoulder is still sore but the doctor optimistically predicted that in time everything will be back to normal again."

"We're so happy to hear that you're coming home, Tom. Let us know when you'll be arriving and Greta and I will meet you at the airport. I'll call John and Velma to tell them the good news and also Harry and Grace.

ANNOUNCEMENT IN *THE WASHINGTON POST*

Senator Fairfield, R-Mass. announces daughter's Betrothal.

Senator John E. and Sharon K. Fairfield announce the engagement of their daughter, Elizabeth to Commander Lars Lundgren, United States Navy. Presently he is serving in Vietnam as a Captain of a U. S. Navy destroyer.

Elizabeth or Beth as she is known, is residing in Hollywood working on a movie to be released later this year.

A June sixth wedding is being planned at the Fairfield summer residence at Chatham on Cape Cod.

SECOND THOUGHTS

From the sublime to the nadir in life.
-Anonymous

Lars had been gone for two months of his six months cruise after the nuptials had been announced. He will return in April. Plenty of time for the wedding in June. Beth would be working in summer stock in theaters around the New England area. When the season ends, she would be heading for Hollywood to begin work on a new movie.

Four months left. She had begun having second thoughts about these six month Navy cruises. Without a husband after marriage. It would be comparable to being single. And if we had a family he would be like a part time father. She decided to call John. He solved their commuting problem by suggesting that Lars request a transfer to a ship based in San Diego.

"John, this is Beth."

"Where are you?"

"I'm in Hollywood working on a movie. I have another problem. I've been thinking about the marriage to Lars. I'm getting cold feet or second thoughts or whatever else it's called. It's those six month separations that bother me."

"Beside that, how's everything in La La land? Is the movie proceeding as planned? He was trying to alleviate her anxiety by changing the subject."

"Everything is great," but she wouldn't be deterred. "I've been agonizing about this marriage. I'm beginning to feel it's a mistake. Also it isn't fair to Lars believing that the plans are progressing smoothly."

"Have you thoroughly discussed this with Lars?"

"The only possibility that we came up with would be for him to resign from the Navy. He doesn't want to and I can understand that.

He hopes that sometime in the future he will be promoted to captain and take command of a bigger ship."

"Have you talked to mom and dad?" Maybe they can offer a solution."

"I doubt it. They're planning on a big wedding in June at our annual get together at the Cape."

"I don't think it would be possible for him to request permanent shore duty. With the war escalating, I imagine the Navy needs officers with his command experience and would be reluctant to retire him. I'm sorry I can't come up with a solution this time, Beth. I would suggest you tell Lars that you're having second thoughts and want to postpone wedding plans. Also, call Mom and Dad and tell them about your thoughts before they become too engrossed in wedding plans."

ENROUTE HOME

The future in trust
-Unknown

Tom was scheduled to fly Pan Am from Honolulu to San Francisco, then on American to New York. Memo to crew on flight 16 SFO-JFK, Lt. Col. Tom Korb, USMC will be a passenger on your flight. Returning from Vietnam. Had multiple injuries.when forced to eject from disabled aircraft. He is also the Chief Pilot in N.Y., VIP treatment. Thanks.

It was a New York based crew and they all knew Tom. The flight attendants, who incidently were the same crew on Tom's trip that almost resulted in ditching. The number one FA said in jest, "I just don't know, Tom you can't stay out of trouble."

"It seems that way. I wrote a letter for your files commending all of you on the excellent job you accomplished in keeping the passengers from panicking."

"Thanks, Tom we appreciate that." They extended a hearty welcome and after being seated in first class was presented with a glass of champagne he managed to sip in spite of his swollen lips. The cockpit crew was occupied with their pre-flight check lists but sent back a note asking Tom if he felt like coming to the cockpit after lunch.

The scheduled departure time was nine o'clock, but due to the three hour time difference it was noon eastern time. The flight attendants began the lunch service after reaching their cruise altitude of flight level 370. Cocktails were served followed by a shrimp cocktail. The entrée consisted of a petite filet mignon with twice baked potatoes, broccoli and dinner rolls. Dessert was a choice of a hot fudge or strawberry sundae and coffee with a choice of cordials.

In spite of his sore lips, jaw and bandaged fingers, he managed to finish the lunch. With his satiety complete, he asked the flight attendant to check with the captain, a gesture of courtesy if it was okay for a visit.

"Hey, Tom it's good to see you. They all shook hands, very gently because of his banadged fingers. He had flown with the entire crew previously. "From what I've heard, that was quite an ordeal you went through in Nam."

"It's amazing we all survived. I got most of my injuries from the ejection. And I can't say enough for the chopper pilots who rescued us under fire without regard for their own lives. I keep repeating that, but it's a difficult situation."

"Sounds like a hairy operation," the captain said. "What are your future plans, Tom? Will you be returning to the company?"

"I'm on a thirty day recuperation leave, then it's the Marine Corps' decision.

Well I'll let you guys get back to work." It was a quick visit.

"We'll be starting descent in few minutes. Hope your return to the company goes well." Tom was wearing his forest green uniform.

"I didn't know he was a Lt. Colonel," the co-pilot observed. "He has enough ribbons to choke a horse. He got most of them in World War II."

They were cleared to descend to flight level 180 and contact approach control on 125.4. Tom had called Kris before departing San Francisco. "I'll be arriving about 5:08. Can't wait to see you and Greta. Got to go. They've begun boarding."

PROBLEM SOLVED

Looking out from prison bars
-Unknown

Security figured the bomb exploded in the space behind the top drawer of the desk. The potential strength of the bomb was only designed to eliminate Heinrich but the blast was strong enough to open a section of the wall injuring Hilda and Erna. After examining them at the hospital it was determined that their injuries were superficial. They were detained overnight as a precaution and released the following day. It was a difficult time for Hilda. Her first husband died from exposure in the Russian winter during the war. Erna had never married and her family died during the Allied bombing.

Due to the scarcity of clues, security was able to isolate a few facts at the scene. They decided it had to be an inside act as someone had access to the office to find an inconspicuous area to attach the bomb. The perpetrator had enough empathy to check Heinrich's calendar as he was supposed to be the only victim thus sparing an innocent person's life.

Security rechecked the personnel names but to no avail. The search was narrowed to those that worked at night and had access to the offices. It included the cleaning crew and their own security personnel. The cleaning crew were all women and a supervisor. They were interrogated as suspects and released.

Security employed part time guards that worked the night shift on weekends. Checking the list, they came across the name Leon Noel. It sounded conspicuous. Checking further it was discovered to be the name of the French Ambassador. Also, it was unique that Leon Noel reversed was Noel Leon. If, in fact someone was using it as a false name it had the opposite effect which prompted security to further check into the situation.

The individual using that name was identified and a photograph of the suspect was shown to Heinrich who identified the suspect as Heinz Steiner. It was decided to put him under surveilance and he was caught selling stolen property in the black market. He will stand trial accused of taking a life and the additional charge of selling stolen property.

GOOD AND BAD NEWS

Be thou the rainbow in the storms of life.
The evening beam that smiles the clouds
away, and tints tomorrow with prophetic ray.
-Lord Byron

Kris and Greta were waiting at the airport when Tom's flight arrived. It was a clear but cold day. A few stratocumulus clouds drifted by propelled by a strong northwesterly wind. A cold front had passed through sometime during the night.

"Here he comes," Greta squealed, as she ran to welcome her father. She gave him a big hug and a kiss. "It's so good to have you home again, Daddy. We're like a family again. How long will you be home? Are you all right? Do you have to go back again?"

"Whoa, one question at a time." Kris caught up to them before he had time to answer all her questions.

"Welcome home again, Marine. It seems as though I've said that a few times in the past." They embraced and held each. She was overjoyed to have him home at least for awhile until she assumed he would be returning to the war.

On the way home Greta was in the back seat. Kris was driving. Tom turned about half way saying, "To answer your previous questions my little inquisitor," he said smiling, "I've felt better but improving. I'm on a thirty day recuperating leave. In regard to the future, I'll be scheduled for a flight physical and the result of that will no doubt decide my future in the Marine Corps."

"What about your airline job?" Kris asked

"I'll be required to take a company physical and there again the results will provide the decision." Silence prevailed for a few minutes. There was so much to say and do.

Kris broke the silence. "We have many calls to make. The families, your son, John and Velma, Harry and Grace."

"I'll check with the flight office but I can't supply a definite answer for them."

"We'll get it all sorted out eventually," Kris said optimistically. "The three of us will have a nice quiet evening at home. I put a standing rib roast in the oven on the timer so it should be ready with baked potatoes and asparagus tips. How does that grab you, Mein Herr?"

"You shouldn't call Daddy names," Greta joked from the back seat.

"Your daughter has a good sense of humor," Kris said.

"She takes after me," Tom bragged.

"So you're saying I don't have a good sense of humor," Kris said feigning hurt feelings. "I think I'll just sit here and sulk."

"Not at all. It just proves there's a little bit of humor in almost everything."

The dinner was a huge success with German chocolate cake for dessert, one of Tom's favorites. They discussed topics of the past and hopes for the future. Greta said she had some home work. "You two lovebirds can be alone. Now I can get a good nights sleep. I don't have to worry about you. Did Mom tell you about her dream?"

"It really was frightening. There was a strong thunderstorm in progress. I woke up, it was more like a nightmare, dreaming that you were injured somehow. It all seemed so real. Coincidently, it was the same time and day you ejected. I've heard of occasions that people had dreams like that. As I recall, it was something about extrasensory communication between minds. I woke up crying and Greta came in to console me. It was all so real."

Tom said, "Whatever you call it, maybe a coincidence."

Tom and Kris were sitting on the couch staring at the fireplace, enjoying each others presence as the shadows from the flames danced in the reflection on the walls from a mirror in the low light. "I really or

I should say we really missed you. Greta is at the age where she needs a father figure."

"Any problems?"

"Not yet. One of the boys in high school wants to date her. I think she's too young to be dating."

"I agree. You want me to discuss it with her?"

"You might casually mention it in addition to other facts of maturing."

"I'll be tactful. What are parents for?"

"She really was concerned about you. She bawled like a baby the day you left. She figured you wouldn't return."

"I'll have a chat with her. She's at the awkward age now," Tom concluded.

They were thinking about calling John and Velma when the phone interrupted there thought. "Kris this is your mother. How's everything up there?"

"Just fine, Mom I was planning on calling you tomorrow. We just picked up Tom at the airport. He has a few hurts but he's on a thirty day recuperating leave."

"Does he have to return to active duty?"

"He won't know until his condition is evaluated at the end of his leave."

"I hope they don't send him back to Vietnam. He's seen more than his share of action in all those wars." Kris started to say something but her Mother continued. "Speaking of Vietnam, I'm afraid I have some bad news. Vietnamese gunboats attacked Lar's ship. A shell exploded on the bridge and he was killed instantly along with the other crewmen on watch at the time."

"Oh, Mom that's really sad. First it was Dad, now Lars. Both killed in the line of duty. We were just about to call John and Velma. Does Beth know about it?"

"Not to my knowledge. Tell them about it when you call them."

"Would you like to come up and stay with us for awhile?"

"That's very considerate of you, Dear, but I have to stay here for all the preparations. Maybe sometime later when everything is settled."

Kris called John and Velma after she received the sad news from her mother. Velma answered recognizing her voice. "Is Tom home yet?"

"He arrived about five o'clock." She went on to explain his condition and a decision will be made when his leave expires and his condition is evaluated. "I was just talking to my mother," she continued, " and I'm the bearer of sad news."

"Maybe I better call John in that case."

"Hey, Kris how's my ol' buddy doing these days?" She explained again about Tom's condition and the prognosis. He sounded cheerful unaware of the bad news he was about to receive.

"My mother just called."

He interrupted, "How is she, Kris? Haven't talked to her for quite a while."

"She's well but we just received some bad news. Lar's ship was attacked by Vietnamese gunboats and a shell hit the bridge. Lars was killed instantly in addition to the other sailors on watch."

"Wow, that is bad news. Your father and now your brother killed in the line of duty."

"Would you call Beth?"

"Sure. Beth was having second thoughts about their marriage plans. In fact, she asked me if I could figure out a solution. The six month cruises were the problems. Ironically, Lar's death was the solution, albeit it's severe and final. Beth is in Hollywood working on a movie. I'll call her. My condolence to you and your mother, Kris. Would you put my ol' buddy on the horn?"

"Hey, John has there been a decision of the bomb release on the A-6?"

"The obsolete M-990-D2 was the culprit. Also the contact fuse in the nose has been replaced with a delayed fuse that explodes after penetrating the ground. I flew the test flight and everything was normal. What's your decision?"

"I'll report to Cherry Point after my leave expires for a physical and evaluation. I don't expect any problems. It's just a question of time until it heals. I assume the XO was appointed as temporary squadron commander until a permanent commander is assigned, or the other possibility would return me to active duty."

"I'll have to call my folks and cancel the wedding plans. They were looking forward to a wedding at the get together. I hope they haven't made any arrangements."

"Glad to hear that Velma is expecting. That was welcomed news."

"She didn't tell me until after I made the decision not to apply for the astronaut program so it wouldn't bias my decision."

"I imagine both sets of parents are happy about the news as I'm sure you and Velma are also."

"I'll give the phone back to Velma so she can tell you."

"Sorry to hear about Lars. As John said it was one way to solve the problem although it was a macabre solution. Good news about your expecting in contrast to Lar's and Beth's problem. Maybe your gene pool needed a little rejuvenation after three miscarriages."

"I imagine John was beginning to think his sperm wasn't good enough for me to conceive successfully. Anyways, is it possible for us to get together sometime?"

"Sounds like a good idea but at present everything is so indefinite. Take care and I'm sure everything will be successful this time," Tom said optimistically.

"I hope everything works out for you after your recuperation also. Regards to Kris and Greta."

Notice appeared in the Washington Post
Senator Fairfield R-Mass. and his wife Sharon
regret to announce the cancellation of the
planned nuptial of their daughter, Elizabeth
(Beth) to Cmdr. Lars Lundgren, U.S. Navy.
He was a destroyer Captain and his ship was
attacked by Vietnamese gunboats. An errant shell
penetrated the bridge and he was killed instantly.
This was the second tragety in their family.
His father, General Lundgren, USMC was killed
in World War II on Okinawa.

THE TRIAL

The truth will out.
-Unknown

With his identification positive, Heinz Steiner was placed under surveilance. When it became definite that he was trafficking in the black market, the time arrived for a confrontation. He was apprehended at seven in the morning after the night shift ended and taken to the Security Office. He sat at a table opposite the head of security for the preliminary interrogation. The trial would convene in the following morning.

Prosecutor: For the record, is your name Heinz Steiner?

Steiner: No, it isn't.

Prosecutor: Then what is your name?

Steiner: Leon Noel.

Prosecutor: Let's stop sparring. We know your name is Heinz Steiner. Your choice of a name wasn't very innovative. Although it's the same reversed.

Steiner: So what. I'm not a complete moron.

Prosecutor: Some parts are just missing. Do you know this man, pointing to Heinrich?

Steiner: No, I don't remember him.

Prosecutor: You knew him well enough as a prosecution witness at the Nuremberg trials. In fact, you accused him of killing your brother. You created an outburst and the judge called for a recess. Isn't that a fact?

Steiner: I don't remember him.

Prosecutor: He remembers you. For revenge you planted a bomb under his desk. You killed an innocent man, thinking it would be Herr Lehndorff.

Steiner: You can't prove that, he said belligerently. It's reasonable to assume anyone could have planted the bomb.

Prosecutor: Ah, but we can. With the assistance and cooperation of the police in your town, I dilute reason with logic. The three threatening notes you sent to Heinrich copied through on the writing pad on your desk.

Steiner: I still think he should be convicted.

Prosecutor: That statement is tantamount to a confession. Would you like to make a statement?

Steiner: No. That's just circumstantial evidence.

Prosecutor: From what you just said, you're still holding a grudge and the evidence presented to a jury I think is enough to convict you for murder one. Also, we have enough evidence to prove you were trafficking in the black market.

Steiner: No way can you prove that either.

Prosecutor: We have your co-conspirator in custody. He has already admitted to the charge and gave us a statement to cut a deal for a lesser sentence.

Steiner: It was an accident. He wasn't supposed to be there, he blurted visibly shaken.

Prosecutor: Regardless, you committed premeditated murder and the penalty is punishable by hanging. In your case, some people are alive only because it's illegal to kill them unless decreed by the People's court.

GOOD NEWS

You number my wanderings, put my tears
in your bottle. Are they not in your book.
-Psalm 56:8

Tom's thirty day leave was inexorably coming to an end. He had received orders to report to Cherry Point for a flight physical and evaluation.

"What are your options, Tom assuming you pass the physical?" Kris asked.

"I don't have an option. It's the Marine Corps' decision. I imagine the XO is the temporary squadron commander until I return. If I can't pass the physical I'll probably be given a job flying a desk or revert to the inactive reserve."

Kris pondered the decision, "If you had your druthers it would be better than going back to Vietnam."

"We'll have to wait and see. I was hoping we'd be able to arrange a get together with John and Mother to be Velma," he said taking the conversation in a different direction. "Also, I'd like to visit Harry and Grace and stop in Annapolis for a visit with number one son. It appears we won't be able to do any visiting."

"What time is dinner? Do I have time to do my homework?" Greta asked.

"It will be ready in about fifteen minutes so you could talk to your father for awhile." Kris suggested.

"You'll be leaving us again, Daddy. Seems like you just got here. Why don't you call in sick?"

"I'm already on sick leave. I'll be reporting to the Commanding General of Cherry Point. He would no doubt take a dim view of the request that my daughter suggested I call in sick," he laughed.

"Why do they have wars anyway? It disrupts peoples lives."

"That's true, but there probably have been wars since the beginning of history for various reasons. History records wars of aggression way back to B.C. In early A.D. Roman hordes almost conquered the world. Wars that had a greater effect on this country were the Revolutionary War, the Civil War and World War I. Then World War II, and the Korean War and now the Vietnam War. One big difference is the weapons became more sophisticated. From throwing spears, it's now possible with the advanced technology, to fire at the enemy when they're not in sight."

"Thanks for the history lesson, Daddy. I guess there will always be wars as long as there are people to start them."

"History repeats itself but apparently no one listens."

Kris came waltzing into the family room, "Time for dinner," she announced. It was a beautiful fall day and the leaves of red, brown and gold covered the landscape like a multi colored quilt.

"Whatever we're having smells good," Tom said. They sat down to a dinner of pot roast, gravy, potatoes and carrots.

"Maybe someday I'll be able to cook like you."

"You will, Dear," Kris advised, "when your father and I were newly-weds, I couldn't boil water. Not quite that inept but it's an acquired art."

"Do you think they'll send you back to Vietnam? It seems to me they should let you sit this one out being you were in the other two wars," was Greta's idea.

"I'll get the answer to that when I return to Cherry Point. If I can pass the physical I'll return to the squadron."

"One of my classmates told me that her father said you're crazy for risking your life on an unpopular war like Vietnam."

"It's my job. I remained in the reserve and I took an oath to help defend the country if necessary. Everyone is entitled to their own opinion."

"You'll be leaving Thursday?" She asked hoping he could stay longer.

"Yes, I'll take a commercial flight to Washington. Then from Anacostia NAS, the Leatherneck express, the Marine Corps shuttle to Cherry Point. Appointment is scheduled at 0800 Friday." They had German chocolate cake and ice cream again for dessert and coffee. Greta had milk.

"If they send you back to Vietnam, would you come home again before you leave?" Greta asked concerned.

"Yes, they will cut new orders for me and a reporting time. The war won't end that soon." At the time, no one could predict the war would continue for another seven years.

Tom's appointment with the general was scheduled after the physical. The bandages had been removed and X-Rays were taken of his fingers and shoulder. After all the tests involving the physical had been completed, he had a conference with the doctor. "Well, Colonel I realize you'd like to hear the results, so I'll begin. The X-Rays look good. Your fingers may be a little stiff but that will wear off. Your shoulder was bruised but nothing broken. Your lips and jaw have healed and shouldn't leave a scar. All the other tests are normal-EKG, blood pressure, urine, eyes. Your condition is excellent considering your ordeal. The ejection was for the most part the cause of your problems. You are still listed as the Squadron CO. Do you have any qualms about returning to Vietnam?"

"No. Truthfully, I'd rather not go but if that's the decision then I'm prepared."

"I was leafing through your record. Very impressive. You've seen enough action to last a lifetime and I can understand your feeling. Physically you're fine but I wanted to check how you felt mentally. My evaluation is that you are capable of returning to duty. So, good luck, Colonel whatever the decision." They shook hands and Tom departed. The doctor remained at his desk for a few moments and the stream of conscious took over his thoughts. The colonel had survived two wars, especially World War II and it appears he will be sent into harm's way a third time.

The general had a luncheon with a group of fellow officers who would discuss and decide the decision of Tom's deployment. "Korb, Thomas J. reporting as ordered, Sir."

"Pull up a chair, Colonel. Would you like some coffee? We seem to run on coffees around here."

"I just had lunch but I could go for another cup. Just cream," Tom added.

The General buzzed for his request and minutes later a Marine sergeant set a tray of coffee and cream on the desk and then departed. "Help yourself, Colonel, then we'll discuss you future. I, or I should say, we delved into your record. Very impressive. You are probably one of the most decorated pilots in the Corps. You were a squadron CO in the reserve and your unit was activated. But a new squadron of A-6's was formed and you were offered the command and a promotion to colonel, due to your extensive carrier experience although you were a fighter pilot. I realize you know all of this but I'm summarizing to explain how we arrived at our decision." They both took a sip of the coffee and Tom figured he would be returning to the squadron deployed on the carrier.

"You have twenty five years in the Corps," he began again, "both active and reserve and I was also informed that you have an airline job when you return to civilian life. Is that correct?"

"Yes, Sir. I was the Manager of Flight-Eastern Region. The country is divided into four regions-eastern, central, southern and western."

"Is there a chance for advancement and do you think you would be in line for the job?"

"Yes, but that's in the future, Vice President-Flight. And there would be quite a few with credible qualifications. That would be in top management. It isn't out of reach as I acquire more experience. In fact the position at present is held by a pilot, although I have a degree in electrical engineering, which is a different field, I'll no doubt acquire additional management experience in my present position."

"You're no doubt anxious to hear the decision," he suddenly announced. Tom was certain he would be returning to the squadron. "The board unanimously decided to return you to the reserve as the CO, all things considered, you have spent enough time in harm's way." It was a complete surprise and relief as he definitely figured he would return to the squadron. "Thank you, Sir, I appreciate that and my thanks to all the board members."

"You have a daughter named Greta?"

"Yes, Sir how do you know that?"

"I received a letter from her."

"I'm sorry. I had no idea she wrote to you."

"Actually it's rather interesting. Would you like to read it?"

> Dear Mister General,
> My name is Greta Korb. You know my father Tom. I'm writing to see if you will please excuse him from going back to the war. My mother said he was in two other wars and he was lucky to come home. We need him to be a family.
>
> Love,
> Greta Korb

"Again I'm sorry, Sir. She never said anything about writing a letter to either me or her mother."

"The innocence of youth. Aside from the coercion by your daughter the decision had already been approved by the board. It was refreshing to see that she felt motivated enough to write. Do you have other children, colonel?"

"My son is in his second year at the Naval Academy, thanks to Senator Fairfield."

"You know the Senator? I hope he will chose the Marine Corps after graduation."

"Yes, Sir his son and I were cadets at Pensacola and we went through World War II together. In fact, the Senator and General Lundgren, who was killed on Okinawa served together in World War I."

"Did you ever meet General Lundgren?"

"Yes, Sir on a few occasions. He flew up from Espiritu Santo to Guadalcanal to present John and me with the medals. Also at the Fairfields. They have a get together every year in June at their summer home *Windmeer* at Chathan on Cape Cod."

"That's very interesting."

"It was through my association with John that I had the opportunity and pleasure to meet some of his friends and relations. My wife is General Lundgren's daughter. My first wife died in an automobile accident when our son was only three months old. I was a student at Georgia Tech at the time."

"I imagine that was a problem."

"Fortunately, her mother, who just died recently bless her, took care of him until I graduated and Kris and I were married."

"You've had an interesting life, Colonel both in the military and socially." The general walked around to the front of the desk saying, "Best wishes for the future." They shook hands as Tom was leaving, the general said, "Tell your daughter I enjoyed hearing from her."

A REUNION

For each one of us there is a desert to travel, a star
to discover and a being within ourselves to bring to life.
-Unknown

Now that Tom was released to the reserves, the first thing he did was call Kris, "Guess what. Good news. They're not sending me back to Vietnam."

"You didn't pass the physical? She asked somewhat concerned that it might effect his airline position."

"Oh ye of little faith who desires to have the truth set forth."

"Okay don't go religious on me."

"In regard to the physical, everything was normal. My fingers might be a little stiff for awhile. Other items were taken into consideration. They were impressed with my previous record. Also, my twenty five years of active and reserve duty. So they figured I shouldn't be recalled to active duty."

"Here's another item that will float your canoe."

"Don't make it too rough. I might get seasick."

"I'll chance it. Your daughter wrote a letter to the general asking that I be excused from going to Vietnam."

"That's hilarious Tom, unless the general took exception to it."

"Not at all, in fact he thought it was refreshing that she was motivated enough to write. Don't mention it to her. I want to surprise her. I just had an idea."

"Is this the idea for the day? You're full of ideas."

"I'll take that as a complement. Previously we figured we didn't have time to do some visiting. What do you think about calling John and Velma? See if they're free for the week-end. I could meet you at

Pax River, and being the great planner that I am, we could visit my son on Sunday if he doesn't have any committents."

"It sounds possible oh great planner. There's one other item to consider. What about Greta?"

"Bring her with you. I don't think John and Velma would object. They haven't seen her for a long time and Velma being pregnant would provide an insight what to expect in later years. She might have to miss one day of school. I was thinking about a visit with Harry and Grace but that would mean taking Greta out of school during the week. Although I'd like to visit them, maybe we better plan on another time. I planned on calling them anyway."

"I'll call John and Velma. If they can't make it that's as far as the planning will go. I'll get back to you." Tom punched in their number and it rang about five times before Velma picked up. "Velma, I thought you weren't home."

"I was outside raking leaves. How's my favorite part time husband?" She had accompanied Tom to Washington when he received the Medal of Honor as he and Mary Jane were at an impass. Several people assumed Velma was his wife.

"It's difficult to get any better."

"You sound as high as a kite. Have you been sniffing the corks in the bar?"

"I just passed my flight physical and I had a meeting with the general. They decided I don't have to return to Vietnam. Several factors entered into their decision but I was wondering if you and John would like some company for the week-end?"

"John is still at the field but we don't have any plans. How are you going to arrange all that?"

"Kris will fly there, will it be alright to bring Greta?"

"Absolutely, we haven't seen her in a long time."

"I'll call Kris and they can make their reservatons. I'm still at Cherry Point and I'm back in the reserves but I think I can talk to the acting CO, until I assume command again, into using one of the F9F

Cougars for a cross country navigation review. Also, if possible I'd like to stop at the Naval Academy to visit my son. Sorry I couldn't give you advance notice but I was certain I was heading back to Vietnam. I'll be on my way to Pax River so Kris will call you with their plans. Got to go. Looking forward to seeing you and John."

Hail! Hail! The gangs all here. It was amazing that everything came together considering the impromptu planning for the occasion. After all the greetings, hugs and kisses ended, the first question John asked, "How did you manage to escape from going back to Vietnam, ol' buddy?"

"It was a complete surprise to me. When the general said the medical report was normal I definitely assumed I was on the way, but then he enumerated all the reasons the board had taken under consideration. My previous record, my actve and reserve time of twenty five years, service in two wars, my age to be flying combat and he also considered my airline job. All considered, I shouldn't be deployed into harm's way, but the deciding factor, the general empathized was a letter from a young girl asking that her father be excused from going back to the war. I wasn't aware you knew the general, Greta?"

"I didn't think he would say anything about that," expecting Tom to make a federal case about it.

"What he did say was despite the coercion by your daughter, the decision had been finalized by the board."

"I'm so sorry I made trouble for you," she apologized.

"Not at all, my dear. The general said it was refreshing that you felt motivated to write a letter." She went to Tom and gave him a big hug and kiss. Greta excused herself to go to the bathroom.

Kris said, after Greta departed, "She really was disturbed about Tom's involvement in Vietnam. So was I," she added, " but it all came to a satisfying conclusion. How many times is it possible to escape the grim reaper?"

"It's difficult to realize you have a teenager," Velma figured, "also do you realize it's about twenty two years since we all met at the World

War II bond rally. Stay young by continuing to grow. You do not grow old, you become old by not growing. I don't know who said that. I guess that might be called sage advice."

"How's everything with your pregnancy?" Kris asked."

"So far everything is progressing normally but I'll feel better when it's time to deliver. I feel fine but it's the anxiety that something might happen. I should be more optimistic but with the history of the miscarriages, I'm a little apprehensive."

"I can understand that but think positive," Kris offered her support.

John and Tom were in the family room bar mixing the cocktails and making a few snacks. "Velma isn't drinking except fruit juice. She has been very cautious about everything in this pregnancy so it's just the three of us and Greta," John explained. He and Tom were delivering the drinks. A scotch and water for John, gin and tonic for Tom and Kris and orange juice for Velma and Greta. "Lets drink a toast to John and Velma for their coming event," Kris proposed. She began again, "With all the good news, Tom being excused from Vietnam." she looked at Greta but she just shrugged, "and John and Velma's pregnancy. The bad news was Lars death when his ship was attacked by the gunboats. Were you able to get in touch with Beth, John?"

"Yes, I think she viewed the news with mixed emotions. Obviously she was distressed about Lar's death but from our previous conversation she had decided to cancel the wedding. It solved their problem but she never figured that death was one of the options."

"Lets talk about good news," Velma suggested, "dinner for example. I took a roast beef filet out of the freezer. It's in the oven, with a green bean casserole. First we'll have a Caesar salad."

"Let me know what I can do," Kris offered

"I can help also." Greta volunteered.

"The more help makes the job lighter," Velma said. "Speaking of jobs, I realize you have a few more years to decide, but is there anything you're interested in now, Greta?"

"I'm planning on college but I haven't decided on a major. I hope something will attract my interest."

"Beth began acting in the plays at college and found her niche in acting."

"And doing well," Kris added. "Velma and I majored in journalism in college. You have a long time to decide on something. It's important to finish college first."

"John, did you take anymore flight tests on the A-6 armament system?" Tom asked.

"The ordinance was ground tested with the new switches and when they were satisfactory, the unit was installed on the aircraft and a bomb dropped. I flew the test flight and the operation was normal. All the A-6s were modified in the fleet."

"Too bad they weren't discovered sooner. It almost cost two lives and loss of an aircraft," Tom recalled.

Just then Velma walked in saying, "Kris and I will have dinner ready in about fifteen minutes. Would you like to set the table, Greta?"

"I can do that," she said happy to be asked to help.

"I will press John into service cutting the roast and Tom will be the wine steward." The dinner was a resounding success with Dutch Apple Pie, cheddar cheese, coffee for dessert and milk for Greta. As they were savoring an after dinner cordial Tom said, "Considering the short notice I gave you, Velma you accomplished the almost impossible. I propose a toast to our hostess. The next time I'll give you a half hour more notice."

"I just knew there would be a catch in there somewhere, Tom Korb and you didn't disappoint me."

"Seriously, Velma you did an excellent job on such short notice. I figured it was worth a try not knowing when we could get together again."

"Speaking of a get together, will you and Kris be available for the annual event in June at Chatham?"

"We would hate to miss it, John. Come hell or high water we'll be there. You being a Naval Academy grad, do the guys get any free time on the week-ends? I was thinking about the possibility of having lunch with my son if time permits. How far is Annapolis from here, John?"

"About fifty miles or so and if he doesn't have any commitments it sounds possible. I just had a thought. We could all go if you like. We haven't seen him for along time. Give him a call and they can get a message to him."

They were enjoying their cordials when the phone captured their attention. "Midshipman Korb could not come to the phone. But he said to tell you, full speed ahead. Looking forward to seeing you."

It was a beautiful crisp fall day for a drive. There had been a light frost but with the help of the sun and rising temperature it disappeared. John drove with Tom riding shotgun. The three girls were in the back seat with Greta in the middle. She said she felt like an oreo cookie and they all got a chuckle from her sense of humor.

They were all chatting, laughing, joking and enjoying the companionship of each other and the time quickly dissolved. At the security gate, the guard seeing the two marine officers saluted and cleared them through. John drove to the visitors area and Tom's son was told that he had visitors. Upon arrival he saluted the two officers according to protocol, then shook hands with his father and John who was more like a second father. There were hugs and kisses with Kris and Velma. "I didn't know Greta was with you," giving her a big hug and kiss. "This is an unexpected surprise and really great to see all of you."

"This whole arrangement was an impromptu adventure," Tom explained. "We prevailed on John and Velma for a visit and they graciously agreed. When I was told that I didn't have to return to Vietnam, I thought it would be a good time for a get together not knowing when we could meet again."

"How's everything so far?" John asked

"It's a very disciplined atmosphere as you know but I've been able to keep up with it. I have you and the senator to thank for this opportunity."

"We did the easy part, you're doing the difficult part," John conceded.

Before they all had an opportunity to discuss things, the Commandant, an Admiral appeared seemingly out of nowhere. John and Tom didn't know if it was protocol or just curiosity. They saluted the superior officer. Returning their salute and extending his hand in greeting, "I'm Admiral Peirson." There were introductions all around. "If you don't have any other plans I'd like to invite all of you to join me for lunch at the officer's dining room."

"That's very accommodating of you, Admiral. It would be our pleasure." John offered a blanket acceptance. He explained later that an invitation from an Admiral was tantamount to an order.

"Are both of you academy graduates?"

"I graduated in the class of '40," John answered.

"I graduated from Georgia Tech class of '49," Tom said.

"What is your position now?" directed to John.

"I'm a test pilot at Pax River."

"And you, Colonel?"

"I just returned from Vietnam. I had just released a bomb and it exploded within seconds and disabled the aircraft. The bombardier-navigator and I had to eject. We were rescued by the chopper pilots under fire from the Vietcong."

"Glad to see you survived, Colonel. Welcome home. Midshipman Korb is your son?"

"Yes, Sir."

"His progress is excellent and I'm sure he will be a fine officer which ever service he chooses." Looking at Velma he said, "You are John's wife. I notice you are expecting so my congratulations and best wishes to both of you. Do you have other children?"

"No, Sir this is my first."

"And you are Tom's wife, Kris? I'm using first names as both of your husbands are colonels."

"I was wondering if you knew my father, General Lundgren? He was killed on Okinawa."

"I knew the name but unfortunately I never met many of the marine officers. And you, Greta is Kris and Tom's daughter."

"Yes Sir. I'm glad he's home from Vietnam."

"I'm sure you are and again, I'm glad he is safely at home. John, your name is Fairfield. By any chance, is your father a senator?"

"Yes Sir, he is from Massachusetts."

"There again, the name is familiar but I've never met the senator."

They had been eating lunch throughout all the conversation with the admiral. They were finishing their coffee when he said, "It's been a pleasure having lunch with all of you." Looking at his watch, "I have a meeting in ten minutes. I don't have the opportunity to meet many of the parents. You impress me as families that have it altogether. Maybe your son would like to show you around the base. It might bring back some memories for you, John."

"Thank you for all your hospitality, Sir." When the admiral departed John said, "There's no doubt you'll ever have lunch here again," John said to Tom's son, "in fact it's the first time for me also."

"Would you like to walk around the base?" Tom's son asked acting upon the Admiral's suggestion.

"The lunch has taken longer than I planned but I think we had better head back to Pax River." Tom explained, "I told the CO I'd return the aircraft today. At least we were able to visit with you for awhile even though the admiral took over most of the time. We didn't have an opportunity to discuss things among ourselves, although the lunch invitation was very gracious of him. I think we'd better say our good-byes and head south." They all considered it was a successful day. Everything planned was accomplished and they were looking forward to the annual get together in June at Windmeer, the Fairfield's summer residence in Chatham on Cape Cod.

When they arrived at home, John asked Tom, "What are your plans when you get back to Greenwich?"

"I'll check with the flight office. I have to take a company physical. My qualification on the 707 is still valid. If not, I'll have to take a brief refresher course, then business as usual."

Tom flew the F9F back to Cherry Point, then jumped on the Leatherneck express to Anacostia, Washington, then caught a flight to LaGuardia. Kris and Greta also flew to LaGuardia but arrived earlier due to Tom's flight to Cherry Point. It was a hectic but an enjoyable week-end, now they had to plan for the coming week.

JUSTICE TRIUMPHS

When ever you have eliminated the impossible, whatever remains,
however probable, must be the truth.
-Arthur Conan Doyle

The International Tribunal at Nuremberg convicted twenty two German
leaders for war crimes. As Heinz Steiner was not in that classificaton he
was tried in the People's Court (*Volksgericht*), the most dreaded tribunal
in the land. It consisted of two professional judges and five others
chosen from among the party officals. There was no appeal from their
decisions or sentences and usually it's sessions were held on camera.
Occasionally, however for propaganda purposes when light sentences
were to be given, foreign correspondents were invited to attend.

There were cases when the proceedings were finished in a day.
There was practically no opportunity to present defense witnesses and
the arguments of the defense lawyers seemed weak to the point of being
ludicrous. From reading the newspaper, which merely announced the
verdicts, most of the defendants received a death sentence which was
carried out two hours after the sentence was imposed.

The case of Heinz Steiner was sent to the People's Court for
adjudication. The charge of premeditated murder, although an innocent
man was the victim instead of the original target, took precedence over
the lessor charge of trafficking in the black market.

The defense lawyer was unable to find any witnesses that were
present at Heinrich's trial before the International Tribual and his
summation lacked any previous thought as though the verdict was
a fore-gone conclusion and it was. The guilty verdict was announced
and the accused was sentenced to death by hanging.

One of the judges asked Steiner if he would like to say anything to the court. His reply was succinct and without remorse. "I'm not sorry for my actions."

The judge admonished him. "You allowed your quest for revenge to guide your thinking. Like your brother whose blatant disregard toward his fellow Germans, chose to participate in the black market. Not only did he disregard his oath as an officer, but also allegiance to the German People. For that he would have been convicted as you were today for following his descent into the abyss of life." It wasn't unusual for the death sentence to occur within a few hours after the announcement was read. For some unknown reason it was delayed until the following morning when Heinz Steiner was hanged at sunrise. It was speculated since Steiner didn't show any signs of remorse, the judges delayed the execution which would permit him to ponder his fate until the hanging at sunrise.

Heinrich was relieved when the guilty verdict was read even though it appeared to be a foregone conclusion. Another chapter ended on his rocky road through life. After the Korean War, Heinrich was getting along in age. His health was deteriorating. The strain in the previous years had begun to exact it's toll. He wasn't flexible in considering and developing new ideas and at that rate the factories would become stagnant. His doctor advised him to slow down or even retire. He resisted both ideas but when a slight stroke occurred, the decision was made.

The logical successor was Hilda, his daughter who had been associated with die Firma since graduating from Oxford University in England before the war. She had the foresight to realize incorporation was the logical path to follow. With guidance from the banker it was accomplished and a research and development department had been implemented.

She also had plans to expand the utilization of the castle. A section of the castle was turned into a bed and breakfast and later became a hotel or gasthof catering to banquets, conventions, parties, weddings et al. It attracted not only the locals but dignitaries were also staying at the castle. With all the expansion, it became necessary to hire more employees. Hanna, Heinrich's wife filled the niche admirably to organize the expansion due in part to her experience at the company hospital and the factory laborer's housing. With the expansion completed and further outlook to the future, Lehndorff Industries, in addition to the castle, became a viable corporation and the Lehndorff Foundation was instituted for the Advancement of Science.

When the Vietnam War ended, Hilda now in her seventies decided to retire. The company was sold to a group of German industrialists who retained the Lehndorff Industrie's name. Hanna had been taking a semi-active part in the company and an active part in the operation of the castle in previous years, retired in reasonably good health and was now in her eighties. Hilda, who had been a widow twice, never remarried and assumed a limited control in the operation of the castle.

FUTURE PLANS

Without future plans life would be like a person who could not smile,
like a summer without flowers, and like a home without a garden.
-Unknown

The impromptu week-end with John and Velma was a success and everything planned had been accomplished to their satisfaction. Kris and Greta arrived in Greenwich before Tom as he had to fly the F9F Cougar back to Cherry Point. He called Kris saying he was still in Washington and would arrive later in the evening. They heard the garage door opening and when he walked in Greta jumped on him saying, "I'm so happy the general didn't send you back to Vietnam," Kris echoed her sentiments and they were a happy family.

"Speaking of the general," Tom said, "you surprised all of us with the letter you wrote to him."

"After I sent it I began to think it would do more harm than good."

"He was very gracious and said it was refreshing that you cared enough to write. When I was leaving his office he said, 'Tell your daughter I enjoyed hearing from her.' "

Morning had broken like the words from the hymn. Everyone had a restful night sleeping, without any worries after the eventful week-end. The night had receded revealing a cloudless sky with a chill in the air. Kris prepared breakfast for Greta, she and Tom gave her a goodbye kiss as she ran out to wait for the school bus happy that her father can remain at home. Tom finished his breakfast and gave Kris the usual good-bye kiss. As he would be driving to La Guardia for a meeting at the flight office, "Hope your meeting goes well," Kris called as he was leaving. "Call me later." Kris remained home with the solitude of the morning.

Morning traffic to La Guardia was heavy as usual. In deference to his position as Manager of Flight he had a reserved parking space near the office as opposed to the employee parking lot. The first person he met upon entering the office was the Manager of Operations. "Welcome back, Tom. We all heard about your ordeal in Vietnam. Appears your recuperation is complete."

"Yes, thanks, Dave. I for one am happy to be here. The issue was in doubt for awhile. I can't say enough for those chopper pilots. They pressed on although receiving ground fire and by some miracle rescued us."

"You've had a difficult year so far. Considering the possible ditching you avoided, which incidentally was an amazing feat of airmanship. I hear you will be awarded the Distinguished Service Medal."

"That's very gracious of the company."

"I hope the coming months will be more tranquil. Your office is waiting for you. For the most part, things have been relatively normal."

Tom's secretary had an office adjacent to his. She was with the airline more years than she cared to remember but it was a good job with many privileges. In her forties, she never married but was attractive in a subtle way with a pleasant personality. One of the retired captains, whose wife died recently, proposed to her and she accepted. It was a surprise as there never was an overt idea he was interested until his wife died.

She entered his office saying, "Did you have an opportunity to read all your memos?"

"No, not yet. Anything important?"

"There's one that might peak you interest. It's from flight training."

"Probably about my 707 qualification. Necessary to take a refresher course."

"Read on *mon Captaine*," she said with an enigmatic smile.

He began reading the memo, exclaiming, "I can't believe this, I just got here and I'm scheduled for 747 qualification at the Boeing factory in Seattle. My wife and daughter will love this bit of news," he said facetiously. "They were overjoyed when I didn't have to return to Vietnam. At least I'll be able to get home for the week-ends. I guess I'll have to accept the fact."

"Looking on the bright side, you'll get a raise," she chided.

"It will buy a few more hamburgers. Speaking of hamburgers," he continued, "whenever we went out for dinner our daughter always ordered a hamburger. On one occasion I said, why don't you order something beside a hamburger. She ordered the most expensive item on the menu, crab legs. After that I never questioned her decision."

"That's amusing. You never know what kids are thinking."

"Incidently, best wishes on your engagement."

"Thanks. That wasn't on an inter office memo, was it? Did you think I was going to be an old maid?"

"No, not at all. Dave mentioned it keeping me informed of the latest happenings in operations. I wondered why someone wasn't eager to corral you in the past."

"I'll take that as a compliment."

"That, indeed was how it was meant. I think I'll call my wife and relay the "*good news*" about the trip to Seattle." He hoped she wouldn't be too disappointed. It's all part of the job. She picked up on the third ring. "Guess who?"

Recognizing his voice, she decided to add a little levity to the call. "You're an old classmate calling to arrange a secret luncheon to discuss old times."

"Now cut that out," he laughed knowing his wife's penchant for humor.

"How come you're calling so early? Everything okay?"

"It's not bad news, just unexpected. The flight training department just sent me a memo that I'll be going to the Boeing factory in Seattle for qualification on the 747."

"I thought you'd be home for awhile. How long does that last?"

"The better part of two months, but I'll be home on week-ends. Just like commuting to Seattle."

"Well that's some consolation you won't be away two months. Greta will be disappointed."

"I'm sure she will but it's better than going back to Vietnam. Also the good news is that I'll be getting a raise." Glancing at his watch, "I have a meeting in a few minutes, Kris. We'll talk about it tonight at dinner."

The meeting commenced at 1000 hours in the conference room. The chief pilots from the four divisions were in attendance in addition to the engineering test pilot from the overhaul base in Tulsa who would chair the meeting. "As you are aware," he began, "we're here to discuss the 747. Although the aircraft will not enter service for at least two years, as usual we prefer to gain an insight into the details as soon as possible. In fact, Tom has been scheduled for a meeting at Boeing later this month, incidentally, Tom welcome back from your ordeal, to acquire an insight into the progress so far." Tom raised his hand to acknowledge the reference to his ordeal.

"The initial order is for sixteen aircraft, five will be configured as freighters. It will be the largest aircraft in our fleet with take off weights in the 700,000 pound range. Gate space will have to reconfigured along with other operational changes."

"In regard to the training, which is primarily your interest as pilots, there will be some changes. For example, the cockpit is thirty feet from the ground which may alter your depth perception in taxiing and also landing where the aircraft will be in a nose high position." He had been talking for about twenty minutes when he noted a few nodding imperceptibly. "Lets take a break. There is some coffee and danish on the table. Then we'll continue and possibly I'll be able to answer some questions you have within my scope of information I've received so far."

During the coffee break, Tom was welcomed back individually.

They were all veterans of World War II or flew in the Air Transport Command who were airline pilots flying cargo and personnel for the military. "What are your thoughts about ejecting?"

Tom considered the question momentarily. "It's was the first time I ever punched out and I hope it was the last. It's a violent experience but it does the job it was designed to do, saved our lives."

Another question. "Are you still in the reserves?"

"Yes. I'm still the CO of the reserve training squadron at Cherry Point. We're flying the F9F Cougars. I flew them in the Korean War."

"Do you plan on staying in the reserve?"

"Yes, at least for the immediate future. I have twenty six years active and reserve."

"What's your rank now, Tom?"

"Lieutenant Colonel. Depending on how long this war lasts, maybe in one of their generous moments they'll promote me to colonel."

They had a fifteen minute break when the pilot conducting the meet said, "Lets continue with our discussion, shall we? To give you a few of the stats in comparing the 747 to the 707."

707	**747**
Wing span 150' 10"	Wing span 195' 8"
Max take off weight 326,000	Max take off weight 710,000
Engines - Pratt Whitney 18,000 lbs thrust	engines - Pratt Whitney 43,500 lbs thrust
Passengers 56 first class 56 Coach	Passengers 66 first class 300 coach

"Initially all of you will receive your qualification at the Boeing factory in Seattle. When it gets closer to the time the 747 will enter service, the ground school for centralized training will be operating in Fort Worth."

"Some items are subject to change especially the passenger configuration. Also with engines that size, the fuel burn will be considerably higher than the 707." He hesitated momentarily. "Before I continue are there any questions that I ought to be covering?"

"How will all that fit into our route structure?"

"Good question. High density routes will be utilized initially. New York-Los Angeles and possibly New York- Dallas-Los Angeles. Crews based in New York and Los angeles will no doubt fly the trips. And later on as we acquire more aircraft a trip through Chicago will be considered." He took a sip of water as his throat was getting dry from all the talking. "Any other questions before I continue?"

"You said that five of the aircraft will be configured as freighters. This is a two part question. Will the same cities be served by the freighters and will the freighter areas require substantial modifications?"

"Yes and yes. The cities previously mentioned are part of the high density routes and also some of the freight carried on our present aircraft will be shifted to the 747 as I understand it can accomodate about 100,000 pound payload."

"Are there any future plans for overseas routes?"

"As you no doubt heard, the company is interested in acquiring routes in the Caribbean. New York -San Juan is a highly traveled route and if successful a 747 passenger and a freighter trip could begin. But there again, the airport and passenger areas would require some modifications to accommodate the larger 747."

"Just one last question? I know you'd like to break for lunch. Is there a time table set when the 747 will enter airline service?"

"The last tentative date I've heard is early March 1970 so that gives us more than enough time to prepare for the inauguration. I'm going back to Tulsa tomorrow morning and at that time I'll be sitting in on some ot the maintenance meetings not only in regard to the facilities but also the aircraft maintenance. So in closing, I'll leave you with this thought. The 707 prototype, as you no doubt know, evolved from the military B-47. The 747 is an entirely new future in jet aircraft. As usual there will be problems associated with any new aircraft but it will be our job to help solve them. Thanks for your attention and I'll be in touch for our next meeting. Just one other thought, the 747 is so big, it's euphemistically referred to as an aluminum cloud."

It was a busy day for Tom at his first day back at work. The meeting occupied most of the morning. After lunch there was a brief meeting due to some of the local operating procedures. Then the revue of the daily reports of engines shut downs, minor incidents, diversions and a crew landed at the wrong airport. The incident in itself was not that serious but the crew exacerbated the problem by taking off without a clearence. A hearing would be held the following day.

It was late when Tom finally arrived home. The sun was trying to restrain the darkness but lost the battle when it slipped below the horizon. Kris saw the car's headlights as they reflected off the windows. She met him at the door. "Sounds like you had a busy day, my love," as they exchanged the usual kiss and hug. "Thanks for calling that you would be late so I held off on the dinner."

Greta had been doing her homework when she heard Tom arrive and also exchanged the usual kiss and hug. "Glad you're home even though you're late," she chided, happy he will be coming home every evening.

"It was a busy day," he explained

"You have time to freshen up a bit," Kris said, "and by that time dinner will be ready." They always had dinner together unless there were mitigating incidents that took priority. And they encouraged the display of affection but not to the point of being overly demonstrative. As Greta was growing up they tried to create a wholesome atmosphere by setting examples that would carry over into the future. Neither of them smoked or swore but she no doubt heard that type of language in school. They had a glass of wine before dinner but never to excess.

Although they were not overly religious, they attended church regularly and took Greta with them.

The sixties had turned into a violent and permissive decade fueled to a great extent by an unpopular war. Greta, who would soon become a teenager was entering a time in her life where the temptation to use drugs, alcohol or sex promulgated by her peers or adults. Both Tom and Kris discussed but not preached to her the pitfalls and fallacy of the drug culture.that would only lead to the degradation of one's lifestyle. They hoped she had the will power to follow the straight and narrow path in life. It would also be difficult when she went off to college. The first time when some of them were away from home, making their own decisions without parental supervision or guidance from the faculty. They weren't concerned about their son who was in his second year at the Naval Academy. An infraction of the rules was cause for immediate dismissal.

"Dinner is ready," Kris announced, "for my hungary family although it's a little later than usual." After they began eating, Kris asked. "What's all this about you going to the Boeing factory in Seattle."

After chewing a mouthful, Tom replied, "It's partially true. An overzealous flight training department assumed it was for the qualification on the 747. I am scheduled for a trip later this month to Boeing's factory but it's only for a short visit on the 747's progress."

"Well we're happy to hear that," they replied almost in unison.

Tom explained the 747 program much the same as it was discussed at the morning's meeting. "An aircraft that size requires a considerable amount of advance planning although the tenative date it will enter service is about 1970."

Now that she was relieved Tom would only be going to Seattle for a short time, she directed the conversation to another subject. "I received a request from our daughter this afternoon when she came home from school," Kris said eating the last bite of the macaroni, ham and cheese casserole.

"Let me tell him, Mom. I'd like to take piano lessons," she said with enthusiasm.

"Considering the fact that we don't have a piano, how would you practice?"

"I was hoping that you and Mom would buy a piano."

"That would be a big investment with no guarantee you would continue to take lessons and practice everyday. From what I've heard about other people's experience with pianos, they lose interest and it just becomes another piece of furniture as we don't play. Although I did learn to play *chop sticks* in my misspent youth."

"Now be serious, Daddy, I would really like to learn how to play the piano and I'll practice."

"What about your other interets," he persisted. "The drama club, the chorus then soccer during the season."

"I could leave the drama club. I don't have the talent Beth has anyway. Please! Please! Please! I really would enjoy it. Could you talk him into it, Mom?"

"I'm sorry, Dear," Kris empathized, "but I have to agree with your father's thinking. The parents buy a piano and the daughter takes lessons for a few months, then becomes tired of the idea and practice is booring thus ending the episode. I'll tell you what," Kris said ending the discussion. "We'll talk about it some more. We would like to be reasonably assured that it isn't just a whim or a passing fancy after spending all that money."

A SURPRISE VISIT

There's a saying: Appreciate your friends.
Life is too short and friends are too few.
-Unknown

All the usual guests had received written invitations for the get together scheduled for the weekend. John and Velma arrived earlier in the week to help his parents with the guest list and other arrangements as necessary. As they were checking the seating list, Sharon said, "There's a call for you from Boston, John. Whoever it is at the other end sounds like an Oriental."

John retrieved the phone from Sharon, "Hello, whom are you calling," thinking someone had the wrong number.

"Are you Lieutenant John Fairfield, United States Marine Corps?"

"Yes," he surmised, it must be someone I haven't seen for a long time referring to the rank of lieutenant.

"My name is Tanaka Omura. Do you remember me, Lieutenant?"

"No, I'm sorry I don't. Where did we meet?" John answered trying to remember the incident.

"I was the captain of the destroyer that rescued you after you were shot down."

"Again I'm sorry. I didn't remember your name. It's been a long time. You really saved my life." Sharon and Velma looked at each other wondering what John had done that someone had saved his life.

"You're in Boston now?"

"I wanted to visit your great country again before I got too old to travel." He graduated from Yale.

A thought raced through John's mind. "How long are you staying in Boston, Tanaka?"

"We leave next Wednesday for Washington after all the sightseeing."

"We have what we call a get together here in June. This is my parents summer residence. It's at Chatham on Cape Cod, If you don't have any other plans, would you like to come here for the week-end?"

"It would be an honor, John. I was wondering if we might be able to meet somewhere. My wife is here with me."

"That's great. Bring her with you. If you will be driving I'll give you the directions. There's also a commuter flight from Boston to Hyannis and we could meet you at the airport?"

"I would prefer flying. It's much faster. That's very generous of you, John."

"We'll make all the arrangement for you. Looking forward to seeing you and your wife."

"Imagine that, after all these years. I don't think I would have survived the night if he hadn't fished me out of the water. When we docked in Sasebo and I departed, I gave him sort of a blanket invitation if he ever got to the U.S. to give me a call. These things don't usually happen," by way of futher explanation.

"We were beginning to wonder," Velma said, "what kind of nefarious activity you were doing that prompted someone to save your life?"

"You thought I was leading a double life," he countered raising his eyebrows like Groucho Marx.

John and Velma were waiting at the airport for the Japanese couple's arrival. "I don't think it will be difficult to identify them," Velma said. "Don't imagine there are many Japanese coming here this morning. I hope they speak English."

"You're so perceptive, my dear. I know Tanaka speaks English.

Don't know about his wife." The cabin door opened and they hesitated for a moment. "There they are," Velma said.

"You're recognition is flawless also," John teased.

"I could hit you, John."

"Tanaka, it's been a long time," John said extending his hand in welcome.

"Ah so, John or should I say Lieutenant, it's been awhile. May I present my wife, Mayume."

"My pleasure," John said, "and I've advanced a few grades. This is my wife, Velma." After all the introductions were completed they walked to the car, John carried Mayume's bag.

"Arrigato, Sir. Sorry, I have to remember to speak English."

"We're very casual here, just call me John."

On the way back to the house, Tanaka asked, "What is this get together we will be attending?"

"Once a year on the first week-end in June we all meet here, that is all who are able and available. We renew old friendship, reminisce about the past, discuss the future and enjoy ourselves."

"And we eat a lot," Velma injected. "You'll probably gain a few pounds."

"We will have some lunch and you being a sailor, Tanaka you'll probably enjoy this, we take about a two hour cruise on our fifty foot sailboat."

"I shall look forward to it. I haven't done any sailing since the war ended."

"Speaking of the war, Tanaka have you heard anything about the officer who interrogated me at the POW camp?" John asked. "As I recall, I was very angry when I was liberated."

"Yes I did. He was sentenced to ten years as a war criminal and I heard he died in prison although I don't know the circumstances."

"Glad to hear it," John said somewhat appeased. "I hope you didn't mind my reaction."

"Not at all. I share your sentiment."

"It will be exhilarating to feel the wind and the spray. In fact that's the name of the boat, *Windmeer*." Meer is the sea. It's also the name of the cottage."

"Have you ever attended a clambake?" Velma asked.

"No, they answered in unison. I don't think I ever heard of one."

"I graduated from Yale," Tanaka explained, "and as I recall, I've heard of them but never attended one."

"Clams, mussels, lobsters, corn on the cob and potatoes are cooked on hot coals in a hole covered in sea weed." John explained, "you probably enjoy a lot of seafood in Japan. That will be our dinner for the evening. You might like to take a walk on the beach afterward."

Arriving back at the house there were more introductions to the immediate family and friends. At the happy hour before dinner, John made all the other introductions en masse. When everyone had their favorite libation, John stood on the fireplace hearth in the family room. "Ladies, gentlemen, friends and some people we're not too sure of, may I have your attention." Everyone groaned. "My special guests, all the way from Japan are Tanaka and his wife Mayume Omura." They waved in response to the applause. "Tanaka graduated from Yale before the war and they're on vacation visiting some of our cities."

He introduced everyone with a few words about each one. "My parents John and Sharon and you already met my wife Velma. My sister Beth who is enjoying a career as a movie actress. Tom and Kris. Tom and I were part of a three strike flight returning from Japan when I was shot down. Kris is General Lundgren's daughter. His son Lars and Beth had announced wedding plans, but Lars was unfortunately killed when a shell hit the bridge of his ship in Vietnam." He introduced a few other local friends but some of the dignitaries would arrive only for the banquet tomorrow evening. The governor, mayor, police chief et al.

"Tanaka is a special person to me. I'm sorry that we could not have met again previously. He was the captain of a destroyer heading back to Sasebo when I was shot down. One of his lookouts spotted my raft and he took me on board. Hypothermia was beginning to have an effect. I don't think I could have survived the night. He treated me as a friend and not an enemy or I should say we were friendly enemies. He even offered me a cup of sake as I recall. If it hadn't been for his humanity, I wouldn't be here tonight. He saved my life." Everyone vigorously applauded.

The Senator proposed a toast. "Although it isn't sake - to the kindness of Tanaka who gave our son back to us."

The following day, after a sumptuous brunch, John, Velma, Tom, Kris, Tanaka and Mayume sat in the gazebo gazing at the ocean. It was almost a cloudless sky with an onshore breeze of ten knots. High tide would be in about an hour as the waves lapped at the shore on the incoming tide.

"I envy you, John this is a beautiful setting," Tanaka observed.

"We come here as often as possible. Actually, I'm based at Pax River. It's not far from Washington. I'm a test pilot and a Lieutenant Colonel now. What did you do after the war?"

Congratulations John, I was referring to your rank as a Lieutenant. I should have realized your progress during all those years. I was based at Sasebo, we were living in Nagasaki when the atom bomb was dropped. I was at sea, but my wife died in the bombing."

"That decision is still being debated, but if the invasion had gone as scheduled there would have been a considerable loss of life on both sides," John offered.

"If you recall our discussion when you were rescued, we were in agreement and it was only a matter of time before Japan would capitulate," Tanaka agreed.

"After the war," he continued, "Tokyo was the place where things were happening so I moved there and fortunately found a job with a law firm that specialized in International Law which was my major at Yale. I met Mayume who was working at a bank and as our friendship developed we were married."

"I met John at a War Bond Rally during the war. I was working for the local newapaper as a writer and also coordinator of events," Velma said. "We were both attracted to each other but decided to wait until the war ended before getting married. I thought our future would never come to pass when he was shot down. Fortunately, fate intervened and thankfully was rescued by you."

"What happened to you after the war, Tom?" Tanaka asked.

"My fiancee and I were married after the war. We had a three month old son when she was killed in a automobile accident. I was in the active reserve and recalled for the Korean War. Kris and I were married after I graduated from Georgia Tech. I just returned from Vietnam. I was forced to eject after the bomb was released and exploded seconds after leaving the aircraft. Now I returned to my job as an airline pilot."

"Both of you have had interesting lives and I'm glad you survived. I thoroughly enjoyed the sailboat ride yesterday, John. Would it be an imposition if we went to sea again for a short cruise?"

"No, not at all. We'll still have a lot of time before the formal dinner this evening."

"Formal dinner," they both gasped. "We don't have any formal clothes."

"Not to worry," John assured them. "We can find a tux and Velma can locate a long evening dress for Mayume. So let's go to sea and we'll have more than enough time to prepare for the dinner."

"I don't know how we can thank you enough, Tanaka and Mayume thoroughly agreed."

"We're happy you called us."

John found a tux for Tanaka and Velma found an evening dress for Mayume, who was about the same size. The tux wasn't a tailor made fit but served the purpose. All the guests had arrived for the cocktail hour and the dinner. The orchester played softly to avoid overwhelming the conversations.

Previous get togethers were held in the cottage but through the years the guest list kept expanding so now they utilized the ballroom in the hotel. There were more introductions at the cocktail hour as old friends reminisced about the past. Many were curious about the connection between the Fairfield family and the Japanese couple. As many of the guests didn't have the opportunity to meet them, John decided to do the honors when everyone was seated.

Johntinkledhisglasssaying, "I'dliketomakeabriefannouncement. Just a few words, as usual a few hundred," that elicited a negative response, "so all you chow hounds can begin eating." More response. Being they were all old friends no one took umbrage to John's kidding. Not realizing it was all in jest, the Japanese couple were concerned until John explained.

"I realize some of you didn't have the opportunity to meet Tanaka and Mayume. They live in Tokyo, Japan and are here on vacation. Incidently, Tanaka graduated from Yale, our friendship dates back to 1945 when I was shot down returning to the carrier from a raid in Japan. Tanaka was the Captain of a destroyer returning to Sasebo." He reiterated the details of the rescue by Tanaka and the cordial treatment he received. "In that short length of time we became friends or one might characterize it as friendly enemies. I didn't believe I would have survived the night. Whether it was chance, luck or fate, I wouldn't be here tonight. He saved my life." The applause was loud, long and sincere.

"Would you like to say a few words, Tanaka?"

"Yes, thank you John. I must confess that I was somewhat concerned when John was speaking and the response he received until I realized it was all in fun. At times I think we Japanese are too reserved. May I present my wife Mayume." Applause but not boisterous.

"This is the first opportunity I've had to visit your great country since my college days at Yale. I didn't get to do much sightseeing then as I returned to Japan between semesters and long breaks such as Christmas, but I hope to see as much as possible this time."

"This is my first visit to Cape Cod. and I thank John for his gracious invitation to your get togethers. When he departed from the ship in Sasebo he said, 'If you ever get to my country give me a call'. Well here I are, he said switching to a colloquial word as an example of Japanese flexibility." Light applause. "I in turn extend the invitation to visit us in Japan. It's been a pleasure." Standing ovation. Tanaka and Mayume bowed in appreciation of the generous reception.

"When I retire Tanaka, I just might take you up on your invitation," John acknowledged the invitation.

ORDERS

Bureau Personnel
Washington, D. C.
Commanding Officer
MCAS, Ewa Oahu
1. Fairfield, John E. III, Colonel, USMC
2. Above named officer will be detached from Patuxent NAS and report to CO MCAS Ewa Oahu, Hawaii to assume command of VMF-211. Further orders will be received in re: squadron boarding of CVW-16.
3. Mil travel authorized. Report no later than 2400 hours 1 Nov 1966.
4. No delay en route authorized.
By direction:
Hartwell, John C. Capt. USMCR

A CHANGE OF DUTY

The chain of human life unrolls as
limitless as the waves in the seas that
lap on the shores.
-Richardson

The Navy has a two year time limit on the duty of a test pilot. When his time expired, John was assigned, due to his extensive aircraft carrier experience as the CO (commanding officer) of a marine squadron deployed on an aircraft carrier.

After a thorough discussion with Velma in regard to the Astronaut Program, he decided against sending in an application much to Velma's surprise and relief. She, in turn surprised John with the welcome news of her pregnancy after three miscarriages.

Relocating to Houston was one of the deciding factors against the decision. They hadn't considered what John's next assignment would involve but were surprised when he received his orders to deploy as the temporary CO of a marine squadron scheduled for a six month tour of duty. Due to medical complications, the CO was unavailable. As John's tour of duty at Pax River ended he was assigned as a replacement. In regard to the timing, he was the logical choice. He had previous carrier experiencce and was qualified on the aircraft. He only required the carrier requalification and that would be accomplished enroute. Also, an impromptu event would look good on his service record as flexible in unplanned situations.

After debriefing the flight he was notified about his new assignment. He hadn't considered anything in particular but neverless it came as a surprise. Velma greeted him with the usual homecoming ritual. During their dinner cocktail, they discussed the day's events and

Velma said, "John my love, you seem rather disconsolate. Anything happen today that you would like to discuss?"

"As you know, my tour of duty as a test pilot will be ending soon and"

She interrupted, "You received your new assignment and you're not happy with it. Am I correct in assuming that."

"You are so right." He explained all the details of the new assignment. "The one consoling factor is that we don't have to move. Also, it's only for six months and I should be home before the baby is born."

"Maybe I can take some time off from the newspaper and visit my folks or they might like to come here for a visit."

John had speculated where his new assignment would take him. It was a possibility he would be assigned as a squadron CO, but not on a carrier which now was a reality. "New orders will be cut for me in a few days," he added.

"All the time we spent on discussing the Astronaut Program," Velma began, "it's a moot point now, it could have solved the problem in the beginning. I almost hate to mention it, but is it possible the carrier will operate in the Vietnam War?"

"It's a possibility," John conceded, "especially as it's a fighter squadron. I'm qualified on the aircraft. I would just have to renew the carrier qualification."

"It was a beautiful crisp fall day when I woke up this morning." The leaves turned the landscape into a kaleidoscope of colors. "Now the news of your deployment has cast a shadow of doubt on our future plans with the possibility of you being sent into harm's way again." She tried to stifle the tears but a few managed to streak down her cheeks. "I'm sorry, John. I shouldn't let this bother me when we don't have all the facts, but the possibility exists. Maybe my condition makes me feel more vulnerable."

"Try not to get too agitated," he cautioned. "We don't want another miscarriage." He held her until her composure returned. Although the surprise news of John's deployment pervaded their home, a stained glass sunset slipped below the horizon as the sun attempted to hold back the night. They continued discussing the change in plans and made a few phone calls. Looking at the time, they forgot about eating. Velma arranged a casual dinner. It had been a tiresome day with the unexpected change in the immediate future. They were mentally tired. It was before their usual bedtime but they decided to retire for the night.

Velma viewed the ending of John's tour of duty at Pax River with trepidation. It had become an obsession when John was sent into harm's way and especially when he was shot down and reported missing in action during the war. Once again she was confronted with the same situation. She decided to call Kris and appraise her of the latest happenings. "Kris, Velma here. How's everything with you?"

"Just fine, how about you?"

"I have bad news, at least disturbing."

Kris assumed she had another miscarriage. "You're having a problem with your pregnancy?"

"No, the news was just unexpected." She explained about John's tour of duty ending at Pax River and the subsequent assignment and deployment to an aircraft carrier.

"Well, that was sudden and unexpected. When will he be leaving?" she empathized.

Velma further explained the chronology of events. "It all happened suddenly. His orders say he has to report the first of the month. This all sounds familiar, Kris.

We've been down this road previously. These wars are our nemesis. The only way to keep our guys at home is eliminate wars or they retire."

"Amen" Velma agreed. "Is Tom home?"

"He's in Seattle on the 747 project."

"When will he be coming home?"

"I don't know for sure. He just left yesterday and usually spends a few days there."

Velma sounded disappointed. "Guess we won't be able to get together before John leaves."

"Tom will be disappointed also. It seems as though our lives are a series of good-byes," Kris said reviewing the past. "Keep us informed, Velma. We have two important events in the future. The get together in June and the birth of your baby. Let's hope for the best."

It was a weepy good-bye when John was leaving for his deployment. He admonished Velma that she shouldn't allow this to become an obsession. She has an important job to stay healthy when the baby is born. "I agree with you, my love but it's difficult to say good-bye again."

"It's only for six months. We don't have to move. You can still work at the newspaper and you still have all your friends here. You can visit Tom and Kris and your folks. The six months will be history."

"Instead of saying good-bye, let's just say see you later."

John's itinerary basically followed Tom's deployment when he left for Vietnam except he departed from Washington instead of New York for the ten hour flight to Hawaii. Although he didn't know the crew they were aware of Tom's position with the airline. John had been talking to the flight attendant about things in general and John mentioned that he and Tom's friendship went way back when they were cadets in flight school. She passed the information to the captain and they invited him to the cockpit for a visit after lunch. After the crew had their lunch, the captain chimed the flight attendant to ask the colonel if he'd like to come up for a visit. They all introduced themselves and the captain said, "We hear you know Tom."

"We were cadets at Pensacola and went all the way from Guadalcanal to Japan. Tom is working on the 747 program, in fact he's in Seattle as of yesterday."

"Where are you heading for now, John?"

"I just finished a duty tour at Pax River as a test pilot. Now I've been assigned as the CO of a squadron to be deployed on a carrier."

"I've heard that carrier flying is tough duty."

"It can get exciting, especially at night in a rain squall." They continued talking for awhile, mostly about flying. "If you see Tom before I do, tell him I had an enjoyable visit with all of you."

After John departed, the co-pilot said, "Did you notice all the ribbons he had.

Must have been awarded everything that's available."

Arriving in Hawaii, John checked in with the CO observing the usual protocol. "Welcome to beautiful Hawaii, Colonel. I'm General Wilson or if you would rather dispense with the formalities in the office, I'm Jim."

"Fine with me, I'm just plain John."

"Leafing through your record, your career has been anything but plain. This has been an accelerated situation as you are aware. You were entitled to some free time between assignments but everything just fit into place except for your carrier requal. Do you see any problems there?"

"None at all, Jim. It's just another checkout except it involves an aircraft carrier."

He pressed a button on the desk and a Navy Commander entered. "John Fairfield, Ray Hunter. Ray is the ship's air boss," he said by way of introduction. "How about some coffee while we engage in some hangar flying?" The captain had been an F-14 pilot.

"I understand," Ray said, "that you just finished a tour as a test pilot at Pax River and you flew the test flight on the A-6 with the premature bomb explosion."

"That I did and the air strike was flown by my ol' buddy."

"You know the pilot?" Jim asked.

"Yes, Tom Korb. We were cadets at Pensacola in '41 and remained together from Guadalcanal to Japan."

"Jim and I were leafing through you records, John. Very impressive. You were a POW in Japan."

"I was fortunate to survive. That was the nadir in my life for several months."

Ray asked, "As this is a temporary assignment, do you have any idea for your next assignment."

"I was thinking about applying for the Astronaut Program. It's about a four year commitment, but where would I go from there? I decided against it."

"I was thinking in that direction at one time also," Ray admitted, "and I even submitted an application but withdrew it. In regard to your carrier requal, you're set up for an 0900 flight. I think three traps should be sufficient and then you can get acquainted with the other pilots. One of the pilots is a woman. Thought I'd mention it so you wouldn't be surprised."

"I've never had any contact with a female pilot but I don't have any objection. I assume she is qualified."

The following morning John's carrier qual proceeded as planned. The air boss complimented John on an excellent demonstration of carrier flying.

All the pilots gathered in the ready room to meet the new CO. Coffee and Danish were available. It was somewhat difficult to describe the female pilot as she was wearing her flight coveralls. The name patch said, ALLISON McCORD, FIRST LIEUTENANT, USMC. Her brown hair was cut short in the typical Marine Corps style and her gaze was somewhat evasive. She was reserved in comparison to the other pilots who were acting boisterous as usual. Carrier flying was difficult to say the least and they figured they were an elite group. It required a considerable amount of skill to land an aircraft on a pitching deck traveling at 130 knots in turbulence at night in a rain squall and have the tail hook catch the usual number three wire. Although those conditions aren't prevalent on every flight, it's essential to be able to cope with the situation when necessary. Also, if the pilot arrives at the carrier with minimum fuel and executes a missed approach for some reason, there's the possibility of depleting the fuel and be forced to ditch.

To become better acquainted, John was talking to the pilots individually to gain an insight into their experience and general attitude. He extended his hand in greeting to the female pilot and her handshake was weak. He didn't expect her to crush his fingers but being a pilot he assumed it would be firm. It resembled a handshake at a cotillion. "Lieutenant Allison McCord," he said reading her name tag. "Is this your first deployment?"

"Yes, Sir. I'm looking forward to it."

"What were you flying previously?" he was curious to hear about her experiences.

"I was flying the F9F's based at Cherry Point and my carrier qual was at Miramar."

"I flew them occasionally. I was a test pilot at Pax River so I flew a variety of aircraft." John's record was common knowledge in the pilot group which may have accounted for her reserve demeanor. Our orders haven't been released as far as I know, but I imagine we'll be operating in the South China Sea. It's somewhat unique having a female pilot assigned to a carrier in a war zone. Do you have any qualms about flying in combat?"

"None at all, Sir."

That was the answer John expected. What else could she say. "What was your motivation in becoming a carrier pilot? You're a member of an elite group and the flying is similar to the precision flying of the Blue Angels."

"I joined a flying club in college and got a private pilot license. I had various pilot jobs to build up my time and applied for flight training and was transferred to Pensacola. I had requested fighters and later on carrier flying. I think that is where the action is and that about brings us up to the present."

John spent more time talking to Allison than the other pilots. She was the least experienced and he was attempting to ascertain if she could perform to the reputation of being a carrier pilot.

All the navy and marine personnel arrived on board the previous day to get squared away. Provisioning the ship would be completed for the departure. After the ship was at sea for a few hours, the navy and marine pilots would fly out to the carrier. It was an expedient way to load the aircraft on board and also served as an operational training exercise.

When Allison was on final approach, the LSO (landing signal officer) indicated she was low. She overcorrected and became high. At that time the ship's bow pitched down and she was too high to land and catch one of the arresting cables. The LSO gave her a wave off and she bolted. She made a successful approach and landing on the second attempt. At the debriefing John asked Allison if she would like some coffee before beginning. It might have a calming effect. He imagined she would be somewhat unnerved about her performance.

"No thanks, I've already had a cup."

"In that case, what happened, Lieutenant?"

"The LSO signaled I was low, so the problem was that I overcorrected. Then I was high and the bow pitched down so I was too high to land and catch a wire, the LSO gave me a wave off and I bolted."

"It goes without saying when you're in close large corrections shouldn't be necessary. At landing speed you're covering a lot of distance in a matter of seconds."

"Yes, Sir. I realize that," she agreed.

"There are legitimate reasons for bolting like a fouled deck for example, but what you did wasn't one of them. If you had to bolt and were low on fuel you might have been going for a swim," he admonished. "Anything you would like to add? Are you having any problems that might be affecting your concentration?"

"No, Sir. I'm sure I will do better next time," she said optimistically.

"Let's call this a learning experience. Carrier flying requires all you attention especially if you return some night in the middle of a rain squall and you're low on fuel and committed to a landing."

"Thank you for your consideration, Sir."

After a few weeks at sea, operations were progressing without incidents, although Allison managed to catch the last arresting wire, instead of the number three wire.

A Grumman E-2 Hawkeye, an early warning and control aircraft picked up a bogey (unidentified aircraft). Probably a Russian Badger on a reconnaissance flight. As it was heading in the direction of the ship, a three aircraft flight was scrambled to intercept. It was cruising at a high altitude so it didn't present an immediate threat. Allison was flying the aircraft to the right and behind the leader. The flight leader radioed the carrier, it was identified as a Badger bomber. They flew along side the bomber and waved at the pilot who in turn waved also.

It was dark when the flight arrived at the carrier. A severe rain squall had enveloped the area. The carrier turned into the wind to accept the arriving aircraft and the deck was pitching in a confused sea. The flight leader and the left wingman made successful approaches and landings, Allison was the last to approach. It wasn't certain that she was selected the last to approach, however if she encountered any problems and fouled the deck, then the other two would be forced to ditch or enter a holding pattern, if they had enough fuel for a brief hold until the deck was cleared.

The aircraft was bouncing in the turbulence. The LSO was trying to tell her to smooth the corrections instead of the abrupt inputs to land on the pitching deck. The LSO recognized the erratic approach and gave her a wave off. She was forced to bolt and the adrenaline was pumping as she tried to remain calm for the second approach. She glanced at the fuel quantity gauge. At least fuel wasn't a problem.

The second approach was a replica of the first attempt and she was forced to bolt again. John was on the bridge apparently watching what could be a catastrophe in progress. In the third attempt, John was relieved to see that somehow she got everything together and caught the last arresting wire. John realized that Allison, being in an agitated frame of mind, it would be to their advantage to delay the briefing until the following morning.

The carrier passed through the squall line during the night and was west of the weather when the morning arrived bright and sunny with a strong wind out of the northwest. Allison was notified to report to the squadron commander's office ASAP. Anticipating the briefing, she arrived in a matter of minutes. She was wearing her khaki uniform instead of her flight coveralls. She had a premonition that she wouldn't be flying today. She assumed there would be some retraining. Standing at attention in front of his desk, "Reporting as ordered, Sir."

"Pull up a chair, Lieutenant. With your cooperation, I'll make this briefing as cordial as possible. In your opinion, what was the problem?"

"The weather. The turbulence. I was trying to compensate for the airspeed and altitude fluctuations and also the pitching deck. The two approaches, I was too high and the LSO gave me a wave off. The third approach, I got things under control."

"Unfortunately, we can't control the weather. Fuel wasn't a problem or you might have been forced to ditch. As I view the situation, Lieutenant, the only alternative I have is to ground you for the present pending the decision of the review board. This is the third time you've had a problem in approach and landing."

She flinched visibly disturbed upon hearing the decision. It's always a blow to a pilot's pride and self respect when told they have been grounded. "I realize there's been a problem, but I know I'm capable of doing a better job. Is it possible to get another chance?"

"Fraid not. You've been consistently having landing problems. Had you crashed last night with fatal results and the aircraft exploded, the ship would have been in jeopardy. The revue board will notify you in regard to their decision."

Assuming the debriefing was finished, she departed without

saying anything which was a gross breach of protocol. She went to her cabin and promptly wrote a letter to the congresswoman from her home state. She was the motivation behind Allison's quest to become one of the first female marine aircraft carrier pilots. Allison received a letter from the congresswoman saying that she was sorry to hear about her predicament. Coincidentally, she and a few other members of congress will be making a fact finding tour to Vietnam and hopefully can arrange a flight to the carrier and possibly reverse the decision of the revue board.

It didn't come as a complete surprise when John was informed of the congresswoman's impending visit in opposition to grounding Allison. Previously, he had asked her what the motivation was in becoming a carrier pilot. She neglected to mention it was at the suggestion of the congresswoman and the favorable publicity it would generate in regard to women serving in the armed forces under combat conditions. The congresswoman requested a woman pilot to fly the helicopter to the carrier for obvious reasons. As she would be remaining overnight the chopper returned to the Army base. It was mid afternoon when the chopper touched down on the carrier's deck. A night operation had been scheduled and she was eager to observe the actual conditions the pilots encountered flying from a carrier.

The revue board meeting with the congresswoman was scheduled for 1600 hours. Members included the ship's captain, the air boss, the Navy's squadron commander and John the Marine Corps' squadron commander. It was figured the meeting would end by 1800 hours for dinner.

The captain convened the meeting by saying, "Welcome aboard, congresswoman." She acknowledged with a wave of her hand. She was an attractive woman in her fifties but appeared younger. She was a trial lawyer and previously was an assistant district attorney prior to entering politics. "This meeting is being held at your request to discuss the grounding of Lieutenant Allison McCord." He continued by explaining the problems she encountered since coming aboard that resulted in her grounding. "Her flying placed the carrier in jeopardy."

"Could you elaborate on that, Captain?"

"The latest incident," he began to explain, "three aircraft were scrambled to investigate a bogey that had been picked up on radar. When they returned a rain squall had developed and the other two landed safely. She bolted after two unsuccessful approaches and finally landed on the third attempt."

"What does bolted mean?"

"An expression meaning she had to go around for another approach."

"Why is that serious?"

"If she had crashed it would no doubt be a fatality, the aircraft would explode and the ship would be on fire. A crash would be a fatality that we attempt to avoid if at all possible."

"You're speculating, nothing happened. I've heard the word *nugget* mentioned, Captain. Is that in reference to a female pilot only?"

"No, it refers to first tour pilots. You can't teach a young *nugget* how to become one of the boys in his or her first squadron. All naval aviators, regardless of their sex, must be bonded into their squadron if they are to survive the emotional and character-building strains they will face on their first real cruise. First tour pilots are traditionally *pushed* by members of their squadron and for good reason. The pressure dished out in the ready rooms is designed to separate the winners from the others. Several male pilots fail to survive their first squadron due to the pressure."

"I've also heard her called 'Gator'. What does that imply?"

"That's her call sign or nickname to make identification easier around the squadron or on a crowded radio circuit. They're chosen from some characteristic associated with the individual. She graduated from the University of Florida, hence the name *Gator* from the football team."

"It's necessary to realize that carrier flying is probably the most precision flying in existence. There isn't any margin for error from the time the catapult sends the aircraft down the deck to the landing when the tail hook catches the arresting wire."

"You're beginning to sound condescending, Captain."

"I'm trying to impress upon you that carrier flying is fraught with possible disasters. Fire is a major calamity. Although the ship is nuclear we're carrying thousands of gallons of aviation fuel and ammunition. Speaking of fuel, it wasn't one of her problems, but there aren't many occasions when a pilot can make three approaches and still have enough fuel to land. Otherwise she would have to ditch with the loss of a multi-million dollar aircraft."

"I think you made your point, Captain. If the press latches on to this the caption could read, 'Female Marine Fighter Pilot Removed From Duty'. It would be a setback to future female pilots aspiring to become carrier pilots."

Conversely, the captain suggested the headline could proclaim, "Female Marine Fighter Pilot Crashes During Attempted Landing On Aircraft Carrier."

"Contrary to everything that has been said, I firmly believe she should be granted another chance. To her credit she has flown fighters without any problems and passed the original carrier qualification."

In opposition to the congresswoman's statement the Captain said, "It was accomplished under ideal conditions. The sea was relatively smooth, it was daytime and the weather wasn't a factor."

"Regardless, I hope you will reconsider and give her another opportunity. Isn't it possible she just isn't attuned to carrier flying and could be assigned to a different type of flying. Every pilot can't be qualified for carrier flying, as every pilot doesn't have the skill to fly with the Blue Angels." The Blue Angels are an elite Navy aerobatic demonstration team who perform at air shows throughout the country. "You said previously that carrier flying is very precise."

"You've made a good point," the Captain conceded. "Let's break for dinner and the revue board will consider your viewpoints." It was a little over an hour before dinner. The board reconvened and decided the congresswoman presented a valid rebuttal. All pilots do not possess the same degree of ability they agreed.

Initially, John's voice was the only dissenting opinion to the idea of giving her another opportunity to fly again. "She consistently has a problem in approach and landing. I don't think she has the *feel* for carrier flying. There's too much at stake here. If she crashes, it would no doubt be a fatality and the loss of a multi-million dollar aircraft. Also if it explodes it puts the ship in jeopardy. From my experience in the war, pilots who were marginal and permitted to fly resulted in unnecessary accidents."

"Your point is well taken, John," the Captain conceded, "but if we deny her this opportunity the congresswoman will make a big issue out of it when she returns to Washington. I can visualize the article; Navy denies woman marine pilot the opportunity to prove her ability." It was a contentious subject but after further discussion they reluctantly agreed to allow her to fly in tonight's operations. The congresswoman was pleased with their decision that she was instrumental in agreeing to give Allison one more opportunity to vindicate herself.

The weather was forecast to expect rain squalls for their arrival. Upon returning to the carrier, similar weather conditions existed when she previously had problems in landing. Prepare to take aboard aircraft, the speakers alerted the deck crews. It was decided to have Allison land last as a precaution if an incident developed the deck would be clear assuming there weren't any problems.

Allison was cleared for her approach. The rain was heavy and the aircraft was being buffeted by the turbulence. On the downwind leg, the pilot extends the aircraft's landing gear, flaps and tail hook, then breaks in a left turn toward the boat. The aircraft should begin the final approach at eight hundred feet of altitude, about three quarters of a mile from the stern of the boat and just fifteen seconds from touch down. On the port side aft is the (Lens). It's a stabilized (against the ship's motion) system of lights to provide the pilot with a visual glide path to the deck. With the proper altitude and sink rate, the pilot sees an amber light (meatball). If the ball is kept centered a row of green lights all the way down will put the pilot in a perfect spot for landing. Any deviation shows red lights.

After the pilot breaks for the final approach, the LSO orders the pilot over the radio to "Call the ball." When the ball is spotted the pilot calls "Roger ball." At this point the final dash to the deck begins and the LSO is judging the approach. He also controls the (Pickle) a series of lights near the LSO platform. If the aircraft remains on course the pilot gets a green (OK), but the LSO can activate more power or wave off lights. If everything is normal the aircraft should be about thirty feet over the fantail with airspeed about 130 knots and a decided nose-up attitude.

The arresting gear brings the aircraft to a stop. Stretched across the deck are four braided steel cables, called wires, numbered 1 through 4 from rear to front. The wires are spaced fifty feet apart and connected to a pair of hydraulic cylinders below deck. If everything was set up properly, the aircraft should contact the deck in the roughly 250 feet by 50 feet rectangle formed by the wires. The favored target is the number three wire which provides the safest landing conditions and the least strain on the aircraft. Catching wires 2 or 4, while acceptable but snagging the number 1 wire is considered dangerous and usually brings the pilot counseling from the LSO. As soon as the aircraft hits the deck, the throttles are pushed to full power. If the tail hook fails to catch a wire, it's called a *bolter* and there is enough speed to fly off the end of the deck and try for another approach. The Vought F-8E Crusader was an interceptor aircraft that saw effective service throughout most of the Vietnam War.

Allison was coming in low again and the LSO advised her. She corrected but an updraft lifted the aircraft higher as the deck pitched lower caused by the winds affect on the sea. The LSO, recognizing the erratic approach gave her a wave off. Due to her intense concentration on the landing attempt and the restricted visibility she never observed the wave off signal from the LSO. Had she noticed the signal, she could have bolted and gone around for another approach. Rapidly approaching the arresting wires she pushed down the nose hoping to catch one of the wires. The aircraft was in a left bank. As she attempted to correct for the turbulence, she hit hard and the left landing gear collapsed as it absorbed the entire weight of the aircraft and slid down the deck with the wing extending over the side. The aircraft caught on fire and exploded in a gigantic fireball as everyone watched in horror as the fire control crew attempted to extinguish the inferno. Now that the carrier had a fouled deck, it had been prudent to land the other aircraft first in the event Allison had a problem.

The congresswoman's questions had been answered by a devastating situation. The newspaper account could begin by saying, "A female marine pilot died in a crash attempting to land on the aircraft carrier's pitching deck in a rain squall." Once the media becomes aware of the crash, they will attempt to uncover the facts leading up to the accident. As this was a major accident, a revue board will convene in Washington to investigate and determine the probable cause.

The fire had been contained and the damage to the deck had been assessed. The burning aircraft was jettisoned over the side and the damage to the deck, due to the prompt action of the fire control crew, did not appear to be severe. Flight operations could be resumed as necessary, after a thorough inspection.

The revue board held a meeting in the captain's cabin when everything returned to normal. After discussing the situation it probably would have been advisable to accept John's dissention against giving Allison another opportunity. There was some apprehension about the accident revue board's decision when it convenes in Washington.

The captain had two options. If he denied Allison the opportunity to redeem herself, he was positive the congresswoman would make an issue out of the situation which would lead to adverse publicity for the Navy especially when the media became involved.

Conversely, by permitting her to fly in the scheduled operation, he was placing the ship in jeopardy as the possibility of an accident existed in view of her past performance. During the meeting, the board began to realize the better option would have been to deny the congresswoman's suggestion to give her another chance. It would no doubt be the accident board's decision that she could have been reassigned to a different type of flying in contrast to the consequences involving the safety of the carrier. An adverse board's official decision in Washington, would no doubt weigh heavily in favor of a transfer, and could possibly have an impact on their future careers.

PRELUDE TO THE ACCIDENT BOARD

When life confronts us with our limits, those who have
lived with the limits all their lives instruct us most profoundly.
-B. C. Lane

The caption in the newspaper article read: Female Marine pilot crashes during ill-fated approach and landing on an aircraft carrier's pitching deck. The official communique was released -Darkness had enveloped the carrier when the squadron returned from an attack on the Ho Chi Minh trail in Vietnam. The carrier was involved in a violent rain squall that diminished visibility with moderate turbulence. The weather was a factor when she turned onto the final approach. Recognizing the erratic approach, due in part to the turbulence, the LSO or landing signal officer gave her a wave off signal. Probably due to her intense concentration and the restricted visibility she didn't observe the signal. Rapidly approaching the arresting wires, she pushed down the nose hoping the tail hook would catch one of the wires. She hit hard in a left wing down position and the left landing gear collapsed as it absorbed the aircraft's entire weight. The aircraft caught on fire and exploded as the fire control crew attempted to extinguish the inferno. After the next of kin had been notified, the pilot was identified as First Lieutenant Allison McCord USMC, from Haywood, Pa.

A letter to John

John, my love,
There was an article in the newspaper involving a Marine pilot and an aircraft carrier accident. I was wondering if it was your ship. It stated that a female marine pilot crashed while attempting to land in a rain squall. It was a fatality but didn't say if the ship was damaged.

Haven't heard from you for a long time but I realize overseas mail is slow. Hope all is well with you. On the home front, I've visited Tom, Kris and Greta for a few days. Tom is busy with the 747 project but we had a good time as usual. Finally talked my folks into spending a week-end here. We even visited Washington for some sight seeing. I was tired when we arrived back home and the doctor said everything was progressing normally. I'll be relieved when it's time for the baby to arrive. Write when you can. Miss you more than words can say. It will be a joyous day when you walk through the door and hang up your jacket in the hall closet. When you're here it's like being warmed by the sun.

Always,
Velma

John finally received Velma's letter and replied.

Hi Mother to be,
The mail finally came through. (The technology of communication at the time had not advanced to the present quality.) Glad to hear that everything is moving along smoothly. We'll be parents soon and we can relax and enjoy our new arrival.

To explain the circumstance leading to the accident, she was having problems with the approach and landing. It was my decision to ground her. Also, the intervention of a congresswoman, who was on a fact finding trip to Vietnam became involved and was supporting the idea to give her another opportunity to redeem herself. I spoke in dissension to the idea. The revue board, in discussion with the congresswoman felt she presented a valid opinion and decided to give her another flight which terminated in disaster.

An official investigation by the Accident Revue Board will be convened in Washington when we return from the six month deployment. In a couple of months we'll be taking up a heading back to Pearl Harbor and I'll be on a flight to Washington. Regards to Tom, Kris and Greta and your family. Also, I haven't written to my folks lately. Would you give them a call to bring them up to date. Looking forward to a get together with everyone.

Luv ya.
Guess who

Two months after the accident, the carrier was under orders to return to Pearl Harbor. The ship had not received major damage from the fire but would require minor repairs that could be accomplished at Pearl Harbor. The entire crew reacted with jubilation when the Captain's PA said they were going home thus ending their six month deployment. It was a familiar sight when Diamond Head appeared on the horizon. The sea voyage would soon be ending. When the engines were shut down, the tugs eased the carrier to the dock. As with any ship returning from the war zone, a clamorous crowd greeted the sailors and marines. When the gangplank was secured they disembarked on the dock en mass. A Navy band provided the welcome home music.

At the first available phone, John called Velma. "It's me."

"Who is me?" She was overjoyed to hear his voice but couldn't resist a short bit of levity. "I'm so happy to hear you're back, but where are you?"

"We just arrived in Pearl Harbor. Can't talk long, there's a big line for the phone. I'll call you later when I have a better idea of the plans."

"Glad you're home. I'll call Tom and Kris. They'll be happy to hear the good news. Talk to you later."

John had packed all his gear in preparation for the short ride to Ewa, the Marine base west of Honolulu. The revue board had a short meeting before departing to reunite with their families. They all agreed that facing the official accident revue board in Washington could involve a few anxious moments. Tell it the way it happened without excuses or embellishment.

Conditions hadn't changed much in Ewa during their six months deployment. He was looking forward to some ice cold pineapple juice and papayas. Active military activity was still evident. The cruise had been punctuated with some anxious moments, highlighted by the crash of Lt. McCord in a severe rain squall. Both the navy and marine squadrons were utilized flying the various sorties to Vietnam. On several occasions Russian built MIG fighters attempted to attack the carrier. When they were observed on radar a three aircraft flight was scrambled and John lead one of the intercepts. The MIG pilot went into a climbing left turn, which was a mistake and John opened fire with a missile and the MIG exploded. He succeeded in flaming one of the MIGs but the other one turned back to Vietnam before his wingman could engage him. It was John's thirtieth confirmed kill. After returning to the boat the pilots had a celebration in the ready room. Everything wasn't peaceful. Some of the aircraft failed to return, victims of ground missile attacks. Others, although damaged were able to return for a safe landing. There weren't any landing fatalities.

John had a meeting with the CO. He was eager to complete the meeting so he could call Velma to let her know when he would be coming home. He had been in this office on several occasions dating back to World War II. The only difference were the COs. John and the present CO knew each other since the beginning of their careers and now they were both colonels. They discussed the details of John's trip back to Washington and he gave the CO a briefing of the six months cruise. They reminisced about the past and three wars later. The CO asked, "Has there been a time set for the hearing with the Accident Revue Board?"

"Not to my knowledge. I imagine I'll be notified sometime during my leave." John gave him a brief summary of the accident before the meeting ended. They wished each other the best of luck in the future like a couple of old warriors that they were.

"I hope everything from the board's decision comes out in your favor, John. I also hope your new assignment will be more to your satisfaction."

John put in a call to Velma. It rang five times before she picked it up. "I didn't think you were home."

"Sorry, I was too busy chasing one of my admirers out the door."

"Are you bragging or complaining?"

"Just speculating, my love. I only have eyes for you. So, when are you coming home?"

"I just had a meeting with the CO who happened to be one of my old friends from way back. They cut new orders for me and I'll be leaving on a military non-stop flight at eleven tonight. There's a five hour time difference so I should be arriving in Washington around three o'clock in the afternoon."

"I'll meet you."

"Do you feel up to it?"

"Oh sure. I had an appointment with the doctor today and he said all systems are go. Sounded like a frustrated astronaut."

"Anyway, glad to hear that everything is normal. I have a few loose ends here and I'd like to take a nap. It will be a long night."

"Have you heard anything about the accident board meeting?"

"No. I'll be notified whenever they get their act together. Got to go. See you tomorrow. Love you."

Velma called Kris after dinner to relay the good news that John was home. They wanted to plan a get together but the date of the accident board was a question mark. Also, Tom was in Seattle again and wouldn't return for a few more days. They decided to wait until the board set a date for the hearing before the plans were finalized for the get together.

A week after John arrived home, he received a notice that the accident board would convene on 6 June 1968 at the Washington Navy Yard. When he opened the notice and saw the date he shouted, "Velma I can't believe this."

"Something wrong, my love?"

"The hearing is set for the sixth of June. It's also the date of our get together. And to further compound things, it's your delivery date. Can you believe this?" he repeated his disbelief.

"We have a real conundrum to deal with, John." she agreed.

"I can't change the board's date and we can't alter the birth date. The only alternative would be to cancel or change the date of the get together. That would present many problems. The invitations have been sent. The catering.has been arranged and the hotel reservations. Some of the out of town guests have made or altered plans.

"Why not call your folks and ask their opinion," Velma suggested.

"Good idea. They may provide an insight to the problem."

Sharon answered the phone. "You're calling to tell me the baby arrived?"

"Not yet, Mom. We have a dilemma." He explained the situation.

"I'll talk it over with your father. When you least expect things like this to happen," she paused, "it must be fate. We'll call you in a few minutes." True to her word, she called about five minutes later.

"What kept you, Mom?" he chided.

"As a courtesy to you, we made a quick decision. Since all the plans are in place, we figured that all considered it would be better to continue with the get together. Some of the out of town guests would have to alter their plans. The baby's arrival is uncertain, but we're looking forward to it and the accident board's meeting is Friday so you still have the week-end."

"Sounds like a logical solution, thanks to you and Dad. We'll call you if the baby arrives before the get together."

THE HEARING BEGINS

Sometimes in the winds of change we find our true direction.
-Unknown

The proceedings were called to order at 0900 on 6 June 1968 at the Washington Navy Yard. The accident board consisted of four admirals and three captains. The senior admiral was the chairman. The admiral made the opening statement. "We're assembled here to discuss the conditions and the decisions leading to the crash of the aircraft on the carrier deck deployed in the South China Sea, involving a fatality." Most of the hearings were "closed door" but there were only a few in attendance. "This is not a court martial although it was considered. Let us begin. Any board member has the option to ask questions."

Chairman: Would the ship's captain take a seat at the table? Were you previously informed of the situation in regard to the pilot's landing problems.

Captain: Yes, Sir by both the air boss and the marine CO who previously had grounded the pilot.

Chairman: And what was your decision?

Captain: I suggested we form a revue board to evaluate her ability as a carrier pilot.

Board: Who were the members of the revue board?

Captain: Myself, the air boss and the COs of the navy and marine squadrons. To anticipate your next question, we agreed she should remain grounded.

Board: Thank you, captain. That was my next question.

Board: We are aware that a congresswoman, who was on a fact finding tour in Vietnam interceded on her behalf.

Captain: She requested a meeting with the board to discuss the pilot's problems.

Board: As the congresswoman is in attendance, I think it would be incumbent upon us to question her.

Chairman: Would the congresswoman please take a seat at the table and thank you for coming here.

Board: Is there any particular reason you interceded for the pilot?

Congresswoman: She is a constitute in my district. I heard she was a marine pilot and interested in aircraft carrier flying. I encouraged her ambition to become one of the first female marine carrier pilots. It was also good publicity for women flying in combat. She wrote to me after she was grounded. I replied that I was scheduled for a fact finding tour to Vietnam and if possible I would try to arrange a meeting with the revue board.

Board: So it was your idea then to coerce the board into giving her another opportunity to redeem herself.

Congresswoman: I wasn't thinking in those terms. I thought it would be adverse publicity for the Navy and the Marine Corps if the media became aware of the situation and proclaimed-female marine pilot denied aircraft carrier opportunity. But I also said that if possibly she wasn't adept at carrier flying and could be reassigned to some other type of flying that wasn't as precise.

Board: What was the result of the meeting?

Congresswoman: We recessed and I would be advised of their decision after dinner.

Board: And what was their decision?

Congresswoman: They agreed that some of my ideas were valid. The captain again stressed that he wanted to avoid any adverse publicity for the Navy. A night operation had been scheduled and after further discussion it was decided to give her one more opportunity.

Board: Had anyone mentioned the possibility of an accident in this case?

Congresswoman: The Marine CO said that accidents exist even in normal operation. Although as a precaution, it was decided she would be the last to land. In her previous flights, even though she was having problems, she managed to make successful landings. I believe they reasoned if there was an incident, the other aircraft could land otherwise the deck would be fouled. The carrier was involved in a severe rain squall. That was the problem.

Board: I don't believe you're qualified to make that assumption as all the other pilots landed safely.

Chairman: We thank you, Congresswoman for your information. Would the air boss take a seat at the table?

Board: You were aware that the pilot was having problems, yet you voted to give her another chance. What was your reasoning?

Air Boss: Being a pilot, it's a serious blow to one's pride to be grounded. Usually if it's a washout the pilot has a final evaluation. I gave her the benefit of the doubt that it might just be checkitis and anxiety.

Chairman: Thank you, Commander, I realize carrier flying can be more stressful at times, but not to the point that the pilots ability is compromised. Would the Navy CO take a seat? What was your reasoning in regard to her ability?

Navy CO: As she was a marine I wasn't directly involved with the situation, but I agreed with the air boss in his reasoning so I voted to give her another chance.

Chairman: You're the last, Colonel and as her CO you grounded her for erratic approaches and landings. As yours was the one dissenting opinion, what was your reasoning?

Marine CO: I've had considerable experience in carrier flying during World War II. The pilots who were having problems were the same pilots responsible for most of the accidents. She had problems on two previous approaches and landings. That was the reason I grounded her. As a precaution we thought it best if she landed last. If she had an accident the deck would have been fouled and most of the returning aircraft would be landing with minimum fuel. Also, there would possibly be damage to the carrier and loss of a multi-million dollar aircraft.

Chairman: Thank you Colonel. That was very enlightening. At this time we'll call for a recess and after lunch I'll announce the board's decision.

THE VERDICT

Keep your face to the sunshine and you will not notice the shadows
-Helen Keller

After lunch the Board Chairman delivered the verdict. The captain sat there nervously fiddling a pencil. The air boss and both COs remained tense, staring at the wall above the revue board. They were fully aware that a negative verdict could affect their future careers.

"As captain of a ship you are responsible for everything that happens under you command." The Captain felt that the decision was not going in his favor. "You hazarded your ship knowing that the possibility of an accident existed from previous experience by permitting the pilot to fly again. The Board decided you would receive a letter of reprimand. The air boss and Navy CO will receive a milder letter of admonition as both of you agreed to the flight fully aware that the potential for an accident existed. There will no charges against the Marine CO as his was the dissenting vote against the flight and through foresight had originally grounded the pilot."

During the board's deliberation they reviewed the officer's records. All their fitness reports were satisfactory, but they were particularly impressed with John's record. Served in three wars and was a POW. Several commendations. At one time was assigned as a squadron commander with about one third of the aircraft out of service. In fifteen months he had all the aircraft and pilots on a full schedule. The commendation read, "By force of his personality he turned the squadron into something special." His record remained unblemished.

EPILOGUE

The secret to happiness is to make
others believe they are the cause of it.
-Unknown

Heinrich von Lehndorff passed through several valleys and plateaus in his life. Some were good but others weren't memorable. He figured the trouble with life, there's no background music to mellow the incidents.

In retrospect his life was punctuated with anxiety. What appeared on the surface to be an asset for die Firma when the factories were converted to produce engines and sub-assemblies for Messerschmitt Aircraft proved otherwise. They were constantly harassed by the Luftwaffe and Berlin to increase production.

His life was in jeopardy on three occasions. The first time, he ended the life of the camp commander when he became aware that Hilda had been raped resulting in a pregnancy. He was exonerated by the People's Court when it became known there were further charges pending against the camp commander for trafficking in the black marked. The second time occurred when he was held responsible for using slave labor in the factories. Again he was found not guilty, but the anxiety had left it's mark. The third time his life was placed in jeopardy when he became the target of an assassin seeking revenge for his brother who had raped Hilda. It was a twist of fate that intervened and an innocent person died from a bomb that exploded in Heinrich's desk. He had scheduled a meeting with Fritz but was called to security. Fritz was sitting in his chair until he returned and absorbed the full force of the explosion.

In the post war recovery, he resisted the idea to incorporate and remained the sole proprietor. Now, in his late seventies with all the pressure of rebuilding in addition to the failed plot on his life, he suffered a stroke. When recovery was certain, the doctor suggested he retire. He was no longer the robust, strong and healthy picture of a man that could destroy the camp commander's office and with a vise-like grip around the commanders neck, thus ending his life. His hair was almost totally white and he walked with the assistance of a cane. It was almost impossible to look into his brown eyes without seeing the depth of sorrow in his spent life. The ghost of a man.

Hilda, recognized for the company to expand, it was necessary to incorporate. Since Hilda was an integral part of the company through the years, she became the obvious choice to assume the head of the corporation. In addition to her expansion plans for the company, she also revealed plans for the utilization of the castle with the help of Hanna. With the company secure and Hilda in her seventies and Hanna in the eighties were both enjoying a reasonably healthy life considering their age. The company was sold to a group of German industrialists.

John agonized over the decision to apply for the Astronaut program. After a thorough discussion with Velma, it was decided an astronauts career would require a drastic change in their life. The Navy has a time limit on the duty of a test pilot. When his time had expired. John was assigned, due to his extensive aircraft carrier experience with the rank of Colonel, as the CO of a Marine Squadron deployed on a carrier in the Vietnam War.

In regard to the accident on board the carrier during John's six months tour of sea duty, an accident review board convened in Washington. At the conclusion of the board meeting, the ships captain received a letter of reprimand, the air boss and Navy CO received letters of admonishment. Eventually the letters were expunged from their records. There weren't any charges against John, due to his dissension in the case, so his record remained unblemished. With his sea duty complete John was then assigned to the Army Command and General Staff School. After completion, his next assignment was a return to the Naval Air Test facility at Pax River as Commandant with the rank of

Brigadier General as Velma speculated when he was considering the Astronaut program. Velma was ecstatic when John decided against applying for the astronaut program.

After three miscarriages Velma delivered a six pound boy much to their relief and thankful for a successful pregnancy. The Senator and Sharon were overjoyed at the idea of a grandson and so were Velma's parents. The Senator vowed to remained in office as long as the people continued to support him. Sharon remained active in the Fairfield Foundation for Education, with Velma's assistance.

Beth, now an established actress received scripts playing opposite some of Hollwood's leading actors. She was described as another Grace Kelly. Rumors linked her with other actors, but was strickly for publicity.

Tom had become completely involved in the 747 program. He flew the first delivery of the aircraft from Seattle to Dallas. On board were company personnel and also those from Boeing and the FAA. Tom requested that Kris and Greta be included and also his mentor Harry Clark and Grace. Harry was retired having reached sixty the mandatory retirement age for airline pilots.

An enormous crowd had gathered to greet the arrival and for a walk through the huge aircraft. Tom flew the inaugural flight from New York to Los Angeles. The following morning, a nine o'clock departure was scheduled for the return flight. Service to other cities was accommodated as other aircraft were scheduled for delivery. Through the years Tom remained in the reserve as the CO of a training squadron at Cherry Point.

Greta was successful in her quest for a piano. If there was any doubt in their minds that she was not sincere, vanished when her exuberance continued all through high school. When it came time to consider a college she chose to attend the Juilliard School of Performing Arts. At that point they were certain her interest in music was genuine. After all the training she became a concert pianist performing as featured soloist with various symphonies. Tom and Kris figured they made the right decision.

Tom and Mary Jane's son was three months old when she died in an auto accident. In her memory, John proffered a scholarship for him from the Fairfield Foundation for Education to a college of his choice or entrance to the Naval Academy, through the Senators recommendation. As he was enrolled at the Naval Academy, the proffer was extended to Greta when she chose the Juilliard School of Performing Arts.

After thirty six years, both active and reserve Tom retired from the Marine Corps. The same general that had discussed Tom's deployment to Vietnam presided over the ceremony. "In view of your exemplary career and one of the most decorated pilots in the Corps, in apprciation of your dedicated service, it's my pleasure to present you with a star, the rank of a Brigadier General."

It took Tom completely by surprise. He figured it would be a plaque denoting his years of service. After the salute and handshake, the general said, "Has your daughter written any more letters?"

Tom explained Greta's progress in her music career.

The general said, "Say hello for me."

John's career in the Marine Corps continued spiraling upward and eventually becoming chairman of the Joint Chief's of Staff as a four star General.

Tom's airline career also continued to accelerate and due to a retirement, he was promoted to Vice-President Flight. It would require a move to the company headquarters in Fort Worth from Greenwich which had been their home for several years. He and Kris discussed the idea. It means a difficult decision. Kris said, "You might just as well grab the brass ring. At least you'll be home every night."

Robert Thomas Korb, Tom's son, graduated from the Naval Academy and was commissioned a second Lieutenant in the U. S. Marine Corps, rather than the Navy, in deference to Tom and John's choice. He applied for flight training at N. A. S. Pensacola, Florida. After receiving his Wings Of Gold, he was assigned as an aircraft carrier pilot before the Vietnam War ended in 1973.

ABOUT THE AUTHOR

Windmeer is a post World War II sequel to his novel Thorn Castle. He and his wife reside in a retirement community in Fort Myers, Florida